Joanna and Sir Rollin were alone,
screened from the others by
the pillars of the little temple.

Suddenly, she felt his arm slide around her waist, and she was pulled against his chest. For a moment, she was so startled she couldn't move. Sir Rollin put a finger under her chin, raised her face to his, and kissed her expertly.

Recovering her wits, Joanna pulled away. "Sir Rollin!" She backed up a few steps. "Someone will see!"

"Ah." He smiled. "You would perfer to continue when they can't?"

She stared at him wide-eyed. Her emotions were in such tumult that she could scarcely frame a reply. Did he really mean what he had said? Was this some sort of unconventional proposal? Meeting his dancing hazel eyes, she knew that it was not. Sir Rollin was not thinking of marriage at this moment. The red in her cheeks deepened. "No, I do not," she said. She had not enjoyed the kiss at all . . .

Novels by Jane Ashford

Gwendeline
Bluestocking
Man of Honour
Rivals of Fortune

Published by
WARNER BOOKS

Your Warner Library of Regency Romance

Rivals of Fortune

a novel by
Jane Ashford

WARNER BOOKS

A Warner Communications Company

WARNER BOOKS EDITION

Copyright © 1981 by Jane LeCompte
All rights reserved.

Cover art by Walter Popp

Warner Books, Inc.
666 Fifth Avenue
New York, N.Y. 10103

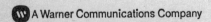 A Warner Communications Company

Printed in the United States of America

First Printing: October, 1981

Reissued: February, 1989

10 9 8 7 6 5 4 3 2

Rivals
of
Fortune

One

Miss Joanna Rowntree sat very straight in the drawing room of her father's house near Oxford, her eyes fixed painfully on the mantel clock. There was nothing in the appearance of this rather handsome timepiece to explain the anxiety in her expression, nor did the room yield a clue. It was an elegant, comfortable apartment, not quite in the first stare of fashion, a Londoner might aver, yet showing taste and the means to command some of life's luxuries. The deep cream of the walls, the dark blue velvet hangings, and the French furniture formed a pleasing contrast to the rolling green fields visible through the long windows.

The slender girl sitting stiffly before the fireplace ignored these familiar surroundings. A diminutive brunette, Miss Rowntree kept her large brown eyes on the clock, which now read six minutes to eleven. Her tightly folded hands had crumpled her pink morning dress, and one of her glossy brown curls had fallen down over her shoulder, but she noticed none of this. It was not until the drawing room door opened and her mother came into the room that Joanna roused a little; but even then, she merely turned her head slightly before going back to gazing at the clock. Her expression became a bit more soulful, perhaps, and her hands twisted in her lap, but she said nothing.

Mrs. Rowntree, also a very attractive brunette who

had retained her figure through twenty years of marriage and three children, frowned slightly and watched her only daughter with lips pressed together. She seemed undecided about something, but finally she said, "Joanna," in a tone calculated to command the girl's immediate attention.

Joanna turned, her eyes growing even larger. "Oh, Mama," she replied in a soft, languishing voice. "I didn't hear you come in."

"Did you not indeed?" said her mother. "And I suppose you also forgot that you were to help Mrs. Harwood with the linens this morning? She looked for you for quite half an hour."

Joanna stared at her in amazement. "Linens? Oh, Mama, it lacks but three minutes to eleven. They are at the church even now, and you talk to me of linens?" She looked down and brought her clasped hands to her bosom.

A spark of sympathy showed in Mrs. Rowntree's eyes, and she sighed. She started to speak, thought better of it, and went to sit down beside her daughter. She took one of Joanna's hands and patted it, but when she spoke, her tone was firm. "Joanna, you are being silly. These die-away airs do no one any good, I promise you. Please do stop. I am going into Longton; come along, and we will see if we can find a new dress length at Quentin's."

"Longton!" echoed the girl, with a distaste for the neighboring village she had never before exhibited. "Mama, how can you be so unfeeling!" The clock struck eleven, and Joanna started convulsively: "At this moment, Peter is being married, and you wish me to go to Longton and look at dress lengths. Oh, Mama!"

Sympathy showed again in Mrs. Rowntree's face, but she answered only, "Well, well, you were not really engaged to Peter, you know, my dear."

Joanna raised her head. "Not engaged? But it has been understood since we were children that we would marry. Indeed, he told me before he went to London in March that we would be married when he returned."

Her mother's lips came together again. "Well, he was very wrong to do so without a word to your father. And you were wrong to listen to him. You see where such behavior leads. A great deal can happen to a young man during a London season, and you would have done better to have told him that you would see about that when you came to town yourself next year."

"Oh, I shan't go now," said Joanna, turning to gaze out the window and avoid her mother's censorious glance.

Her diversion was successful. "Not go? Of course, we shall. You have been eighteen these two months, Joanna. Naturally, I shall present you in London next season. Indeed, I would take you now if it were not already June."

"Mama, I *could* not. *He* is there. With his . . . his wife."

"Well, I daresay they will both be here very soon, if it comes to that," responded her mother unencouragingly, "so you had best become accustomed to the idea of meeting them."

"Here?" cried the girl, horrified.

"Yes, of course. I suppose Peter will wish to show her his house."

Joanna leaped to her feet. "Oh, what shall I do? You must take me away, Mama."

"Nonsense. You will meet Peter and his wife calmly and with dignity. Do you wish to set the whole neighborhood talking? Have a little conduct, Joanna, and stop acting a Cheltenham tragedy."

"But, Mama, I love him!"

Her mother smiled skeptically. "You do not, you know. You have no more idea of love than Frederick does."

"Frederick! Why he is only a—a grubby little schoolboy."

Mrs. Rowntree nodded equably, accepting this characterization of her youngest child without demur.

"He—he is a perfect toad," her daughter went on, nearly inarticulate with outrage. "How can you compare my feelings to his? I do love Peter, I do!" She stamped her foot.

The older woman's lips twitched. "I know you think you do, Joanna, but in a few weeks, you will see that it was all a take-in. Calf love."

The delightful pink in Joanna's cheeks deepened. She was about to pour out an impassioned defense of her feelings when the drawing-room door opened once more and one of the maids came in. "Excuse me, Ma'am," she said to Mrs. Rowntree, "but a gentleman has brought Mr. Frederick home. Covered with dirt, he is, and he's hurt his ankle."

"Oh dear," said her mistress, getting up. "I wonder what he has been at this time." And leaving her daughter fuming, Mrs. Rountree walked quickly out of the room.

Joanna stood tapping her foot for a full minute, then curiosity got the better of her anger, and she went out to the landing and looked down into the hall. Her thirteen-year-old brother was indeed covered with dirt, and his face showed that he was in some pain. A footman had just lifted him and was starting up the stairs. Her mother was talking to a stranger in buckskin riding breeches and a brown coat. Joanna wrinkled her nose in disdain. His appearance was so far from being fashionable that she could not imagine where he had purchased his clothes. Even in Oxford, there were tailors who could manage a better cut.

"Do come upstairs," her mother was saying.

Joanna quickly retreated to the drawing room again.

The others entered soon after. "This is Jonathan Erland, Joanna," said Mrs. Rowntree. "Only fancy, he is our new neighbor at the Abbey. Mr. Erland, my daughter Joanna."

The gentleman made a rather awkward bow, his eyes showing clear appreciation of Joanna's petite good looks, and she surveyed him with more interest than before. The abbey was the largest house in the neighborhood, though sadly run down at present, and since its owner's illness and death last winter, there had been much speculation as to whom it would fall.

Mr. Erland was an open-faced young man, just above middle height. His complexion was ruddy, his hair brown, and his eyes a clear gray. He had none of the airs of a fashionable exquisite, but there was something in his manner that Joanna found unfamiliar, almost foreign. He seemed about five and twenty.

"Tell Mr. Rowntree we have a visitor," her mother was saying to the maid. "Ask him to come up." They all sat down, and Mrs. Rowntree continued, "I collect you have only recently arrived in the neighborhood, Mr. Erland. My husband would certainly have called if we had known."

The gentleman smiled, his rather commonplace countenance lighting charmingly. "Just this week. The news of my uncle's death, and of my cousin's which I had not previously heard, did not reach me till then. I was rather out of the way."

Joanna started to ask where he had been, but her mother spoke first. "I thank you again for rescuing Frederick. What a poor introduction to our family you have had."

"Not at all," answered Erland. "Frederick seems a very promising lad—full of pluck."

Mrs. Rowntree shook her head. "He is that."

"What happened to him?" asked Joanna.

"The tiresome boy took it into his head to trespass at the Abbey. He fell from a crumbling wall in the ruins and sprained his ankle. I've sent Nurse to see to him." Mrs. Rowntree turned back to their guest. "You mustn't think me unfeeling, Mr. Erland. Frederick comes home injured more often than not. I have concluded he is indestructible."

The man laughed. "He is certainly durable at any rate. It was quite a fall he took."

"Well, if he will climb everything he sees, he is certain to fall," said Joanna severely. "Why did he wish to poke about in the ruins of the abbey?"

"He tells me there is a rumor going about the neighborhood that my Uncle Thomas buried his fortune somewhere there," answered Erland. "Would that it were true."

Mrs. Rowntree smiled. "All boys long for such a chance. It is all nonsense, of course."

He made a wry face. "I fear you are right, and it is most unfortunate for me. The place has gone to rack and ruin since I saw it ten years ago, and a treasure is clearly required to set it to rights. I wish that my uncle had left one."

"Oh, but he was such a clutchfist; did he not leave you a fortune?" asked Joanna before she thought. She colored as Erland turned to her.

"Joanna!" said her mother.

"No, no, it's quite all right. I'd rather everyone knew just how I'm placed; I like to have things out in the open. My uncle left me the estate and a competence, nothing more. I would like above all things to renovate the Abbey, but I doubt that it will be possible. I hope the neighborhood will not be disappointed." He smiled again.

"How funny," said Joanna. "We always made sure he was excessively rich. How mistaken one can be in people." This reflection reminded her of her melancholy, and she sank into a brown study.

Her mother was about to speak when the drawing-room door opened slowly and a tall thin man with pale brown hair and abstracted gray eyes came into the room. "Hello, dear," said Mrs. Rowntree. "Here is Jonathan Erland, the new resident of the Abbey. Mr. Erland, my husband George Rowntree."

Mr. Erland stood and bowed.

Mr. Rowntree murmured something unintelligible, standing beside the open door as if puzzled; then his brows drew together and he struck the palm of one hand with his fist. "Of course," he said decisively, "sulfate of ammonia." His eyes lit, and he turned as if to leave the room.

Jonathan Erland cast a perplexed glance at Mrs. Rowntree.

"George," she said firmly, "come and sit down, dear."

Mr. Rowntree started and turned again. "Emma," he said, as if surprised. "I have solved it, the problem I was explaining to you at breakfast. It is sulfate of ammonia. You see . . ."

"That's wonderful, dear. I'm so pleased. But here is Jonathan Erland to see you. He has just come to live at the Abbey."

Mr. Rowntree seemed to see their guest for the first time. "The Abbey, is it?" he replied, with no sign of embarrassment over his unconventional welcome. "Splendid. Perhaps we can persuade *you* of the pressing need to document the contents of the ruins there. It is vital, you know, to investigate such sites scientifically. Careless curiosity seekers destroy countless things every day. Even now, much of it is utterly spoiled. One must have method, order, or all is lost. Surely you agree?"

"Why, ah, yes," said Erland, "but I'm not sure I . . ."

"Capital! Old Tom Erland would never listen to me. Hidebound and closed-minded, he was. He had one or two ideas, and he held to them, no matter what harm came of it. Inflexible. It's the worst of faults, perhaps." His gaze shifted. "We can get up a digging party next Thursday. Young Templeton will be overjoyed. And I suppose Carstairs will want to come along, though he's a sloppy thinker." His voice trailed off as he frowned in concentration.

Mr. Erland was looking a bit lost.

"We are so glad to have you at the Abbey," put in Mrs. Rowntree. "It will be a pleasant change to have a young man there. Do you have a family?"

Turning to her gratefully, Erland started to speak, but Mr. Rowntree looked up at that moment and exclaimed, "Jonathan Erland. The old man's nephew?"

Their guest nodded, looking slightly apprehensive.

"We have met, have we not?" continued Rowntree. "It's been some ten or fifteen years, I daresay, but you are the young man who was to go to the colonies, aren't you? Or perhaps there was another nephew?"

"No, sir. That was I. I have lived in Canada for nearly ten years." He turned to smile at Mrs. Rowntree. "I have had no time to think of marrying; too busy trying to make my fortune. Unsuccessfully, I fear, though I had a fine time at it." He looked back to his host. "We must have met when I stayed at the Abbey just before I sailed, Mr. Rowntree. I was but fifteen when my uncle paraded me about the neighborhood."

"Of course, of course," replied Rowntree abstractedly. "Canada, now. That is most interesting, most interesting. In what area did you reside?"

The younger man smiled again. "All parts, at one time or another, sir. Through the good offices of my uncle, I had a position in the eastern settlements for some time. But for the last several years, I have lived in the Northwest Territories."

Mr. Rowntree leaned forward and put his clasped hands on his knees. "Really! The territories, you say— fascinating. You have been a member of the exploration parties, I take it?"

Erland nodded. "I was with Thompson."

His host's pale eyes glowed, and he seemed scarcely able to keep his seat. "Thompson! Why he is one of the greatest explorers now living, and you have traveled with him? You must tell me all about it, *everything*."

Mr. Erland laughed. "That would take me some time. But I confess I am surprised. Few Englishmen have heard of Thompson, I believe, and fewer still would be interested if they did."

"My husband is a scholar," said Mrs. Rowntree.

Waving her explanation aside, Rowntree said, "Tell us about Thompson."

"I am happy to tell you whatever you like. I have the greatest admiration and respect for David Thompson.

He taught me more than anyone else in my life. He just completed a long river expedition in the Northwest, you know, on which I was privileged to accompany him. I have never seen such country. We were right in the midst of the Rocky Mountains."

Mr. Rowntree's eyes sparkled. "Indeed. Did you find the Northwest Passage at last, perhaps?"

"No," laughed Erland. "I doubt that anyone will find that mythical route. We must still sail north or south, into the ice or the storms. But we found a river route into the interior of the continent, albeit a difficult one, and saw a great many marvelous things. Thompson is a friend of the native tribes in that area, and they help him find his way, you see."

"The Indians," breathed Joanna, her interest caught at last.

"Yes," responded Erland, smiling at her warmly, "do you . . ."

"Tell me about the country," said her father. "It is coniferous forest?"

Erland nodded, turning away from Joanna a bit reluctantly. "For the most part." He paused, and his eyes grew faraway. "The river we traveled this trip was called the Kootenay by the natives. I don't recall what that means; I am not well acquainted with the native language unfortunately. But the water was unlike anything you can see in England: pale green because it comes down from the ice fields and glaciers. Snow and ice stays the whole year on some of the mountains, yet the valleys are green and lush." He sighed. "It is beautiful."

Joanna echoed his sigh; Mr. Rowntree nodded wisely. "The elevation," he murmured.

"Yes," agreed the younger man. "The mountains rise almost straight out of the plains to the east, an amazing sight, and the river is right among them. I can't describe it properly, it is so breathtaking. I wish you could see Thompson's journals. He tells everything so well."

"Ah, wouldn't that be splendid," cried his host. "I

must tell you, Mr. Erland, that ideas are the chief joy of my life. To exchange opinions and observations with a man such as he would indeed be exciting."

As always when her father began to go on in this way, Joanna felt bored. Her thoughts turned back to London. It was nearly twelve and Peter would be married now and they would be at the wedding breakfast. She wondered what his wife was like and whether she was prettier. I hope she is not very tall and blonde, she thought. If she is, she will make me look like a wretched little dab of a thing, and I shall feel even worse. She knew very little about the woman Peter Finley had chosen over her. They had received the news via an announcement in the *Morning Post,* and they knew only that Adrienne Denby, now Mrs. Finley, was the sister of Sir Rollin Denby, a man one of their neighbors characterized as an "ugly customer," whatever that meant. He had added that Miss Denby's portion was substantial and that young Peter was doing very well for himself in that regard, though he might still regret the match.

Joanna frowned. She had not understood why he said that either, though several others in the room at the time had looked at each other significantly. But she indignantly rejected the idea that Peter had married for money. He did not care for such things. Had he not been ready to marry her, with next to no fortune at all? Joanna sighed. No, Peter had simply fallen out of love with her when he met someone he liked better. And hard as this was to bear, she hoped he would be very happy. She herself would dwindle into an old maid, she supposed, looking after her brothers' children and, possibly, knitting. I must learn to knit, she decided. She assumed a martyred expression and sat up a little to catch a glimpse of her reflection in the drawing-room mirror. It was very affecting. She sighed again, then noticed that Mr. Erland was looking at her with a smile on his lips, and blushed fiercely, looking down.

Their guest stood. "I must go," he said. "I am sorry,

but I was with my bailiff when I heard Frederick calling for help. He will be impatient."

Mrs. Rowntree rose immediately. "And we have kept you from your business. You should not have allowed it. But I hope you will come to dinner one day soon."

Mr. Erland professed himself grateful for the invitation. "My uncle's old housekeeper is not much of a cook."

"Mrs. Smith?" Mrs. Rowntree laughed. "I daresay not. Do you get on with her?"

"I am terrified of her," replied Erland, and everyone laughed.

Any other father might have inquired why his youngest son had been calling for help, but Mr. Rowntree said merely, "Come whenever you like." His tone was very cordial. "You're a great addition to the neighborhood. An intelligent man. You must attend one of my meetings. I have recently formed a Philosophical Society to discuss topics of general interest, you know. Several fellows of the Oxford colleges attend. My eldest son is trying for a fellowship at Magdelan this year. A very bright lad, if I say so. Has some wonderful ideas. Thursday nights. Just come along."

"Why not come to dinner this Thursday?" asked his wife. "Then you can join the meeting afterward." She smiled at him. "Or not. Just as you like."

"Of course he will join us," said Mr. Rowntree. "A splendid idea. Do come."

Mr. Erland bowed his thanks and accepted, then took his leave of them. When he was gone, Mr. Rowntree said, "A fine young man. Not at all like most of the frippery fellows these days, interested in nothing but some ridiculous oversprung vehicle or the height of their collars. I approve." He turned toward the door. "I must go back to my study, my dear. I am working on a very interesting little problem, very interesting indeed."

His wife nodded. "Of course, George. The sulfate of ammonia."

He whirled. "What? What did you say?"

"Sulfate of ammonia?" repeated Mrs. Rowntree. "You said when you . . ."

"That's it!" cried her husband. "Sulfate of ammonia!" And he rushed out of the room without shutting the door behind him.

Mrs. Rowntree looked startled for a moment, then shook her head and laughed. She went back to sit beside her daughter on the sofa. "I agree with your father," she said, "though for different reasons, I fear. Our new neighbor is a very pleasant young man. Didn't you think so, Joanna?"

The girl shrugged but said nothing.

"Really, Joanna." Her mother frowned at her. "You were very quiet. You should try to talk more when we have guests."

Joanna looked at her reproachfully, but the older woman did not notice. She was looking thoughtful. "Perhaps we will give a dress party to welcome him to the Abbey. He could meet all his neighbors at once, and we could give him a proper welcome. Yes, I think that would be nice." She glanced at her daughter. "You would like that, would you not, Joanna? We can have some of the young people and perhaps organize a bit of dancing. After all, you are to come out in the spring. You should learn how to go on in a crowd."

"I couldn't dance," answered Joanna dramatically. "I pray you won't ask it of me, Mama."

"Don't be silly. You love dancing."

"No more." The girl looked down and shook her head. "I shall never dance again."

Her mother made an exasperated noise. "I have no patience with you when you are in one of your romantical moods, Joanna. Try for a little common sense, I beg you, and do not be mooning about the house all day. Go for a walk, or take your mare out for a good canter in the fields. I must go and see how Nurse is getting on with Frederick." And with that, she left Joanna alone again.

The girl leaned back on the sofa once more. But her

motive for watching the clock was gone, and it was indeed a fine June day. The scent of early roses drifted in through an open window. After a few minutes, Joanna jumped up and went to fetch a sunshade. She would go for a walk down to the stream and look at the water lilies. They would match the melancholy of her mood precisely.

Two

The next day was Sunday, and though Joanna tried to convince her mother that she was too ill to attend church, Mrs. Rowntree would have none of it. She and her parents set out in the gig at nine and reached the Longton village church as everyone was going in. There was no time to chat before the service, for which Joanna was grateful. Though most of their friends had seen the announcement of Peter Finley's engagement, and many had known of the vague agreement between her family and his, Joanna felt somehow worse now that he was actually married. It made everything so final. She dreaded facing the neighbors after church.

Reverend Williston's sermon seemed woefully short to Joanna, by no means a usual occurrence, and all too soon the family was filing out into the churchyard again. Her father stopped to remind the rector of the meeting on Thursday, and Mrs. Rowntree fell into conversation with one of her friends; all Joanna's hopes of rushing directly to the gig and driving straight home were dashed. As she shifted impatiently from foot to foot beside her mother, there was a tug at her sleeve. She turned to find her best friend, Selina Grant, standing behind her and followed the girl a few steps away.

"Oh, Joanna," said Selina in a dramatic undertone, "are you all right? I was thinking of you all through

21

yesterday. I wanted to come, but Mother kept me at lessons and errands the whole day."

Joanna hung her head and looked stricken. Selina, a romantic damsel one year younger than herself, had entered actively into her feelings during this difficult time, and it was into her sympathetic ear that Joanna poured all her troubles and anxieties.

At her downcast expression, Selina pressed her hand.

"Well, I think it is all very stupid," said a sturdy voice behind them. They turned to find Georgiana, Selina's younger sister, standing there. A young lady of only fourteen summers, she had as yet little interest in affairs of the heart and found her sister's airs tiresome. "Who would want to be married, after all?"

The two older girls looked at her reproachfully, and Selina said, "Keep your voice down, Georgiana, please."

"Huh," sniffed Georgiana.

Selina pulled Joanna a few steps away from her. "Joanna, I must speak to you," she hissed. "I have news."

"What is it?" asked the other girl.

Selina pressed her hand again. "Oh, my dear! If you can only bear it."

"What nonsense," said Georgiana, who had followed them blithely. "You know, Selina, Mama says that if you don't soon outgrow these missish freaks, she'll have to send you to Miss Rich's academy for a year to have some sense put in your head. I heard her tell our aunt so only last week. Who cares a fig whether Peter Finley comes home, I say? He's nothing but a slowtop. He doesn't even ride well. Remember when he was thrown into the horse pond at the Annandale's hunt? He . . ."

"Comes home?" Joanna interrupted. "Here?"

Glaring at her sister, Selina nodded. "We heard of it only yesterday evening. Our housekeeper is very friendly with his. She has had orders to prepare the house. They are arriving this week."

Joanna put a hand to her mouth. "Oh, no."

22

Selina nodded sympathetically. "I thought you would wish to know immediately. To prepare yourself, you know."

"What rubbish!" exclaimed Georgiana, and she flounced away in disgust.

Watching her go, Selina shook her head. "I cannot think how I came to have a sister so lacking in sensibility. Can she be a changeling, do you think?"

But Joanna had no time for Georgiana. "Oh, Selina, what shall I do? I am bound to meet them sooner or later; this is such a small neighborhood. How can I face him?"

The other girl clasped her hands before her. "Oh, I know how you must feel. But you must be strong. You must not allow your feelings to show. They say *she* is very proud and unpleasant, you know, and I'm sure she would be rude to you if she knew of Peter's attachment."

"Attachment," echoed Joanna, laughing hollowly.

"He *was* attached to you," insisted her friend. "Anyone could see that. I am certain she entrapped him. I daresay Peter will be miserable in his marriage." Her expression reflected satisfaction with this notion.

"Oh, no," replied Joanna softly. "I could never wish that."

"Well, it will be his own fault. They say she has a sharp tongue and is used to her own way. We shall see." She looked wise.

"Who says? Where have you heard these things?"

"My Uncle William. Did I not tell you? But no, I have not seen you since their visit last week. I meant to come Friday, but Mother insisted that I go with her on some stupid errand in Oxford, and we returned too late. And then yesterday, I told you . . ."

"But what did he say?" asked Joanna impatiently.

"Well, I have told you most of it. My uncle says the Denbys were a very rich family. Her father was a nabob, in India, you know. He made piles of money there—in trade of some kind." Selina's pug nose tried to point superciliously. "And he left his two children very well off.

But the son, Sir Rollin, gambled all his money away. And they say his sister wouldn't help him at all. She kept all her money for herself."

"How horrid!" exclaimed Joanna. "If Gerald or Frederick needed money, I should give it to them instantly." She imagined herself doing so, with great magnanimity.

"Of course you would," agreed Selina. "But she is very proud and hard, you see. And my uncle said that she has been hanging out for a husband these three years at least. She is older than Peter."

"No!" said Joanna, shocked. "How old is she?"

"Five or six and twenty, my uncle says. And no one in London wished to marry her because she is so disagreeable. I am sure she ensnared Peter in some low way."

"Your uncle told you all this?" asked the other, wide-eyed.

Selina colored. "Well, no, not precisely," she admitted. "I heard him talking to Mama. I couldn't help it—the drawing-room door was wide open, and they were speaking quite loudly."

Joanna disregarded this, shaking her head and murmuring, "Oh dear, poor Peter."

Selina was about to go on when they were joined by Constance Williston, the daughter of the vicar. Constance was some months older than Joanna, and whether because she had been at school in Bath or because she was a slender willowy blonde, Joanna and the short, freckled Selina disliked her. Constance had been home from school for a month, and they had resolutely ignored her overtures.

"Good day," said Constance pleasantly. "Isn't the weather splendid?"

"Yes, indeed," answered Selina quickly, moving closer to Joanna. "Not at all hot."

"No. In fact, I was thinking of taking a walk this afternoon, to see the flowers in the fields. Would you care to come with me? We could have tea afterward at my house."

24

"I'm sorry," said Selina, "I can't today."

This ungracious reply made Joanna frown a little, but she also said, "I—I can't either. I promised Mama I would help her with, ah, something." Joanna flushed and felt guilty.

Constance's eyes dropped. "Ah, too bad. Another time perhaps." And she turned and walked away.

"Oh dear," said Joanna. "Perhaps we should go."

"Why? She would only go on and on about some weed or other, and we could not talk about anything *important* with her there. No, we must hold a conference and decide what to do."

"There is nothing we can do," sighed Joanna.

Before Selina could protest, a male voice interrupted them. "Good morning, Miss Joanna," said Jonathan Erland. "A lovely morning, is it not?"

Joanna turned to face him and agreed without much enthusiasm. Mr. Erland wore a different, newer coat of dark blue superfine today, but it was hardly more modish than the other she had seen. Everything about him bespoke his provincial travels.

Selina inched forward, and Joanna presented her. Her friend's sandy brows went up when she heard who the stranger was. "You are going to *live* at the Abbey?" she cried. "Oh, how can you? I am sure it is haunted. All those crumbling ruins behind."

Jonathan laughed. "Well, the ruins may be haunted, to be sure. Perhaps the old monks, or nuns—I'm not precisely certain which it was—are still angry about being evicted. But I doubt they come into the house. It's such a dashed uncomfortable place, no sensible ghost would set foot in it." He grinned engagingly at the girls, but they returned his gaze blankly.

Then Selina shivered. "Well, I do not understand how anyone could live with acres of crumbling ruins practically in one's back garden. Why hasn't someone cleared them all out, I wonder?"

"What? And spoil the atmosphere of mystery that surrounds the place?" asked Erland, still smiling.

Selina seemed much struck by this. "Would it? Yes, I suppose so. But still, all those old walls and pits; does it not make you shudder to see it every day?"

"I fear my sensibilities are too hardened," he replied. "But Mr. Rowntree may grant your wish. He plans to get up a group to clear it out, I understand." Erland turned to Joanna. "Or at least so thoroughly categorize it that no ghost will be left an inch of space. Isn't that so, Miss Joanna."

"Oh, I—I don't know," stammered Joanna.

"He does. Will you join the digging party, perhaps?"

The corners of Joanna's mouth turned down. "I shall not be asked. Father thinks me quite heedless and silly." There was a trace of bitterness in her tone.

Erland blinked. "Ah. Well, I daresay it will be a dull dirty job." Sensing constraint, he changed the subject. "I believe your mother mentioned that you are fond of riding, Miss Rowntree?"

Joanna nodded.

"I, too," he continued. "Perhaps one day soon you will join me and show me the best rides hereabouts. I should be grateful; I am quite bored with the ones I know."

Joanna shrugged. "All right," she said rather ungraciously, "if Mama approves." Privately, she thought that she would not. Joanna had never been allowed to join such expeditions.

"Of course. And you must come also, Miss, ah, Grant."

"I hate riding," said Selina positively.

"Ah."

"Selina," called Georgiana from behind them, "we're going."

Her sister turned with an angry sigh, then shrugged and said goodbye. "I shall walk over to see you later this afternoon, Joanna," she said as she left.

"I see that your parents are also ready to leave," said Erland when she was gone. "May I escort you to them?" He offered his arm, and Joanna took it, but her

26

mind was far away, wondering when the Finleys were coming home and how she could greet them with even the appearance of calm.

When they reached the gig, Erland bowed. "Good day. You won't forget, I hope, Miss Joanna?"

"Forget?"

"About our ride."

"Oh, oh no."

As the gig drove off, Jonathan Erland watched it with a combination of amusement and irony showing in his face.

Selina Grant arrived at the Rowntrees' about three o'clock. The two girls went directly to one of their favorite haunts, an arbor at the back of the garden overgrown with white roses. Here, they had played with their dolls and sat through long summer afternoons talking, reading, or writing letters. And here this spring, they had excitedly begun to plan Joanna's wedding. On this sunny June day, the place was fragrant and filled with the humming of bees.

"Oh, Joanna," said Selina when they were alone, "they are coming this very week. It may even be tomorrow!"

"What, so soon after the wedding?"

Selina nodded. "She wants to see the house right away and start the workmen redecorating. That's what the housekeeper says. The servants are in a worry, wondering what changes she plans to make."

Joanna sighed. "Mother will make me go when she calls on her. I know she will. She doesn't understand at all."

"Couldn't you pretend to be ill?"

"She wouldn't believe me."

The two girls contemplated this grim prospect in silence for some moments. After a while, Selina said, "I wouldn't come into the country on my honeymoon. What a slowtop Peter is. I should go to Paris."

Joanna bridled.

"I daresay it was all her notion," added Selina hur-

27

riedly. "She wants to take over the household as soon as possible." There was a short pause. "I was never more surprised in my life than when Mr. Erland joined us this morning," she continued. "When did he arrive at the Abbey? I had no idea."

Listlessly, Joanna repeated what she had learned during his visit.

"No money!" exclaimed the other. "Well, what a take-in. After the way old Mr. Erland squeezed every penny, I should think there would be piles of it." When Joanna made no reply, she added, "Do you think he is handsome?"

Roused, Joanna stared at her. "Mr. Erland?"

"Yes. He has a kind of masterful manner, does he not?"

The other girl was speechless for a moment, then she burst out, "Masterful? Selina, whatever can you be thinking of? He has no style at all. His coats look as if they were made for someone else. He has never even been to London, I believe."

"Well, of course he does not compare with men of fashion," Selina responded hurriedly. "How could he after all, if he has been abroad for years and years? I only meant he seemed a pleasant, well-mannered man."

"As well-mannered as one can be who has never had the advantages of mingling with the *ton*," said Joanna haughtily.

Selina began to giggle. "Oh, Joanna, you should have seen your face when you said that. You looked the picture of disdain, just like my Aunt Arabella from London."

This idea did not displease Joanna. "He is well enough," she continued in measured tones, "but he has missed the finer things of life and will never be truly cultivated."

"Will you really go riding with him?" asked Selina. "Do you think your mother will allow it?"

Joanna frowned. "I don't know. She said yesterday

that I might dance at the dress party. I'm to come out in London next season, you know." Suddenly recalling, she added, "Or I was to have come out. I cannot go now, of course."

"What dress party?" asked her friend eagerly, for once ignoring Joanna's plight.

"Oh, Mama plans to give one to welcome Mr. Erland to the neighborhood."

"With dancing?"

"Yes."

Selina clasped her hands. "Oh, if only Mother will let me dance." Her face fell. "I don't suppose she will, though. She is always scolding me for being pert and forward." She grimaced. "How I hate not being out!"

Joanna was looking at the garden wall and did not appear to hear.

"But you, Joanna, you will dance. That means you are practically out already. You will be invited to everything once that is known. How lucky you are."

"I shan't come out," said Joanna sadly.

"What!" cried Selina, aghast. "Not come out? What do you mean?"

Joanna shook her head. "My hopes are blighted. I shall dwindle into an old spinster like Miss Snell at Longton."

"Well, yes, of course. But not go to London? Joanna!"

Before Joanna could explain to her friend why it was impossible for her to go to London, even with Peter Finley removed from it, they were interrupted by the approach of her brother Frederick, limping down the path with the aid of his father's stick. He came up and lowered himself beside them in the arbor.

"What do you want, Frederick?" asked Joanna impatiently. "We are talking."

"I could see that," retorted the young gentleman. "That's why I came out. It's dashed dull inside—nothing to do but read."

"How did you hurt your foot?" asked Selina, and Joanna glared at her. Asking Frederick questions was no way to get rid of him.

Enthusiastically, Frederick launched into the story of his adventure at the Abbey. "I was just walking along the top of an old wall in the front part of the ruin when two of the stones gave way, and I fell. What a stupid accident." He looked at his ankle. "The doctor says I shall be hobbling for weeks—worse luck."

"But why did you wish to climb the walls of the ruins?" asked Selina. She shivered. "I don't like it there."

Frederick eyed her with contempt, then leaned forward conspiratorially. "I was looking for the treasure," he whispered.

Selina's eyes widened. She stared at him for a moment, then said, "What treasure?"

"Old man Erland's treasure. I wager it's in the ruins, though Jack Williston thinks it's in the house. I might have found it that very day, and now it will be ages before I can hunt again. Someone will probably get in ahead of me."

Selina leaned back and smiled condescendingly. "You cannot really believe there is treasure buried at the Abbey. It is *too* ridiculous."

Frederick sat up straighter. "What's ridiculous about it? Old man Erland was the greatest clutchfist in nature. Why shouldn't he have hidden his money? Misers do, you know."

"But he would have told someone before he died."

The boy shook his head. "Not he. They never do. Can't stand the idea of anyone else getting their hands on the money. I know it's there. I was looking for a place that had been dug. I'll find it, too, when my cursed ankle heals."

"Well, you wouldn't be allowed to keep a treasure, if you did find it," snapped Joanna. "Frederick, do run along and look for Mama. I daresay she will play a game with you."

30

"Not keep it!" cried her brother, outraged. "And why should I not? If I find it, it's mine by right."

"Nonsense. It would belong to the estate."

Frederick looked defiant. "Then I shan't tell when I do find it. I shall hide it again and use it when I'm older. To buy my own curricle."

Joanna turned away with an exasperated exclamation, but Selina and Frederick argued spiritedly for some time over the relative merits of his plan. By the time they had finished, it was five, and Selina had to go. Thus, the two girls had no chance to work out a plan, and Joanna was left to discover for herself how she should face the new Mrs. Finley.

Three

Joanna heard no further word of the Finleys before the Thursday that Jonathan Erland was to dine at the Rowntrees'. As she dressed for dinner that evening, she wondered yet again when they would arrive. Waiting for the event was worse, she thought, than experiencing it could possibly be.

As she brushed her brown curls into clusters over her ears, her mother came into the bedroom. "Oh, Joanna," she said immediately, "not the blue dress. It's so old. You must wear your new white muslin with the yellow ribbons."

Joanna stared. "The new dress? But, Mama, you said I was only to wear it on special occasions."

Mrs. Rowntree's eyes dropped. "Well, this is a special occasion, is it not? How often do we have a dinner guest? And your father's friends will be coming later. Do change, Joanna."

Joanna frowned, then shrugged, turning to allow her mother to unbutton the blue dress. "I thought to wear the white at our dress party," she said as she struggled out of it. "It is my best. But I suppose I can still do so."

"Oh, no. You must have a new gown for that."

Joanna stared. "Another new gown?"

Her mother laughed. "You will need a great many new dresses for your coming out, my dear. You must get used to them."

33

Joanna frowned again, started to speak, then turned away to get the white dress from her wardrobe.

A quarter of an hour later, she went down to the drawing room. Both her parents were before her. Her mother, looking splendid in deep rose pink, sat on the sofa before the fireplace, knotting a fringe. Her father, whose blue coat and bluff pantaloons looked a bit disarranged, was at a small table in the corner, leaning over a scrap of paper and talking to himself. When Joanna came in, Mrs. Rowntree looked up and smiled. "Very pretty, my dear," she said. "The yellow ribbons were a good choice. Doesn't Joanna look well, George?"

Her husband did not respond until she repeated the question. Then, he gazed vaguely in Joanna's direction and murmured, "Ah, yes, just so."

Mrs. Rowntree smiled and motioned for Joanna to sit beside her. The girl did so, but she was not smiling.

"Where is Frederick?" she asked.

"I thought he might eat his dinner in his room this evening. He will walk about on that ankle, so it is not healing as fast as it should. I have told Nurse to keep him in bed tonight. If anyone can do it, she can."

Joanna nodded absently, and silence fell again. Her father continued to mutter. She heard him say, "Divided into three, and then six parts, one to be combined with saltpeter, another with sulfur, and so on." She watched him for a moment with a wistful expression.

Mrs. Rowntree gazed thoughtfully at her daughter, as if trying to solve some abstruse problem of her own.

As the mantel clock was striking seven, the maid brought Jonathan Erland to the drawing room. He was dressed in his blue coat again, and Joanna thought his neckcloth ridiculous. It was almost as clumsy as her father's. Mr. Rowntree came out of his corner, and they all sat down together.

"How comfortable this is," said Erland immediately, leaning back in the armchair with a sigh. "You cannot imagine what a week I have had. I do not believe that there is a chimney at the Abbey that does not smoke, a corner that is not piled with dust and cobwebs, or a decent joint or bottle to be had. Mrs. Smith utterly cows me when I venture to complain. I do not understand how my uncle tolerated that woman." He smiled to take the sting from these words, but it was clear that he meant them.

Mrs. Rowntree returned the smile. "Your uncle had a very limited and unusual conception of a housekeeper's duties, I believe, Mr. Erland. He wished only to curb expenditure. Mrs. Smith excels at that, I think."

"Only too well," agreed their guest. "I think she buys spoiled meat because it is dirt cheap. And I know she tried to cheat the baker; he has complained to me. There's no help for it; I must pension her off and find a new housekeeper. I can't go on as I am."

"No indeed," put in Mr. Rowntree unexpectedly. "A man must not be distracted by domestic problems. It is fatal to the logical faculties. You must be surrounded by a smoothly running household to allow the mind to run smoothly as well."

Mrs. Rowntree laughed a little, and Erland agreed with a smile. Only Joanna made no response. Glancing at her, Erland was surprised to see an almost resentful look on her face.

"Tell us more about your Canadian travels," said Rowntree jovially. And Joanna resigned herself to boredom until dinner was announced.

Conversation over dinner consisted of Erland's praises of the food and his answers to Mr. Rowntree's questions about the wilderness. Joanna was glad to rise at her mother's signal and retreat to the drawing room once more. She was heartily sick of Canada, she thought defiantly, and she hoped that rather than joining them, the gentlemen would go directly to the library, where her father's society was to meet at nine. When her mother made an innocuous remark about how unfortunate it was that Gerald could not come this evening, Joanna said only, "Humph."

She got half her wish. Her father did not appear

after dinner. But Erland came in soon after them and sat down beside her mother on the sofa. He complimented her yet again on the dinner, then turned to Joanna with the air of a man who meant to become better acquainted. "I have not forgotten your promise, you know," he said lightly. "And I mean to hold you to it, as soon as I can find the time."

"Promise?" echoed Joanna blankly.

"Yes. Have you forgotten we are to go riding together?"

"Oh. Oh, no."

He smiled at her, his gray eyes lighting. "I think perhaps you did. But as I say, I hold you to it. Perhaps on Saturday?"

"Well, I am not sure . . ." Joanna looked to her mother.

Mrs. Rowntree nodded. "That sounds like a splendid scheme. You have not taken your mare out all week, Joanna."

"It's settled then. You must come. Your mare will be wanting the exercise." He looked into her eyes. "And I am sorely in need of guidance. I know there must be some charming rides in the neighborhood, but I have lost myself four times searching them out. You must show me."

Joanna smiled at the idea of Erland lost in the fields. "All right," she said, though she was not certain she really wished to go.

Erland opened his mouth to say something further, but at that moment, one of the maids came in and announced, "Mr. and Mrs. Peter Finley, ma'am, and Sir Rollin Denby." And before Joanna and her mother could do more than open their eyes in astonishment, the three callers were walking into the room.

Joanna's eyes were drawn first to Peter, in spite of herself. He stood between the two strangers, looking somehow small and rather uncomfortable. His pale blond hair had been cut in London and was brushed into a modish Brutus. But it was his clothes that made Joanna blink. Peter had always been interested in fashion and had driven his Oxford tailors nearly frantic with constant requests for the very latest in London styles. Joanna had admired his clothes excessively. But she had never seen anything so magnificent as the outfit he now wore. His coat was pale blue and his pantaloons the palest fawn—the cut was exquisite. And the height of his shirtpoints, the arresting pattern of his waistcoat, and the mirror gloss of his high Hessian boots nearly overwhelmed her. She swayed slightly and was hardly able to stammer a reply when her mother greeted the trio and made the necessary introductions.

Joanna sat down again and tore her eyes from Peter to study his wife. She had received the impression of height when the callers came in, and now she saw that, as she feared, Adrienne Finley was tall. Indeed, she appeared to be slightly taller than Peter, who was a slight gentleman. Her figure was statuesque and her blue evening dress magnificent, especially since she wore it with a stunning string of sapphires around her neck. But when Joanna raised her eyes to Mrs. Finley's face, she felt some slight relief. The newcomer was not beautiful, and she was not truly blonde. Her hair was a light brown, as was her complexion, and her rather prominent eyes were green. With a start, Joanna realized that her scrutiny was being returned, and she dropped her eyes. Adrienne Finley smiled.

As Joanna looked at the floor, Peter greeted her mother and nervously apologized for their unannounced call. "We were just—just passing by, you see," he stammered. His eyes avoided theirs.

"Peter darling," drawled his wife in a deep careless voice. "You may as well tell the truth." She smiled brilliantly at Mrs. Rowntree. "It is completely my fault that we intrude on you. I am so eager, you see, to make the acquaintance of all Peter's neighbors, *our* neighbors now, and to get everything comfortable and clear." Her emphasis on this last word made. Joanna jump. When the younger girl looked up nervously, she found that Mrs. Finley's eyes were still on her face. She dropped her eyes again.

Mrs. Rowntree made a rather unintelligible reply.

"I do think it's important for neighbors to understand one another, don't you?" Adrienne went on sweetly. "One can be made so miserable by misunderstandings when one lives so close."

Joanna's mother had by now recovered her poise, and she agreed blandly, ignoring the edge in her guest's voice. Mrs. Rowntree expertly turned the conversation to London and addressed Peter again. The rigid set of her mouth revealed what she thought of this unusual situation.

Adrienne joined the conversation, and though she continued to express strong opinions, it seemed that she felt she had made her point. After a while, Joanna was able to raise her eyes once more. She turned with some curiosity to the party's third member.

Sir Rollin Denby did not much resemble his sister: he was a tall man with the shoulders and bearing of an athlete and the careless arrogance of one who usually got his own way. His hair was black and his complexion dark, almost swarthy. His eyes were a sparkling hazel. At first, Joanna thought Peter the better dressed, but as she looked again, she realized that the cut of Sir Rollin's dark blue coat was far more subtle and complex, his less noticeable neckcloth much more elegant, and his waistcoat a marvel of understated fashion. She raised her eyes again and met his. He smiled at her, and a chill seemed to run quickly down her spine. She had never before seen such a man.

"Yes," Peter was saying, "just got in last night. The house is hardly ready, but Adrienne—we all—wanted to come right down."

"I think servants must be made to see, as soon as possible, what is expected of them when a change is made," added Adrienne. "Don't you agree, Mrs. Rowntree?"

"It is always wise to be open," replied the latter coldly. Joanna marveled at her mother's politely distant manner. "You are established in the country for some time then?" continued the hostess.

"Oh, yes," answered Adrienne quickly. "The household will require a great deal of work. Bachelors never know how to manage servants." She looked at Peter from under lowered lashes, and he both smiled and seemed to wince.

"You also will be staying with us, Sir Rollin?" asked Mrs. Rowntree, trying to draw the third guest into the conversation.

"I don't quite know," he responded in a deep resonant voice. "My plans are not fixed. In fact, I must take some of the blame for disturbing you tonight. Peter has told us so much about your charming family, you see, that I insisted we call straightaway. My visit may be cut short, so I wished to make your acquaintance as soon as possible." He smiled again. Joanna was suddenly reminded of the cook's cat, a ferocious beast, though she couldn't think why.

"You are going to your own house perhaps," said Joanna's mother, without marked enthusiasm.

Sir Rollin made an airy gesture. "Most probably not. I shall go to Brighton at some point. Prinny expects me to dance attendance during the summer."

Joanna breathed an audible sigh. "The Prince Regent?" she murmured, then blushed fierily.

Sir Rollin nodded as he and his sister exchanged a smile.

"So," interjected Peter, with a heartiness that rang false, "you're the new owner of Erland Abbey. Very happy to meet you. When did you arrive?"

"Very recently," replied Jonathan Erland. His calm disinterested tone sounded strange to Joanna. She had almost forgotten he was there.

"Glad to see it," continued Finley. "Your uncle was a poor landlord, I have to say. Everyone will welcome a new man at the Abbey."

Erland bowed courteously but said nothing.

"Is the Abbey the large house we passed as we drove in?" asked Adrienne. On being told that it was, she smiled graciously at Erland and said that he must come to dinner when they were settled. Until then, she had paid little heed to the undistinguished young man in the corner seat.

The drawing-room door opened abruptly, and Mr. Rowntree strode into the room. "Erland," he said, "come along. Nearly everyone has arrived and we're ready to begin." He seemed to notice the others in the room then, looked at them vaguely, then turned to his wife.

"It is Peter Finley, dear," said Mrs. Rowntree helpfully, "returned from London with his wife and her brother, Sir Rollin Denby."

Her husband frowned as he surveyed the guests again. "Wife?" he repeated, as if mystified.

Peter moved uneasily; Adrienne raised her eyebrows and returned Mr. Rowntree's gaze; Sir Rollin smiled sardonically.

Their host started. "Well, that is of no consequence. Are you ready to come down, Erland?"

Jonathan Erland scanned the faces around him. "In a moment," he said. "You begin without me, and I will join you later."

Rowntree frowned. "It is very difficult to follow a discussion from the middle, you know. You'd best come now."

"A few moments only," answered Erland firmly.

His host shrugged and started to turn away.

"What sort of discussion?" asked Sir Rollin.

Rowntree looked at him as if he could not quite recall who he was, but he explained his society and its purposes eagerly. "The topic this evening is the relation of natural science to ethics," he finished. "All interested are welcome." He looked at Sir Rollin.

"I fear that is a bit beyond my depth," replied that gentleman. "Another time perhaps."

But Rowntree had already forgotten him and was walking to the door. Sir Rollin smiled wryly and glanced at his sister. They exchanged an amused look; and Adrienne shook her head very slightly.

Joanna blushed again. Suddenly, under Sir Rollin's sardonic eye, she saw her hitherto infallible father as eccentric and slightly ridiculous.

Silence fell. Mrs. Rowntree seemed annoyed and said nothing to break it. Peter appeared to be searching in vain for something to say. And Adrienne and Sir Rollin surveyed them all with amusement.

Jonathan Erland was also watching the group, though no amusement showed in his eyes. When his gaze met Sir Rollin's, he said, "Is this your first visit to this neighborhood also? I take it you live in London?"

"Yes on both counts," drawled the other man lazily. "Frankly, I cannot imagine living anywhere else."

"Ah. You are fond of town life."

Denby raised his eyebrows. "Is there any other sort?"

Erland's answering smile held some mockery. "Well, I think so, of course, but I am by no means an expert, never having lived in town."

"Indeed? I can scarcely credit it." But Sir Rollin's eyes, moving slowly up and down Erland's unfashionable figure, said just the opposite.

Joanna's eyes widened, and she expected the younger man to retort angrily. Denby's implication had been clearly insulting. But to everyone's surprise, particularly Sir Rollin's, Jonathan Erland burst into hearty laughter. He was so amused, in fact, that it took him a moment to regain his composure. Joanna, Peter, and Adrienne stared at him incredulously, the latter seeming to doubt the stranger's sanity. Mrs. Rowntree frowned slightly at first, then smiled. Sir Rollin's eyes narrowed, and he looked at the other man more closely than he had before.

Gradually, Erland recovered, though his eyes remained crinkled with amusement. "Pardon me," he said at last. He rose. "I must go down and join Mr. Rowntree," he said to his hostess. "Shall I see you after?"

Joanna's mother also rose, shaking her head. "George's discussions go on very late. We shall all be in bed long since."

"Ah, too bad. Then I shall take my leave of you now. Miss Joanna, do not forget our ride." He bowed. "A pleasure to meet you all." And with that, he left the room.

They all gazed at the door for a moment. "What a very unusual young man," murmured Adrienne.

Joanna started visibly when the door opened again, but it was only Mary with the tea tray, a welcome diversion. Mrs. Rowntree served tea and initiated a determined monologue on the beauties of the neighborhood. She was feebly seconded in this by Peter, his wife occasionally putting in a word and Sir Rollin maintaining an air of mildly bored attention. It was with obvious relief that Mrs. Rowntree rose to see them out later that evening, and when she returned to the sofa, she sighed quite audibly. "What an uncomfortable evening," she said to her daughter. "What can Peter have been about, to descend upon us in this way? It was quite monstrous."

"Perhaps she made him do it," suggested Joanna.

Mrs. Rowntree opened her mouth, then shut it again. "Perhaps," she replied shortly.

"And Sir Rollin," added Joanna.

"Yes, indeed. More than likely he hoped to make some mischief; that seems his style."

"Do you think him handsome?"

"Sir Rollin?" The older woman looked at her daughter sharply. "Not particularly. He is too dark."

"Yes," replied Joanna slowly, "but he is quite distinguished, is he not? Such an air. And I have never seen a more elegant coat."

Mrs. Rowntree sat back on the sofa and raised a hand to massage her forehead.

"Peter looked very modish, of course," continued

Joanna, "but Sir Rollin had much more, ah, polish, did he not?"

"Yes, he did," agreed her mother heavily.

"I have never met anyone like him."

"No."

Joanna suddenly remembered her broken heart. "It was very hard to see Peter again, of course. I thought my heart would stop when he was announced. He has changed. He seems much more, ah, quiet. Don't you think? And his wife is not what I should have expected."

Mrs. Rowntree shrugged.

"I suppose we will have to call on her?"

"Of course."

"Well, I am not certain I shall ever be able to like her. But I shall be polite."

"Of course," said her mother again.

"Do you suppose Sir Rollin will stay long?"

Mrs. Rowntree sighed. "I imagine not," she said. "He seemed the sort of man who will be bored with our country neighborhood quite soon."

Joanna nodded. "Yes. He will go to Brighton, I daresay." She sighed. "The Prince Regent," she murmured once again.

Mrs. Rowntree's heart sank.

Four

The next morning, Joanna was up betimes, and as soon as she had dressed and breakfasted, she set off across the fields to Selina Grant's house. The path through the rolling, walled meadows was well-worn; she and Selina had used it almost daily for more than ten years, and Joanna hardly needed to look down as she strode swiftly along. She thought instead of the encounter last night. It had not happened at all as she expected, but it had been embarrassing enough. What an awful creature Peter's wife was!

It took only half an hour to reach Selina's, and Joanna was soon seated in the garden, pouring out the story. But Selina was less surprised than she had expected. "Oh, yes," her friend replied, "I knew they were here. They called on the vicar yesterday afternoon and left cards at the Townsends' and here. She is certainly wasting no time in showing herself to the neighborhood."

Joanna nodded. "But you did not meet her?"

Selina shook her head regretfully. "We were out. Mother would go to visit old Mrs. Ives. Is she very horrid?"

"An odious managing female."

"Didn't I tell you!" cried Selina triumphantly. "She trapped Peter into marriage, and now he will be quite miserable."

"Selina, don't," said Joanna.

"Well, it is his own fault. What is the brother like? Is he odious also?"

Joanna looked away. "Oh, no. He is, well, magnificent. I have never seen anyone like him."

"My uncle says he is very attractive to women," added her friend. "He says that all sorts of girls fall in love with Sir Rollin. But he is hanging out for a rich wife, so he only flirts with them and then ignores them." She lowered her voice and looked about the garden to see that her mother had not come out. "He is a—a rake," she whispered.

Joanna's eyes widened, but she tried to look superior. "I daresay," she answered.

Selina gaped. "Did he flirt with *you*, Joanna?"

The other girl raised her eyebrows. "Would that be so astonishing?"

"Well, no, but . . . but did he?"

Joanna looked tempted, but she was obliged to say, "No, not really. My mother was there, you know, and the others."

"Yes, that is fortunate. We must take care not to be alone with him, ever." Selina looked both pleased and excited by this idea.

"Why?"

"Well, because, because . . ." Selina stopped, finding herself at a loss for words.

"Why should I not flirt a little?" asked Joanna defiantly. "After all, my life is blighted. Why should I not have some amusement after my disappointment?"

"But, but Joanna," stammered the other, "he is a dangerous man. My uncle said . . ."

"Nonsense. What could he do to us here?" She gestured around the garden, which did indeed look very peaceful and safe. "I am only talking about a little flirtation."

"But he is a rake."

"What do you know of rakes?" answered Joanna, in such a loud voice that her friend was startled.

"Nothing," retorted Selina. "and neither do you, so you needn't look so haughty. But my uncle does, and he told my mother . . ."

"Oh, I am sick of your uncle and what he says," cried Joanna, jumping up. "I daresay he is quite mistaken in any case. He is so odiously starched-up that he thinks he knows everything, but he is nothing but a hanger-on at court, after all. I heard Mr. Townsend say so."

"Joanna!"

Joanna was surprised and rather ashamed at her outburst, but for some reason, she felt it was imperative to divert her friend from the question of Sir Rollin Denby's character. "He did say so," she repeated, sounding more like a sulky child than a young lady of eighteen.

"Well, it was monstrous mean and spiteful of him, and it is mean of you to repeat it."

Joanna drew herself up. "If that is what you think, perhaps I had better go." She turned and started toward the gate that led into the fields. She expected every moment to be called back, but Selina made no move. As she walked rapidly along the footpath, Joanna listened for steps behind her. Selina had never allowed a quarrel between them to last more than a few minutes. But this time, she did not follow, and when Joanna was half way home, she realized that she would not. Her steps slowed, and she hung her head a little. She had been rude, she supposed, and unreasonable. Why had she spoken so? Thinking back over their talk, Joanna really could not tell. What had made her so angry? She *had* been silly. But could Selina not see that she didn't wish to hear her uncle's silly gossip?

She walked on more slowly, her mood alternating between chagrin and defiance and her eyes focused unseeingly on the grass at her feet. She did not see the figure picking flowers in the field to her right until she was hailed and turned to find Constance Williston beside her.

"How deeply occupied you were," said Constance. "I hope I do not disturb your thoughts."

"No," replied Joanna, but her tone was not welcoming.

The older girl reddened slightly. "I was picking wild flowers," she added, showing her basket of blooms. "My mother loves them so. But she is too busy with the children to look for them. So I try to make up a bouquet now and then for her room."

The delicate blues and yellows in the basket attracted Joanna in spite of herself, and she bent to smell. "They're lovely."

Constance smiled, her rather narrow face lighting. "Aren't they? I found one bluebell, down by the stream. It's so late, but all the more beautiful for that, don't you think?" She pulled out this flower and held it up.

Joanna nodded but said nothing.

"Are you going home?" asked Constance. "I must pass by old Mrs. Rouse's on my way, to leave some liniment Mother made for her. I could walk along with you." She sounded both eager and uncertain.

Joanna blinked. Since Constance had returned from school, she had thought little about her beyond twinges of envy at the older girl's apparent assurance and graceful height. Now, the tone of her voice made Joanna examine her more closely. Constance looked like someone who expects a rebuff, yet is still hopeful. And suddenly, Joanna realized that Constance must be very lonely in this neighborhood. She and Selina were the only girls near her age; Constance's sisters were all much younger. And the two of them had shut her out completely. Some of Joanna's envy melted, and she said, "Of course, do come along. I am very stupid this morning and have been quarreling. You must forgive me." She frowned as soon as she had said this, for she did not at all wish to tell Constance that she had quarreled with Selina.

But Constance said only, "Splendid," as she dropped into step with Joanna. And immediately afterward, she began to talk innocuously of flowers once more.

Joanna listened more attentively than she might otherwise have, thinking that Constance was very understanding. She asked a few questions about the flowers in the field around them, and the other girl answered with a surprising amount of knowledge. This had gone on for some minutes when Constance abruptly stopped speaking and said, "But you mustn't let me prose on in this way. Father says that I am mad on the subject of flowers. I didn't mean to bore you."

"You did not," said Joanna quite truthfully. "You certainly know a great deal about wildflowers. Did you learn it at school?"

The older girl nodded, her cheeks reddening slightly. "The senior teacher interested me in the subject, and I—I took it up on my own. You must think me very silly."

Joanna's eyes widened. The idea that she could think this very superior girl silly startled her. "Not at all. I only wish I had gone to school. But my father wished to educate me himself." She sighed as she remembered the long sessions in his study, where she had understood perhaps a quarter of the things her father said.

"Oh, it is you who were lucky," replied Constance quickly. "My father says that yours is one of the most brilliant scholars he has ever met. How much you must have learned that the rest of us will never have the chance to know."

Joanna smiled ruefully, but did not disillusion the other girl, who had sounded quite rapt. She was not averse to being thought wise by the self-possessed Miss Williston.

A silence fell, but before it could become uncomfortable, Joanna suddenly remembered something. "I believe I heard that the Finleys called at the vicarage," she said.

Constance started. "Yes." She looked at Joanna sidelong.

"They called on us also," said the other, unheeding. "I found Mrs. Finley a bit overpowering."

"Y—yes. She seems very sure of herself." Constance sounded wistful.

"Yes, well, she is older."

Constance stared at her, seemingly unable to think of a reply.

Joanna noticed her expression and continued, "You have heard, I daresay, that there was once some talk of Peter and me making a match of it. Indeed, he has always been one of my best friends. I do so hope he will be happy." She allowed a hint of doubt to creep into her voice.

Constance seemed impressed. "You are magnanimous," she murmured. "I hope that I could be so."

"Oh, well," replied Joanna vaguely, feeling very noble. "Did you meet Sir Rollin Denby also?"

The other girl wrinkled her nose. "Yes. But I must say I did not like him overmuch."

"Did you not?"

"No. He has that kind of sneering, careless manner that I find insufferable. There are many such men in London; it is the fashion. But I do not care for it."

Joanna looked at her. She sounded so positive. She knew that Constance had already spent three weeks in London at her aunt's house and that she was to return for next season, when Joanna was also to be in town. "Why not?" she asked.

Constance frowned. "A good question, since I believe Sir Rollin's type is often thought to be very attractive to women. I think it is because they lack kindness and humanity." She paused and laughed self-consciously. "At least to my eye. But I am by no means knowledgeable on this subject."

That was true, thought Joanna. "Perhaps one must know them well before one sees their kindness," she ventured.

Constance bowed her head. "That may be. Many of them have a large circle of male friends, I think. And I do not wish to condemn a stranger." She looked about them; they were near Joanna's house by this time. "Here is where I turn off for Mrs. Rouse's. I enjoyed our talk very much, Joanna. I hope we may repeat it." The diffidence was back in her voice.

"Indeed, I hope so, too," answered Joanna warmly. "Let us do so soon."

Constance smiled brilliantly. "Yes, please." And as she turned to walk away, she waved gaily.

Joanna was thoughtful when she entered the hall. It seemed to her that much had happened during the morning. It was scarcely time for luncheon, yet she had perhaps lost a friend and gained one in the space of a few hours. When her mother came to ask Joanna about some sewing she had promised to do, she had to speak twice before the girl heard.

Five

By the next morning, Joanna had resolved to apologize to Selina. She concluded that she had indeed been unreasonable, and her behavior now seemed demented. But as she was putting on her bonnet before leaving the house, one of the maids came to her bedroom to tell her that Mr. Erland had arrived to fetch her for their ride. With a muffled exclamation of annoyance, Joanna put down the hat. She had completely forgotten about this appointment. For a moment, she thought of putting him off, pleading a headache or some other trifling illness, but then she shrugged and began to unbutton her morning gown. She pulled her riding habit out of the wardrobe and put it on, and in the space of ten minutes was ready to go downstairs. But her expression as she descended showed more resignation than anticipation.

Jonathan Erland was talking to her mother in the drawing room; he rose when Joanna entered. His gray eyes were appreciative, and indeed, Joanna made a charming picture in her rose pink habit. Her eyes looked almost black against the bright background, and they seemed large in her heart-shaped face.

Her mare had already been brought round, and they set off immediately, Erland's groom following behind. The day was warm but not hot, and the scents of summer filled the air. Before long, Joanna began to feel glad to be out and trotting through the country lanes, and she smiled at her companion happily.

"Ah, that is better," he said. "I had begun to fear that you didn't want to go riding after all."

"Oh, no, I love it."

Erland smiled. "Indeed? I would scarcely have credited it, seeing your face when you came into the drawing room. You looked like a child reluctantly doing some onerous duty."

Joanna colored a little. This came a bit too near the mark. "Nonsense," she said airily, "I was simply thinking of something else."

"Thank God for that. I should hate to think I was the cause of such an expression."

Joanna was unused to this sort of banter. "Why?" she asked.

Erland laughed, throwing back his head and letting his hands drop. "You are the most refreshing girl I have met in England," was his only reply. "You know, after living in Canada, one finds most English girls very stiff and starchy. But you are not. I like that."

"Are the girls so different there? What are they like?"

"Ah, now I am caught in my own snare." Erland grinned. "Well, they are not all alike, of course. And I am wrong to make sweeping generalizations about them, especially since I am not at all expert on the subject. But I do think that the women who have had the courage to cross the sea show a freer spirit." He paused, thinking. "That does not sound precisely right. I do not mean to imply any criticism." He shook his head. "I am certainly making a mull of this. Let us say only that girls I met in the territories seemed less hypocritical and fenced round with foolish restrictions. While not at all improper, they seemed freer." He smiled again. "And with that, you must be satisfied, Miss Joanna, for it is the best answer I can give."

Joanna's interest was caught. "I suppose they lead a very different sort of life. More exciting and dangerous."

54

"A few of them, perhaps. But most men would never take their wives and daughters into the real wilderness. I do not speak of the natives, of course."

The girl's eyes widened. "Did you meet Indian girls, too?"

The skin around Erland's eyes crinkled. "Yes, you may say so. Although one does not exactly *meet* Indian girls." When Joanna looked inquiring, he continued, "There are no formal introductions in the forest, Miss Joanna." Something seemed to amuse him, and he laughed again. "It is difficult to explain that world to you. But I have talked with Indians of both sexes on occasion."

"What are they like?"

"What an interrogator you are. Frankly, I cannot answer that question. I doubt there are five men in the West who could, truthfully. I know only enough to know that I cannot."

"Oh." The girl considered this. "Well, I suppose it is all more complex than it appears. That is what my father always tells me, when I don't understand something or can't explain what I mean."

"That is exactly it," agreed Erland appreciatively. "But let us talk of you. Tell me about yourself."

Joanna dimpled. "Well, that is not complex, at least. It may be done in a moment."

He looked inquiring.

"There is really nothing to tell," continued Joanna, thinking of Peter. "I have not traveled or done exciting things, as you have."

"Traveling is not everything. I believe I was told that your father had charge of your education. That must have been most interesting. What was your favorite study?"

Joanna frowned. "None of them," she almost snapped. "Why does everyone expect me to be a scholar, just because my father is? I am not."

He raised his eyebrows. "Does everyone? How clumsy of me. I apologize."

"Oh, I didn't mean, that is, you went to one of his meetings. You saw how it is."

Erland's eyes danced. "How it is? I must have done, but I confess I'm not certain what you mean."

"Did you *like* the meeting?" said Joanna incredulously.

"Well," he replied wryly, "I fear I did. But they let me do a great deal of talking, you see, and that no doubt accounts for it."

The girl sighed and looked out over her horse's head. "If that is the way of it, you will never understand. You will be just like Gerald."

Erland suppressed a smile. "How can you say so before you try me? I'm sure I am more understanding than, er, Gerald. That is your brother?"

Joanna nodded. "Gerald thinks I am a simpleton."

"Then I protest absolutely your comparison. I think nothing of the kind."

Looking at him narrowly, Joanna saw no signs that he was mocking her. "It is hard to explain," she said hesitantly.

"Please."

"Well, everyone admires my father so."

"Can you blame them? He strikes me as a brilliant man."

"Oh, no," answered Joanna quickly. "I admire him, too. I think he is wonderful. But I am not at all like him, you see, and when people expect me to be very learned and wise just because I am his daughter, well, it is vexatious, because I cannot. I never understand half of what Papa says, and no matter how hard I study, it is always so." She looked dejected; she seemed to have almost forgotten her listener. "He is very disappointed in me."

"He cannot have said so."

Joanna started. "Of course not," she said hurriedly, shocked at her confidences.

"And I am convinced he would never think so either. He seems singularly without prejudice in that re-

56

gard. My mind is by no means as good as his, yet, he listened to my views with attention."

"Oh, yes." For some reason, Joanna felt impelled to add, "But you should hear him speak of Canon Weyland's daughter. She is very learned; she reads Latin and Greek and probably lots of other languages as well." Joanna sighed. "I hated Latin. Papa thinks she is a ... a harbinger of the future."

"Does he?" asked Erland. "How so?"

Joanna wrinkled her nose. "Well, I do not understand it completely. But he believes that everyone should have all the education he wishes. I heard him tell Mr. Grant so. Georgiana wishes to go to school."

"And have you had all the education you wish?"

"Oh, yes," said Joanna feelingly.

"Well, then." He smiled at her.

The girl frowned, then nodded, but she looked unconvinced.

Erland continued to smile as he watched her for a moment, then said, "You have brought me back past the Abbey. Remember, you promised to show me some pleasant rides."

Looking up, Joanna saw that they had indeed reached Erland Abbey. Its tumbledown stone wall ran along the right side of the road, and the great, rusted iron gates leaned just ahead. Joanna rode up to them and looked down the avenue to the house. The Abbey was built of brown stone and heavily overgrown with ivy. It was difficult to make out its outlines through the shrubbery and tall elms that lined the drive.

"Not exactly a pretty sight, is it?" asked Jonathan Erland, who had stopped beside her. "My uncle let everything go shockingly. And now, I cannot repair all the damage."

"I haven't been inside the park in years," said Joanna reminiscently. "I used to play here sometimes when I was a child. All the neighborhood children explored the ruins, though your uncle used to chase us out when he caught us."

57

"Did he? I should like to have seen that."

Joanna dimpled. "He rarely did. Maurice, your cousin, used to let us in at the back gate."

"Did you know Maurice well then? I never did."

Joanna shook her head. "He was four years older, and went off to school when I was very young. Gerald knew him, though." She gazed into the park again. "I was always convinced that something mysterious and romantic would happen to me in the ruins. You can hardly see them from here."

"But it never did?"

"No," replied the girl regretfully.

"Well, I shall have to see what I can do about that," said Jonathan, but she did not appear to hear him.

The sound of another horse approaching the gate made them turn, and they found that Sir Rollin Denby was riding along the road toward them, mounted on a magnificent black. He raised a hand.

"The deuce," said Erland.

"What?"

"Nothing, nothing."

Sir Rollin reined in beside them. "How fortunate to meet someone I know in this neighborhood," he said smoothly. "Are you going to look over the Abbey?"

"No," said Joanna. "I am showing Mr. Erland some of the rides hereabouts."

"Really? How lucky for me. That is just what I want myself. May I join you?"

Joanna agreed, though Erland did not second her, and the three of them turned back to the road.

"Lead on," said Sir Rollin. "We are in your hands."

Stifling an impulse to giggle, Joanna directed her mare to a path a little further along and led the party out across the fields. They soon came out on the top of a small hill, from which they could see the whole of the Abbey, the ruins behind, plus a pleasant prospect of hedges and fields.

"This is charming," said Sir Rollin. "I should never have found it myself. I am in your debt, Miss Rowntree."

Joanna stole a glance at him. His resplendent top boots and elegant coat quite threw poor Mr. Erland in the shade. She had not seen it before, but Erland's riding dress was worn and outmoded.

"How about a gallop?" said the younger man, seeming to sense Joanna's changed mood. And without another word, he was off across the country. He rode very well indeed, she noted.

"Such an energetic young man," murmured Sir Rollin. He made no effort to spur his horse. Joanna watched Erland a bit nervously. It seemed equally rude not to join him and not to remain with Sir Rollin.

This gentleman watched her face with a small smile. When she turned back to him, he said, "We were so pleased to meet you and your family, Miss Rowntree, particularly my sister. She has heard so much about you."

Joanna's chin came up. "Has she indeed?"

"Oh, yes. Peter sings your praises continually."

Joanna took a breath. She did not understand what this man was about, but some instinct made her reply coolly, "We have always been good friends, like brother and sister. We grew up together, you know."

"Very good, Miss Rowntree."

She looked up, her eyes briefly meeting Sir Rollin's before they dropped again. "I beg your pardon?" she said.

"I was merely complimenting you on your presence of mind," he answered. "I hadn't expected it, frankly."

Feeling lost, Joanna said nothing.

Sir Rollin watched her for a moment. He ran one finger along his lower lip meditatively. An ironic light came into his hazel eyes, making them dance, and he smiled. "You have not yet been to London, I believe, Miss Rowntree?" he asked.

This unexceptionable question relieved her. "No, not yet."

"But you are to go, I hope."

Nodding, Joanna told him of her mother's plans.

"Ah, good. I can look forward to the pleasure of

59

seeing you then. May I claim your hand for your first dance at Almack's?"

Joanna smiled. "You are roasting me, sir."

Denby spread his hands. "Why do you say so?"

"It is more than eight months before I go to town."

"And so? I wish merely to put in a claim ahead of the legions of young bucks who will no doubt surround you after you arrive. I am becoming too old to jostle with the sprigs."

This sort of conversation was wholly new to Joanna. She found that she liked it, but she could think of no reply.

Sir Rollin took another tack. "You will like London, I think." And he began to tell her of the main amusements of society and the places they frequented.

Joanna was soon enthralled. Among the delights of Almack's, Hookham's, Rotten Row, and Vauxhall all her previous statements about not going to town dissolved. She listened with wide eyes and parted lips as Sir Rollin expertly captured the scene at each place and brought it alive for her.

"Oh," she sighed when he paused, "it sounds splendid."

He smiled. "There is splendor in it, on occasion."

Joanna looked at him shyly. "And you are a friend of the Prince, Sir Rollin?"

Something in her question made him grimace, but he said, "Yes, I have that honor."

She sighed again. "*He* is very splendid. My mother saw him at a ball once; she has told me."

One corner of Denby's mouth jerked. "Oh yes, Prinny is the most splendid of us all. And when your mother saw him, I daresay, he was even more so."

His tone brought Joanna up short. "Don't you like him?" she inquired, shocked.

He raised his eyebrows. "But naturally, my dear Miss Rowntree."

Joanna met his eyes, and he held her gaze for a long minute. She felt almost as if he had physically grasped her wrist. She could not look away until he turned to gaze over the fields. "Ah," he said, "here comes our energetic friend back to us."

Jonathan pulled up before them and began to urge them to join him. This time, Joanna agreed before Sir Rollin could speak, and she spurred her horse at once. Soon, all three were flying over the meadow. Sir Rollin rode as well as Erland, and Joanna's seat was also good, so they kept even for some time. Then, Denby pulled ahead, his black clearly the strongest mount. But as he approached the hedge at the end of the field, Erland spurred his chestnut, seeming to want to catch Sir Rollin. The two men rode furiously side-by-side for a short period. Joanna could see that both were grinning as they leaned over their horses' necks. Fascinated, and slightly frightened by their intensity, she slowed her mare.

They came up to the hedge very fast, and at the same moment precisely, both horses lifted and flew over it. Their form was flawless, and Joanna drew an admiring breath before she too cleared the bushes. On the other side, the men waited for her. Erland looked exhilarated, but somehow a bit disappointed as well, and Sir Rollin showed his habitual sardonic amusement.

The rest of the ride passed without much conversation. Joanna pointed out various paths and shortcuts to the two gentlemen, and they were properly appreciative. But she spent most of the time deep in thought. Did Sir Rollin know of her engagement to Peter, she wondered? He had certainly sounded as if he did for a moment. As Joanna's thoughts went to Peter, a man who puzzled and intrigued her. Erland completely slipped from her mind as she thought of him.

Both men escorted Joanna home, but they did not come in. When she had dismounted and walked up the steps to the front door, she turned and watched them ride off together. Only when they had disappeared around the bend in the drive did she go in, and then she was so abstracted that she did not even notice her mother's sharp look as she ran up the stairs to change.

Six

On Sunday, Joanna apologized to Selina, and all was well between the two girls again. Selina came home with the Rowntrees to spend the afternoon and to hear the story of Joanna's ride. She found it very exciting. "And so they both went over the hedge together?" she asked more than once. "How thrilling it must have been. Oh, Joanna, you are so lucky."

"Why?"

"Well, simply to have *been* there." Selina leaned back in the arbor where they were again sitting, and sighed. Her freckled face creased. "Oh, if such a thing would only happen to me!"

A silence fell while Selina contemplated this glorious prospect and Joanna looked out over the garden. Gradually, Selina came back to earth. She blinked, then said suddenly, "Oh, Joanna, I meant to tell you first thing. Have you heard what *she* has done now?"

"Who?"

"She. Peter's wife."

"No, what?" asked Joanna with more interest.

Selina's eyes widened and she leaned forward. "She went to Reverend Williston and positively insisted on becoming head of the relief committee. She told him that she wanted to take her place as the 'chief lady of the neighborhood' and do her part in helping others. Can you credit it? Chief indeed. I wonder what Mrs. Townsend and your mother will have to say to that?"

Though shocked, Joanna tried to be fair. "Well, it is true that Peter's house is the largest in the neighborhood, except the Abbey, of course, though that hardly counts now. And was not Peter's mother the head of the committee?"

"Oh, I daresay. She may well have the right, Joanna. But to go to the rector and say so! I think she is quite vulgar. What can one expect, after all, from the daughter of a merchant?"

Joanna began to giggle. "Highty-tighty," she said.

Selina looked indignant, then she too laughed. "Well, I still think it was horrid. And of couse, Reverend Williston is so persuadable that he agreed at once. Mrs. Williston is to give way."

Joanna shook her head. "Where do you hear these things, Selina? I declare, you always know everything that happens."

Selina flushed a little. "Our housekeeper . . ." she began.

"Is a friend of the Williston's housekeeper," finished Joanna laughingly. "How lucky that Mrs. Jenkins is such a friendly soul."

A little resentful, the other girl said, "You are very merry today, Joanna. What has become of your broken heart?"

Joanna sat up straight and frowned. "There is no need to fly into a pelter. I was only bamming you." She considered for a moment, then added, "You know, I begin to wonder if my heart is broken."

"Joanna!" gasped her friend.

"Well, I do. I cannot believe that it is, for I no longer feel that my life is over, or that I shall never be happy again, or any of those things. Sometimes I feel quite happy. And I often forget about Peter for hours at a time."

Selina clasped her hands. "Can it be that you mistook your heart?"

"Perhaps. When I saw his wife, do you know, I felt only a kind of pity for Peter. I didn't like her, of course, but I didn't hate her either. Do you suppose my mother was right and I shall recover now that he is married?"

Selina frowned. "It seems so, so . . ."

Joanna nodded, and both girls contemplated the garden. They had not yet solved the problem when they were joined by Joanna's mother, who came out of the French doors from the morning room with a sheet of paper in her hand and walked toward them. She was also frowning.

"Joanna," she said when she reached the arbor, "what is the Townsend boy's first name? It is ridiculous, but I cannot recall."

"Jack," answered Joanna.

"Of course. It is unaccountable how one can forget the most familiar things. I *could* not remember." She turned as if to go back into the house.

"Is that your guest list for the party?" blurted Selina.

Mrs. Rowntree looked up. "Oh, hello, Selina," she said. "I thought you had gone. Yes, I am just preparing the invitations. It is to be Tuesday this week." She turned to Joanna. "Your father is starting to organize his digging at the Abbey, so we must have the thing soon if we are to have it at all. He will be too engrossed within a very short time, I imagine, to tolerate any interruption."

"Oh, it is so exciting," exclaimed Selina. "I hope my mother will let me come."

Mrs. Rowntree smiled. "I do not see why she should not. It will not be a formal evening. A little dancing, perhaps, among childhood acquaintances."

"Oh, Mrs. Rowntree, you will tell her so, won't you?" said the girl. "If you ask her, she is bound to approve."

"I shall tell her what I plan," laughed the woman, "and she will decide for herself."

"If only I may come," repeated Selina. "Dancing!"

At that moment, Mr. Rowntree's voice was heard calling to his wife, and she went back toward the house.

Selina also rose. "I must go," she said regretfully. "I promised to be home in time for tea."

"I shall walk with you part of the way," said Joanna.

The two girls set out accordingly, after bonnets and shawls had been found and donned. They strolled across the fields, chatting lazily. When they were about half-way to the Grants', Joanna stopped and said goodbye. She had turned to start home again, when someone called her name and she saw Constance Williston approaching from the other side. "Hello," called Constance. "Are you walking home? I am on my way to Mrs. Rouse's again."

The two girls waited until she came up with them. Selina seemed both surprised and a little annoyed.

"How lucky," continued Constance when she reached them. "I was just thinking what a dull walk I had ahead. Or are you going the other way?"

"No, I am going home," said Joanna. "I was just walking part way with Selina."

"Splendid."

There was a pause. "Well, goodbye again, Selina," added Joanna. "I shall see you soon."

"You might come home to tea with me," said Selina suddenly. "I am sure Mother would be glad to see you."

"I cannot," replied Joanna, surprised. "I am expected at home."

"We could send a note round."

Puzzled by her friend's insistence, Joanna shook her head. "I cannot today."

"Oh, very well," snapped Selina, and she turned and flounced away.

The other two stared after her. Constance was silent, but Joanna said, "What can be the matter with her?"

They walked for a time in silence, then Constance ventured that it was a lovely day, and they agreed that the spell of perfect weather could not last. These commonplace remarks eased the atmosphere, and soon they were chatting easily. Joanna asked Constance about her school and was told what it was like, and in her turn,

Constance inquired about some of the young people in the neighborhood. She had known them as a child, of course, but Joanna had seen them grow up through the past four years, so she had much to tell. To Joanna's surprise, she found that Constance had a lively sense of the ridiculous.

"Do you remember," asked Constance, "when your brother Gerald and Gregory Townsend took one of the Townsends' farm horses and tried to make it jump the Abbey wall? I never laughed so much in my life. The horse was so large and stolid and wholly uninterested in anything but the grass by the roadside, yet Gregory and Gerald kept mounting up and urging it to try the wall." Her laughter began to overcome her.

Joanna smiled. "I had forgotten. How silly they were. Anyone might have known that that horse would never jump."

"Yes," gasped Constance, "but they were forbidden to take out the hunters because they had lamed Falcon on another wall. I shall never forget their solemn discussion about whether their 'word' included the farm horses also. They had promised not to go riding for two weeks, remember?"

Joanna shook her head. "What a memory you have. I had forgotten it all. But now I recall that the old horse finally just walked back to her stable, after she had eaten all the grass she wanted."

Constance nodded with brimming eyes, and the two girls dissolved in laughter.

When they had recovered their breath, Constance said, "Gerald is still at Oxford, I believe?"

"Yes, he is trying for a fellowship, and Gregory has gone into the army. How long ago it all seems."

"He is, ah, studying classics?"

"What? Oh, Gerald? Yes, classics. Can you imagine how dull it must be?"

Constance looked down. "It is fortunate, though, that he is so close. You can visit him."

"I?" said Joanna, amused. "He would not be over

glad to see me at his chambers, I daresay. He thinks me quite silly."

Constance flushed a little. "I meant that he could visit his family now and then, and, and get away from his studies."

"As if he would wish to. But yes, he does come to see Papa and join in his Philosophical Society. They go on for hours about the most ridiculous things."

Constance made no reply, and soon after, they reached the place where she was to turn off the path. The two girls said goodbye, Joanna thinking to herself that she liked Constance much more than she would have expected. She was invited to the rectory for tea the following week and accepted happily, glad to further her acquaintance with this pleasant girl.

When Joanna reached her own house and went into the hall, she nearly collided with Jonathan Erland, who was just coming out of the study. "Oh, hello," she said, startled.

He bowed slightly. "Good day. I have been with your father, discussing his plans for my grounds. They are extensive. I fear you will find me under foot here often in the next few weeks."

"Ah, well," was the only reply Joanna could think of. "Will you come upstairs?" she added. "My mother is probably in the drawing room."

"Thank you," replied Erland, "for a moment, perhaps."

They walked up the stairs, but Mrs. Rowntree was not in the empty drawing room. Joanna felt extremely awkward. She took off her bonnet, but could not decide where to put it. She looked about nervously and at last set it on a table by the door. Hesitating again, she finally went to the sofa and sat down. Why had she asked the man to come up, she wondered?

Erland joined her. "Your father is very eager to begin his scheme," he told her. "He wants to go over the entire ruin, clear it out, and catalogue the contents of each section."

"Why?" asked Joanna before she thought. She flushed a little.

But he smiled. "Perhaps the untidiness offends his scientific sensibilities," he suggested.

Joanna looked at him dubiously, then giggled, shaking her head.

"No, you are right. He wishes to see what has been left there, and perhaps find out something about the lives of the monks. It was monks, by the by; one of the Oxford gentlemen has ascertained that. Indeed, this whole scheme owes much to his enthusiasm. Do you know him? Templeton, the name was."

Joanna shook her head again.

"Ah, just as well perhaps." His eyes twinkled as he smiled at her.

"Why?" asked Joanna again, returning his smile with real amusement.

"You are always eager to know why, are you not? I think you are more your father's daughter than you know. Well, young Templeton is awfully wrapped up in his studies. He is writing a book on English life in the time of Elizabeth I, and as far as I can tell, thinks of nothing else. He would not pay proper attention to a lovely young girl if he were forced upon one. I'm certain he would prose on for hours about Spanish diplomacy and the economic purposes of royal progresses."

Joanna had blushed a little at the compliment, but now she laughed aloud. "And what were they?"

"What were what?"

"The—the economic purposes."

Erland shrugged comically. "I haven't the faintest notion. I must confess I deserted him when he began on that. You must ask your brother Gerald; he listens to Templeton, I believe."

Joanna thought this very likely. "I can't bear students," she said.

He laughed. "Indeed? Why not?"

"They are so young and silly. None of them has the least polish or address. And though that is only what one may expect from gentlemen who have never been to London, I suppose, still it is so uninteresting." Feeling very grown-up, Joanna tossed her head.

Erland's smile had faded a little. "You think a sojourn in London is vital then?"

"Oh, yes. No one can be truly elegant and assured without."

"And that is important?"

His tone was so odd that Joanna stared at him. "Of course." She suddenly remembered that Mr. Erland had never been to London. "Now that you are back in England," she added kindly, "you will have the opportunity to see what I mean."

"Undoubtedly." He smiled ruefully. "Though a trip to town is very expensive, I believe."

Joanna leaned forward. "But indispensible."

"Indeed."

There was a pause. Joanna, a little abashed by her own vehemence, sat back, wondering what to say next. Erland appeared deep in thought. Some new idea seemed have occurred to him. But at last, he looked up. "Talking of fashion, I wanted to ask your advice on something, Miss Joanna."

Joanna raised her eyebrows, but before he could go on, the drawing-room door opened and Mr. Rowntree hurried in.

"Erland, thank heaven!" he exclaimed. "I thought you had gone, but one of the maids said you had come upstairs. Something has just struck me."

The younger man had risen and now replied politely, "Yes, sir?"

Rowntree distractedly ran a hand through his thin brown hair and blurted, "Shovels."

Joanna and Erland blinked.

Seeing that they didn't understand, Rowntree repeated, "Shovels. And I daresay trowels and rakes and all manner of other things. Where are we to get them?"

Erland's face cleared. "Ah, for the digging, you mean."

"Of course. It came to me just now. We shall need a great many tools, I suppose, and some workmen. We can do some of the digging, but not all." He frowned and shook his head.

"There is quite a pile of gardening tools in a shed at the Abbey," said the other. "It looks as if they had an army of gardeners years ago. Some of them are a bit rusty, but I daresay they will do."

"Splendid," cried Mr. Rowntree.

"As for workmen, that is more difficult. Old Ernst, my gardener, will help us now and then, I suppose, and perhaps your man also. But other than that, I do not know. We may pay some workmen, I daresay?" This last remark was tentative.

Rowntree frowned again. "No, no, we cannot do that. My other experiments require all of my extra funds at present." He thought for a moment, then made an airy gesture. "Well, we shall simply have to dig ourselves," he said. "There is nothing for it. I daresay it will be good for us all." And having reached this conclusion, he turned and left the room without another word.

When he was gone, Erland smiled ironically. "I wonder how Templeton will like that," he said. "He did not seem to me the sort of young man who likes to dig. I wonder if he has ever held a shovel?"

"Have you?" asked Joanna.

He turned back to her, his smile gone. "Indeed, I have. Do you forget that I am a colonial? I have held and used a shovel, an axe, a long rifle, and many other very ungenteel implements. I shall be your father's chief digger, I wager." He looked directly into her eyes.

For some reason, his cool gray gaze made Joanna uncomfortable. "Father did not mean . . ." she began.

But Erland held up a hand. "I have the greatest respect for Mr. Rowntree."

Joanna found this reply somewhat unsatisfactory, though she did not know why. But before she could speak, he went on. "And now, I want your advice."

She stared at him. No one had ever asked for her advice before.

"Your mother has been telling me, you know, about this party she plans. It sounds splendid, and I am very grateful. Indeed, I should like to repay her hospitality and entertain my neighbors, perhaps. So, I have evolved a scheme."

"What?" said Joanna when he paused.

He smiled. "I thought I would stage a picnic at the Abbey, perhaps next month. We might wander about the ruins, you see, and eat our dinners sitting on mossy old stones." He looked at her expectantly. "What do you think?"

"I?" Joanna was nonplussed.

"Yes. I want your opinion. Do you think it a good idea? Will it be suitable? The interior of the house is so run-down, I cannot hold any gathering there. This seemed just the ticket. But will it do?"

"Oh, yes. It sounds splendid."

He eyed her narrowly. "There's no need to be polite, you know. I have been out of the country for so long that I know nothing about fashionable amusements." He grimaced. "Never did, if the truth be told. So, I wish to know if a picnic is all right."

Joanna had recovered from her surprise. "Oh, yes," she assured him. "It is all the crack just now. Everyone will like it excessively."

Erland looked at her, then nodded. "Good. I will set things in motion. Mrs. Smith will no doubt have the vapors."

Joanna laughed, a vivid picture of the old housekeeper's probable reaction in her mind.

"Exactly," said Erland, "but have no fear, I shall win through."

"When will it be?"

"Well, your mother's party is next week, I believe, so mine shall not be for another two weeks after that. I do not wish people's memories of your mother's perfectly-run household to be too bright. The contrast will be shocking, I fear. So, say the middle of July, then."

"Perhaps the ruins will be cool," offered Joanna.

"Precisely. I shall put that on my invitation cards."

"How absurd you are."

"I?" He feigned astonishment. "Not at all. I am the most commonplace of men."

Joanna merely shook her head, and Erland rose. "I must go," he added. "I have neglected a great many unpleasant duties already this morning, and now I must attend to some of them."

Joanna rose also, and they started toward the door.

"By-the-by," continued the man as they reached it, "I do not wish to reveal my plan for a picnic just yet. I must see first whether it can be done. Can we make it our secret for a while?"

Joanna cocked her head. "If you wish."

He smiled. "You must help me with the arrangements, and when they are complete, we shall unveil the scheme to the world."

The girl did not know exactly how to take this. She wondered if her mother would approve of her planning a party for a single gentleman. But she could think of no reply, so said only, "I will not mention it."

Erland bowed slightly, then took his leave. Joanna watched him run lightly down the stairs before she picked up her bonnet and went up to her bedroom to put it away.

Seven

The next few days were very busy ones for Joanna. She had little time to herself as she helped her mother prepare for the dress party, fidgeted through fittings for her new dress, and spent long hours listening to Selina's laments. The latter's mother had decreed that she could not attend the Rowntrees' party, being only seventeen and not nearly out. Selina did not take the decision well. In fact, she was outraged, and took Joanna's every spare moment to express her emotion. By the day of the party, Joanna was heartily sick of the subject. She looked forward to the evening not only as a source of amusement, but also as an end to Selina's complaining.

As she dressed that evening, Joanna thought of Peter and his wife, who perforce had been invited. Somewhat to her surprise, she felt no great emotion at the idea of seeing them. What was wrong with her? As she fastened a silver bangle on her wrist, a gift from her mother, she thought of the third member of that household. Sir Rollin Denby would also be present tonight; he had promised to come. A memory of his wild race with Jonathan Erland and the jump that ended it floated through Joanna's thoughts, and she smiled slightly. It would be a little exciting to see Sir Rollin again. Her cheeks flushed becomingly.

Joanna stood up and turned before the long mirror

above her dressing table. The new dress was perfect: the palest jonquil muslin, with tiny puffed sleeves and one long flounce at the hem. Trimmed with deeper yellow ribbons, it glowed against her dark brown hair and gave her dark eyes a brighter sparkle. Her mother had also bought her new kid slippers to match, as well as the bracelet, and Joanna had done her hair in a mass of ringlets tied with yellow ribbons. Altogether, she had never felt so elegant and grown-up as she did in this moment. The girl looking back from the mirror might be a London miss, she thought, ready for an outing at Vauxhall or Almack's. Her reflection smiled, cherry red lips curving upward. Surely tonight would be a night to remember. And all her vows of eternal seclusion forgotten, Joanna skipped down the stairs to meet her mother in the drawing room.

Mrs. Rowntree awaited her there, also looking very fine. She wore a gown of deep red and her grandmother's ruby necklace. Her dark hair was twisted in a knot on the top of her head with curls falling over her ears. She might have been Joanna's sister rather than her mother, and she looked nearly as excited as the girl. The Rowntrees seldom entertained, Mr. Rowntree being utterly uninterested in such frivolity, and his wife had resigned herself to that fact. But before her marriage, she had been extremely fond of parties and dancing, and her eyes were bright with anticipation now.

"Perfect, Joanna," she said as her daughter entered. "The dress is lovely."

Joanna pirouetted before her. "Oh, I do like it," she replied.

Her mother nodded, smiling, but before she could speak again, the door opened and Mr. Rowntree came in. He looked rather awkward and uncomfortable in his evening dress. His neckcloth seemed too tight for him and his shirt points too high, though neither would have drawn a second disdainful look from one truly interested in fashion.

"Emma, this is intolerable," he said, running a finger

around his neck. "Why must I make a spectacle of myself in this ridiculous way? I have work to do, important work, and you know I am no good at these occasions."

His wife smiled again. "If you want to be on good terms with your neighbors, George, you must see them occasionally."

Mr. Rowntree sighed miserably and went to sit at his table in the corner. "I am too uncomfortable to argue the point," he said, putting his head on his hands. "Let them come."

Mrs. Rowntree exchanged an amused look with her daughter.

"Oh, but you look splendid, Papa," said Joanna coaxingly, "and Gerald is riding up for the evening. You will be able to talk with him and his friends." Mrs. Rowntree had recruited several of the Oxford students to fill out her numbers.

Mr. Rowntree raised his head and turned to answer his daughter, but paused with his mouth open and simply stared at her for some moments.

After a while, Joanna moved nervously. "What is wrong, Papa?"

He recovered himself, but shook his head as if mystified. "You are different, Joanna. You are grown-up, I suppose." This idea seemed to both astonish and displease him. Joanna looked to her mother.

"She looks lovely, does she not, George?" said Mrs. Rowntree.

The man continued to look at his daughter, frowning, and his wife had to repeat the question before he heard her. "Eh?" He started. "What? Oh, so she does. Lovely." His brow cleared, and he added warmly, "You are beautiful, Joanna. I can't think why I haven't noticed before now. You're the image of your mother when I met her. You'll be a credit to us both tonight, though I'm sure I'd little to do with it." He ran a distracted hand through his sparse brown hair and smiled. His thin, rather austere face softened, and Joanna was overcome by the knowledge that her father cared for her.

"Th–thank you Papa," she stammered. "I shall try to be, always."

The maid came in then to tell them that a carriage had arrived, and the family moved to the landing to receive their first guests. They were Mr. and Mrs. Grant, but Joanna greeted them in a daze, her father's praise still ringing in her ears.

By eight-thirty, their drawing room was filled, with only the Finley party yet to arrive. Joanna stood with Constance Williston in the corner of the room and looked out over it. Her brother Gerald stood opposite with her father and a group of young men, all talking at once. Her mother sat at the other end of the room with the Grants and some of the other neighbors, and another group of young people chatted further down the side where Joanna stood.

She turned to Constance, who looked cool and pretty in a gown of pale green muslin, embroidered at the waist and hem with a row of dark green leaves. "It is getting hot, isn't it?" said Joanna, putting her hands to her glowing cheeks.

Constance started, pulling her eyes from the opposite side of the room. "What?" she asked, blushing.

Joanna repeated her remark, and Constance agreed.

"I do not see how we can dance," continued Joanna. "We should melt in this heat."

"It is hotter in London rooms," said Constance absently. "Girls sometimes faint from the closeness of the air."

"I can well believe it. I cannot imagine . . ." But Joanna's imaginings were interrupted by the arrival of the Finleys and Sir Rollin, the former full of apologies for their lateness. Adrienne Finley blamed her brother in a penetrating voice. "He would not hurry. I told him that a country party is not at all like London. One may not wander in at any hour and expect a welcome. But Rollin is too used to being cosseted. Hostesses have spoiled him. They are so glad to see him enter their drawing rooms that they forgive him the most cavalier behavior."

Adrienne was glancing sharply around the room as she spoke, nodding to the people she knew and subjecting the others to close scrutiny.

Mrs. Rowntree came forward and began introductions. Most of the guests were already acquainted, but only a few had met the new Mrs. Finley. Adrienne enjoyed being the center of attention, and her voice carried throughout the room as they progressed around it. Several conversations paused. "How do you do? Yes, just married this month and arrived here soon after. A lovely neighborhood. So rustic. How do you do? Quite a romance, yes, all in the first weeks of the season. How do you do?" This went on for some time.

Joanna made an impatient gesture. "Must she talk so loudly?" she murmured with annoyance.

Constance glanced around them, but no one was near. "Perhaps she is nervous," she suggested.

The two girls looked at Adrienne, who was telling Reverend Williston of a superb preacher she had heard at Bath. Adrienne was brilliant in emerald silk with masses of pale green ribbons and a green and gold enameled fan. "Do you truly think so?" asked Joanna skeptically.

Constance watched Adrienne move on to Mr. Townsend and begin to rally him on his flowered waistcoat, saying that it was almost as striking as one she had seen the Duke of Cumberland wear in London last season. Mr. Townsend was obviously torn between complacency and outrage. "Well, perhaps not," agreed Constance. She smiled wryly. "I begin to wish I had not chosen to wear green," she added. "I shall be quite overpowered."

"Nonsense," replied Joanna fiercely. "How can anyone like *her*?"

"Like whom?" drawled a lazy voice behind them. Both girls jumped guiltily and whirled. It was Sir Rollin Denby.

"I . . . I didn't hear you come up," stammered Joanna.

"Obviously," answered Sir Rollin, "else you would not have been gossiping. It is never so amusing when one

79

is overheard. But tell me, whom can no one like?" The wicked twinkle in his eye suggested that he already knew the answer.

Joanna could think of nothing to say; she swallowed nervously.

"We were speaking of old Mrs. Rouse," put in Constance cooly. "It is a very sad case. She is in need of assistance, but she is so unpleasant that few people want to visit her." Her calm blue eyes met Sir Rollin's hazel ones with no sign of wavering. Joanna looked at her with amazed gratitude.

"Ah," said Denby, his smile widening. "But I can hardly believe that that is true of *you*, Miss Williston. You are not the type who lets such superficialities guide her behavior."

"I hope not indeed," replied Constance, her chin high.

"And you, Miss Rowntree?" he asked mockingly. "I take it you are not quite so charitable?"

"I . . . I fear not," stammered Joanna, wishing she were somewhere else.

"A pity. Harboring ill feeling can lead to such very unpleasant consequences." There was a hint of steel in his voice, and both girls looked up, surprised. He made a gesture and smiled. "It is always best, I have found, to forgive injuries and forget them."

Constance raised her eyebrows. "Of course."

To Joanna's vast relief, they were interrupted at this moment by her mother, who was endeavoring to start a few couples dancing at the end of the room. Besides Joanna and Constance, there were two other girls from some distance away, and there was a wealth of young men to partner them, thanks to the colleges. The governess from the Townsend's had agreed to play.

"Come Joanna," said Mrs. Rowntree, "you and Constance may start. I have young Townsend eager to dance and . . ."

"And I," interrupted Sir Rollin. "Will you honor me, Miss Rowntree?"

Joanna's mother did not look overly pleased at this development, and the girl herself felt a quiver of unease. Still, she could do nothing but accept. Soon, she was standing up with Sir Rollin for a country dance, Constance and Jack Townsend beside them, and the two other girls partnered by Jonathan Erland and one of the Oxford students.

There was some commotion behind them; then Joanna heard Adrienne Finley exclaim, "La no, Mr. Townsend, I protest I will not dance. Why, I am an old married woman now." The gentleman made some remark that Joanna could not hear, then Adrienne continued. "Well, if you insist, but I do protest. What will Peter think?" Peter evidently thought nothing at all, for in a moment, the new couple had joined the set.

The piano began. Joanna watched her feet for the first few minutes. This was the first time she had danced in public, and though she knew the steps, she felt a little nervous. But finally, she saw that she was not going to make a mistake or tread on her partner's foot, and she looked up. Sir Rollin smiled. "You are looking very pretty tonight, Miss Rowntree," he remarked.

"Thank you," answered Joanna. Sir Rollin was very splendid himself, in his dark evening coat and pale pantaloons. Indeed, he was the most elegant man in the room, and Joanna felt rather in awe of him. It was not only his magnificent appearance; he seemed in the habit of saying the most unsettling things. She searched for something to say. But Sir Rollin did not allow the pause to lengthen. When the dance movements allowed, he chatted pleasantly, gradually putting the girl at her ease.

"I have tried some of the rides you showed us," he said later in the set, "and I enjoyed them very much. You made good choices. Yesterday, I rode to the top of Brent Hill. The view is splendid, particularly of Erland's ruins. They are really extensive, are they not?"

"Yes. It was a very large abbey, I believe."

"Alas for Henry VIII."

"I beg your pardon?"

"Nothing." He smiled slightly.

There was a pause. Feeling awkward, Joanna asked, "Do you go to Brighton soon?"

Denby's smile seemed to stiffen. "I really cannot say, Miss Rowntree. That depends on many things."

"You must miss your fashionable friends, here in the country."

He raised his eyebrows. "Doubtless. But do they miss me? That is unlikely."

Joanna did not understand his tone, and she frowned.

"Brighton, my dear Miss Rowntree, is an odd place," he continued, "and a preeminently expensive one. Unless one has friends with a house, it is really too expensive. At least for such as I. And so, I stay, for a time." His lips quirked. "My sister desires my company," he finished.

Joanna felt uncomfortable and had some idea that she had made a social error, though she did not know just what it was. She was generally silent through the rest of the dance. Sir Rollin stared out over her head, as if his own thoughts were far more interesting than the gathering at which he found himself.

When the set ended, there was a pause while the young people rearranged themselves. Sir Rollin drifted off, and Jonathan Erland approached Joanna. Adrienne Finley called her husband who came a bit reluctantly into the dance,

Constance had moved toward the corner of the room, near where Mr. Rowntree and the Oxford students were talking; she looked uncomfortable. Joanna went over to her. "Do you have a partner?" she asked.

Constance started, then shook her head.

Joanna looked around. Jack Townsend was paired with one of the other girls; his father had gone back to his chair; Sir Rollin was nowhere in sight. She turned back to the group in the corner. "I know," she said, "I shall get Gerald. You can tell him that you remember his prank with the horse." And she started forward without hearing the slight sound Constance made.

Gerald Rowntree was standing beside his father, both listening to another young man hold forth. Like Mr. Rowntree, Gerald was tall and thin with light brown hair and blue eyes. He wore his evening dress negligently, but his face glowed with interest as he heard his friend's argument.

"Gerald," said Joanna, tugging at his sleeve.

He turned impatiently and looked down at her.

"Come and dance, Gerald. Here is Constance Williston; you remember."

Her brother did not glance at the slender blonde girl who winced slightly as Joanna spoke. "I have no time for such nonsense, Joanna. We are having an important discussion here."

"This is an evening party, Gerald," insisted Joanna, "not a meeting of Papa's society. Come and dance. You know Mama wishes you to."

This last point seemed to have some effect, and to Joanna's surprise, her father turned and added his support. "Yes, go and dance a bit, Gerald," he said. "It will please your mother."

With a resigned shrug, Gerald gave in.

By this time, Constance was blushing furiously. Joanna led her brother up to her and repeated, "You remember Constance Williston, Gerald."

"Of course," said Gerald, bowing politely. But it was not at all clear that he did. He was four years older than Joanna and had been away at school for most of his life.

Constance's flush deepened. "Come along," said Joanna impatiently. Gerald was impossible, and she was beginning to be sorry that she had inflicted him on her new friend.

They joined Jonathan Erland as the music started, and the four began to dance. Joanna was frowning. "What are you thinking of so grimly?" asked her partner.

"Brothers!" exclaimed Joanna, in strong accents of disgust.

He smiled, raising his eyebrows.

"They are the most infuriating things in nature," added the girl by way of explanation.

"Are they? Having no brothers, I had not noticed."

"Well, they are." Joanna turned to look at Gerald. To her surprise, he was talking animatedly to Constance, even missing steps in his eagerness. "Why, how funny," she said.

"What?"

"My brother." Joanna shook her head. "It is just like him. I had to positively drag him from his discussion to dance, and now he seems to be having a fine time. There is no understanding him."

Erland laughed at her disgusted expression. "Perhaps he found Miss Williston charming, after all."

"Oh, yes, but Gerald would not care for that. He is interested only in Latin and Greek and fusty old poetry. I only hope he is not boring Constance about Virgil. The last time he came for a visit, he went on about him all through dinner."

Looking at the other couple, Mr. Erland doubted that either party was bored, so he was able to dismiss this worry from his mind without difficulty. "You will be interested to hear, I hope, that I am getting on very well with my plan for a picnic," he said.

"Yes?"

"Absolutely. 'Tis to be in two weeks' time. I mean to send out the invitations tomorrow."

"And Mrs. Smith did not object?" asked Joanna teasingly.

"On the contrary. I have hopes of making her leave my service over the issue. She is outraged."

Joanna laughed. "And may I tell about your scheme now?"

He nodded. "Have you really kept it secret?"

"Of course I have." Joanna was indignant.

Erland apologized, and the rest of the set was taken

84

up with talk of his plans—where the tables were to be, what was to be served, whether there should be games. He asked her advice about each detail, and by the end of the dance Joanna felt very superior and knowledgeable.

Mrs. Rowntree had had a cold supper laid out in the dining room, and the young people soon followed some of the older ones there. Joanna was surprised to see Constance and Gerald go in together and sit down, still talking eagerly. She grimaced a little; Constance would get no supper if she relied on Gerald to fetch it. She and Erland joined Jack Townsend and his partner, and supper was a noisy, jolly meal.

After she had eaten, Joanna did an errand for her mother, then returned to the drawing room. Many of the guests were still at table, and the room was half empty when she came in. As she hesitated in the doorway, she heard someone call her name softly, and she whirled to face Peter Finley, who silently had come up behind her.

"Peter!" At once, Joanna's heart began to beat faster. Though she had astonishingly almost forgotten about Peter during this evening, standing face-to-face brought back a flood of memories and confused emotions.

"How are you, Joanna?"

She stared at him, fascinated by his face, his modish blue coat. This was the man she had thought to marry. It made her feel peculiar. "Well," she stammered.

"I meant to write you," he went on quickly. "I know I should have, but it was . . . "

"Peter," exclaimed a sweetly venomous voice from the drawing room. "And Miss Rowntree. How fortunate."

As one, they turned to face Adrienne. Peter looked both annoyed and a little uneasy.

"Peter, I seem to have lost my fan," continued the woman. "Would you be a darling and look in the dining room? Perhaps I left it there on the table."

Peter nodded curtly and turned away without a word. His wife looked at Joanna. "So silly of me," she murmured. "I am always misplacing my things."

Joanna was silent. Mrs. Finley's tone made it clear

she was not pleased; and though Joanna had done nothing, she felt a little nervous.

"Well, Miss Rowntree, a delightful little party. I simply must compliment your mother."

"Thank you," said Joanna, a bit stiffly.

"And you also. You look charming in that sweet little dress." The smile that accompanied this remark was so patronizing that Joanna could not bring herself to reply. She started to excuse herself, but the older woman stopped her by adding, "You go to London next season, I believe, Miss Rowntree?"

Joanna nodded.

"Ah, your first season! How I envy you. I remember mine with such fondness."

"It was some years ago?" responded Joanna sweetly.

Mrs. Finley's eyebrows went up, and she wagged a finger. "Now, now, you mustn't ask that of an old *married* woman." The bunches of light green ribbon on her gown fluttered as she moved. "If you like, I can write a note to one of my friends in town. It is vital to have introductions, you know, and not be *completely* unknown." She smiled.

"You are *too* kind," said Joanna through gritted teeth. "Fortunately, my mother has several old friends living in town, so we need not trouble you."

This elicited a flood of questions as to who these friends were, where they lived, and how her mother knew them. Without being insolent, they were prying, and Joanna lacked the social address to turn them all aside. She did have the satisfaction, however, of knowing that Mama's friends were unexceptionable and probably more fashionable than Adrienne's. Indeed, the woman appeared to be impressed.

When she had found out what she wished to know, she changed the subject abruptly. "You know Peter's housekeeper, I suppose?" she asked Joanna.

"Yes."

"A kindly woman, but dreadfully old-fashioned. I

have had to speak sharply to her several times since I arrived."

Joanna made a noncommital sound.

"The entire establishment is positively quaint, I vow," continued Adrienne, oblivious to Joanna's expression. "But bachelors are such helpless creatures. They never make changes in the house they grew up in, though I think Peter might have; his mother has been dead for years." She shrugged. "But I should not complain. It leaves me more to do, and I am having a grand time. We mean to do the place over in the latest modes."

She seemed to expect a reply. "Really?" said Joanna.

"Oh absolutely. I am particularly interested in the park. I have a positive passion for gardening, and Peter's garden is so antiquated. All those straight paths and square flower beds! We shall have them all pulled up and a cunning wilderness planted. And the shrubbery must go; it is so close and dark. You know Repton's plans, of course?"

Joanna, thinking that she had spent countless happy hours in that shrubbery and that garden as a child, and never found the least fault, shook her head.

Adrienne raised her eyebrows. "No? But *everyone* talks of them." She shrugged again. "I think them too perfect. And I am determined to get a hermit. They are all the crack, you know."

"A hermit?" echoed Joanna, mystified.

"Oh, yes, my dear Miss Rowntree. Have you not heard of that, either? So fashionable. We mean to construct a grotto with a cave, and there is nothing more engaging than having a hermit to live in such a place. One's guests just catch glimpses of him, you know, as he goes about his business. It is terribly affecting. The Duke of Devonshire has one."

"But a—a hermit, that is, where does one find a hermit?"

Adrienne gave a long silvery laugh. "Oh, my dear,

you are too amusing. He is not *really* a hermit, of course. One hires some local to put it on. I daresay there may be any number of old men in the neighborhood who will be delighted to have the place."

Joanna was astonished by the idea. "D–do you?" she said weakly.

Adrienne made an airy gesture. "Naturally. What have they to do, after all? It is not as if it were difficult work. The man need only wear suitable clothing and wander about the grounds." She frowned. "He will have to grow a beard, of course, and let his hair hang long, but he can be compensated for that." She looked down at Joanna. "Do you know anyone who might want the place?"

"I? Oh, no, I don't think so."

"Well, no matter. Peter will find someone."

Joanna tried to imagine Peter asking one of the neighborhood workmen, say old Mr. Jenkins, to take on such a role. She could not.

"And in the house," Adrienne was going on, "I shall have new carpets and hangings, of course, and I think I shall pull out the wall between those two cramped front parlors and make them into a billiard room. So much more fashionable. It will mean that we cannot entertain on any scale for some time, but I don't care for that. Our neighbors will understand, I daresay, and when we are finished, we shall have a gala day to show the new additions. How delightful it will be!" She paused to savor this idea, then carried on in the same manner for nearly a quarter of an hour, detailing all of her plans for Joanna.

The younger girl was both bored and rather overwhelmed at the extent and nature of these, and she said little in reply. She was heartily grateful when they were interrupted by her mother, who came in to start the dancing once more. Mrs. Finley gushed over her, no doubt remembering her creditable London connections.

Joanna took this opportunity to escape. Seeing Constance opposite, she went to her, eager to vent some of the outrage she was feeling. "What an appalling woman," she said softly when she reached Constance's side. "I came within an inch of telling her so, too."

"What?" said Constance dreamily.

Joanna looked at her. Clearly, Constance was not listening. Her eyes seemed to be on some faraway object, yet when Joanna looked in that direction, there was nothing unusual to be seen. "Is anything wrong, Constance?" she asked.

"Wrong? Oh, no," replied the other, with such emphasis that Joanna did not know what to make of it.

"Well, but you seem abstracted."

Constance turned toward her, but did not really look at her. "Thank you, yes," she said, and then drifted away across the floor.

Joanna frowned as she looked after her, but at that moment, Jack Townsend came up to beg her to start the dancing again as his partner, and she forgot Constance in the organization of a set.

There were several more dances before midnight, when the guests began to depart. Joanna had the last dance with Jonathan Erland again, and he was most enthusiastic about the evening. "I have never had such fun in England," he told her. "Your mother is the best of hostesses."

"Ah, but you must try to outdo her," teased Joanna.

"No thought is further from my mind. I hope merely to repay her, and perhaps amuse her a bit."

Joanna nodded absently.

"Will you go riding with me another day, Miss Joanna?" said her partner somewhat abruptly. "I very much enjoyed our outing last week."

"If you like," said Joanna.

"Perhaps Miss, ah, Williston would like to come also? We might make up a party."

Joanna began to look more interested. "I don't know if Constance rides. I suppose she does."

"We shall ask her."

The set ended on this note, and Joanna was called away by her mother, to say goodbye to the Grants. As they were talking, the Finley party came up to take their leave as well. Sir Rollin had reappeared from wherever he had spent the latter part of the evening; he looked bitterly sardonic. As Adrienne was bidding her mother farewell, Joanna looked at Peter. They had not danced and had hardly spoken to each other. How strange that seemed. Since their childhood, they had been inseparable at every neighborhood gathering they attended. And now, she had had a perfectly pleasant evening without him.

Peter looked down at her. "I am sorry we could not talk more," he blurted. "I meant to."

Joanna was surprised at his awkwardness. She had always thought of Peter as an immensely polished gentleman. But beside Sir Rollin Denby, he seemed a boy. "Yes," she replied easily. On impulse, she held out a hand. "Another time, perhaps."

Peter nodded, but his eyes slid nervously toward his wife. Joanna stared. How could she have thought herself in love with him?

Adrienne finished her goodbyes quickly, gathered Peter, and went out, with a sharp glance at Joanna. Sir Rollin bowed over Mrs. Rowntree's hand, to her evident amazement, and then turned to Joanna. "What have you done to set Adrienne's back up?" he asked softly.

"I?"

He smiled. "So innocent. I wager we both know. Young Peter is not worth the battle, you know." He looked at her. "Yes, I think you do."

Cheeks flaming, Joanna blurted, "Where did you go?" Then berated herself for sounding like a ninny.

Denby raised one eyebrow, then smiled again. "Alas, I have not been a model guest, have I? I confess I went out to the garden."

"The garden?"

"Yes. To brood on my wrongs."

The girl smiled back uncertainly. "Not really?"

"Really. Brooding is good for the soul, you know."

"I thought it was just the opposite."

"I suppose it depends upon the soul in question."

Joanna looked up at his tall, elegant figure, not knowing whether to laugh. Before she could decide, he took his leave and followed his sister out the door.

"How strange he is," said Joanna to herself.

She did not realize she had spoken aloud until a voice replied, "He strives to give that impression, certainly, the Byronic agony."

Joanna turned to see Jonathan Erland's ironic smile.

"It is irresistibly attractive to some females, I understand," he added.

Joanna did not quite like the way he looked at her when he said this, so she answered only, "You are going, Mr. Erland?"

He nodded. "Yes, but I . . ." He paused. "Yes. Good night."

"Good night."

Bidding her mother farewell also, he went out.

Only the group around Mr. Rowntree remained now, and Joanna's mother gestured toward them with a smile. "They will be talking for hours yet. We may as well go to bed, Joanna."

The girl nodded.

"Are you tired?"

Joanna considered. "No," she said, "not at all."

Her mother laughed. "Well, I am. Come let us go." And arm in arm, they walked up the stairs and toward the bedrooms.

Eight

The next morning after breakfast, Joanna returned to her room and sat down at the window, gazing thoughtfully out over the fields. She had been wondering at herself since last night, puzzled by her own reactions. It had always seemed to Joanna that she understood her feelings very well. But now, she was not so sure. Could her mother have been right after all? Had she never really loved Peter? Last night, when she had spoken to him for the first time in weeks, she had been amazed at her relative indifference. After a moment of tumult and embarrassment, she had felt almost nothing. She pitied Peter and wished him well, but that was all.

This realization led her to another less welcome one. If she had so misunderstood herself over this very serious matter, could she trust her own evaluation of any of her feelings? The possibility that she had no very clear knowledge of herself made Joanna distinctly uneasy.

She tried to talk this over with Selina when she came for a visit that afternoon, but the younger girl wanted instead to hear the details of the party she had missed. "Tell me everything," she insisted as they sat together in the rose arbor. "My mother noticed nothing important, I declare. She spent the whole evening talking with Mrs. Townsend."

Joanna obligingly told her what had occurred and with whom she had danced.

"Sir Rollin first," sighed Selina. "And was he very elegant?"

Joanna nodded. "The most modish man at the party."

The other girl clasped her hands. "To lead off with the most modish man present," she sighed. "Did Jack Townsend wear his spotted neckerchief?" When Joanna shook her head, Selina smiled. "I knew his father would forbid it. Jack insisted it was the latest thing, but his father says the kerchief makes him look like a groom. I knew he wouldn't wear it, whatever he said."

Joanna shrugged.

"Did *she* dance?" added Selina portentously.

The other girl nodded, not having to ask whom she meant. "Several times. First with Mr. Townsend and later with Mr. Erland and Jack."

Selina's eyes bulged. "Was she very splendid? I daresay she overdressed and could not dance nearly so well as you, Joanna."

Joanna considered. "She wore emerald silk and ribbons, a bit too much trimming, perhaps. But she danced very well, I must say."

Selina shrugged. "I'm certain you were much prettier in yellow. What a fine gown that is. I should like one just like it."

Privately thinking that yellow might not become her sandy-haired friend, Joanna nodded. "Yes, it is pretty. Poor Constance chose green, and she was put out that Mrs. Finley wore it also. Though her dress showed more taste, I thought," she added generously.

Selina tittered. "Poor Constance, I daresay," she added.

Joanna did not notice the venom in her tone. "You know," she continued, "Constance is really quite nice. I'm beginning to like her very much. I am to go to tea at the vicarage today. It is nearly four; I must think of getting ready."

Selina bridled. "Tea at the vicarage? But I thought

we would take tea together. Perhaps here in the arbor, as we used to."

"Well, that would be delightful, but I cannot today," replied Joanna, still unheeding.

Selina stood. "Well, I do not mean to keep you, to be sure. Do not concern yourself with me. I shall go immediately."

Joanna looked up at her, astonished. "Why, what is the matter, Selina?"

"Pray think nothing about it," retorted the other dramatically. "I'm sure my feelings do not matter in the least."

Nonplussed, Joanna stood also. "Of course they do. But whatever is the matter?"

"If my friendship means so little to you that you cannot see it," declared Selina, "then there is no more to be said." She made as if to turn away. "I shall go."

"You will do nothing of the kind," answered Joanna, getting a little angry at her friend. "You will sit down and tell me what is wrong."

"You are occupied. You must go out."

"Not for half an hour yet. Come, sit down."

Selina sat reluctantly on the extreme edge of the seat. "Well, I certainly do not want to interfere with your other, more important friendships," she said petulantly.

"What other friendships? You are making no sense, Selina."

"Am I not?" cried the other. "I suppose if you wish me to abandon my friendship for Constance Williston, I should simply slink away quietly and never bother you again?" She rose again. "Well, I shall."

Joanna stared at her. "Selina, there is no question of abandoning anyone. Are you acting this way because I said I like Constance? Do be reasonable."

Selina burst into tears.

Amazed and appalled, Joanna went to her. "Selina! You *are* my best friend and always have been. There will never be any question about that. Do stop crying."

Selina gulped down a sob. "Th—then you will not go?"

"Not go? To tea you mean? Of course I shall. Selina . . ."

But the younger girl burst out sobbing anew and ran from the garden.

Joanna looked after her, perplexed. The fact that she was beginning to like Constance had nothing to do with Selina. What was the matter with her? As she thought more about the incident, Joanna became a bit annoyed. Selina really was being silly; no doubt she would see it herself before she got home, and they would make it all up tomorrow. Joanna shrugged and started inside to change.

Dressed in cherry-striped muslin and a chip straw hat, Joanna arrived at the vicarage just at four-thirty. Constance greeted her at the door, seeming very glad to see her. Mrs. Williston awaited them in the drawing room, and it was not many minutes before the rest of the family joined them, including the four Williston children who were not away at school.

Constance's parents received Joanna kindly, Reverend Williston inquiring about her father and Mrs. Williston chatting amiably about London and the likelihood of their seeing each other in town next season. But when tea had been drunk and Constance urged Joanna to come up to her bedchamber for a good talk, Joanna was happy to agree.

"Wasn't it a splendid party?" exclaimed Constance as soon as they reached her room. "I don't think I ever had such fun."

A little surprised at her rapturous tone, Joanna nodded.

Something in her face seemed to catch Constance up. "Did you not have a good time?" she asked.

"Oh, yes," said the other, "of course."

"Yes," sighed Constance. "I shall never forget it."

By this time, Joanna was thoroughly puzzled and

rather intrigued. She had thought Constance a very reserved, and even perhaps a rather cold girl but now she was speaking with amazing intensity. Joanna wondered what the reason could be. "What did you enjoy most?" she asked, attempting subtlety.

"Oh, the dancing," responded Constance without hesitation, "and the talking, and, oh, everything." Her blue eyes glowed.

"My mother took particular care with the supper," said Joanna. "Did you like it?"

"Oh, yes!"

"What did you like best?"

"Oh, well, the, the . . ." Constance looked perplexed, then laughed aloud. "Oh, Joanna, I was having such fun that I do not even remember what I ate. But it was all wonderful."

Joanna watched her new friend with astonishment, for *she* remembered that Constance had gone in to supper with Gerald. Had Joanna been forced to eat with her brother, boredom would have made her pay the closest attention to her food. Indeed, she still shuddered at the memory of a dinner alone with Gerald when they had traveled together to her aunt's house. He had prosed on and on about some ancient Greek through the meal, so that though she had been scarcely ten years old, she could still name every dish she had eaten. "I hope Gerald did not weary you with talk of his studies," she added tentatively.

"Weary me?" exclaimed Constance. "Not at all. I could never tire of hearing such marvels. Did you know, Joanna, that the comedies of Aristophanes contain many echoes of Aeschylus? It's a small point to be sure, but reading in translation, one would hardly know it. Gerald says . . ." She stopped, blushed, then added, "but you don't care for that, I daresay. Pardon me."

Joanna's mouth had fallen open a little, and she remained speechless under the onslaught of several astonishing ideas. That Constance should be genuinely interested in what she herself would not have hesitated to label the dryest of dull subjects was surprising enough. But she was beginning to realize something even more incredible. It really seemed that Constance had more than a casual interest in her brother Gerald! That any girl could like him was a new idea, but that the slender superior Constance Williston did so left her unable to speak for a full minute.

Constance moved nervously under Joanna's stare. "I, ah, I have always been interested in ancient literature," she murmured, shame-faced.

Joanna recovered herself. She started to speak, then decided she would not add to the other's embarrassment by referring to Gerald again now. They did not know each other well enough for that sort of confidence, perhaps. But later . . . . Joanna smiled. "Have you?" she asked in a carefully neutral voice. "I confess I am very stupid about such things. I prefer novels, though I know they are inferior."

Looking relieved, Constance hastened to say that she also enjoyed novel reading, and the awkwardness was passed off in an animated comparison of a book they had both read and liked.

When a pause came, Joanna turned the subject by telling Constance of the picnic being planned at the Abbey. "Mr. Erland has decided to have archery and games, too," she said, "and the luncheon is to be quite grand." She giggled. "Unless, of course, old Mrs. Smith makes such a fuss that he cannot have any gathering at all. He says she is outraged by the idea even now."

Constance smiled. "I remember Mrs. Smith, I think. Was she not old Mr. Erland's housekeeper?"

"Yes. And she is driving the new Mr. Erland into a decline, he says." She repeated to Constance some of the tales Erland had told her.

The other girl began to giggle. "She truly threw a roasting pan at the baker's boy? You are not bamming me?"

Joanna shook her head. "The baker has sworn he will not take bread to her any longer. One of the other servants must fetch it from the village."

Constance laughed again. "What is Mr. Erland going to do?"

"He wishes to pension her off and get a new housekeeper, of course, but he says he is afraid to tell her so."

They laughed together. "I like Jonathan Erland," said Constance then. "At least, what little I have seen I like. He seems a very sensible, kind man."

"Oh, yes." Joanna shrugged. "It is a pity he spent so much of his life in the colonies."

Constance raised her eyebrows. "Why?"

"Oh, well, he has never been to London, and I daresay he is five-and-twenty at least. He has had no chance to become cultivated or to learn the manners of a man of fashion."

The other girl considered this. "I suppose you are right. But I find his manners quite acceptable, for my part. Many so-called men of fashion might learn from his consideration for others."

It was Joanna's turn to look inquiring.

"Indeed," continued Constance reflectively, "I'm not sure but that I prefer the slight lack of polish that Mr. Erland exhibits. I confess I do not trust a man, or any person, who does not occasionally show some uncertainty. It is usually a sign either of intolerable conceit or utter stupidity."

Joanna blinked.

"No one lives who is not at some time uneasy or clumsy," Constance went on more positively. "To pretend otherwise is hypocrisy, don't you think?"

Feeling a little out of her depth, Joanna nodded. What Constance said sounded true, though if it meant that one must prefer the dowdy Mr. Erland to a London beau, she emphatically did not agree. However, Joanna could not formulate what she felt in words smooth enough to match Constance's. She changed the subject. "Do you know that Mrs. Finley means to hire a hermit?"

Constance had been lost in thought, but this jerked her back to the present. "What?" she said incredulously.

Joanna nodded. "She means to build a grotto, and she wants to hire an old man to play hermit within it."

The other girl stared blankly for a moment, then collapsed in peals of laughter. "That is the most ridiculous thing I have ever heard," she gasped.

On this subject, at least, they were of like mind, and the two spent an agreeable half hour discussing the Finleys' plans for their estate and the obvious flaws in them. Joanna began to enjoy herself again.

It was by now nearing six, time for Joanna to think of going home. She said as much, and though Constance protested, they were soon standing together in the downstairs hall as Joanna tied the strings of her bonnet. When she took her leave, Joanna held out her hand and said, "Thank you so much for asking me. I truly enjoyed myself very much."

"Oh, so did I," replied Constance. "I hope we may do this again soon, and often." Her genuine emotion was clear in her face.

"I, too," said the other, once more flattered by this girl's interest. Even if it stemmed partly from Constance's feeling for Gerald, as Joanna now believed it must, she could see that more was involved. Constance did seem to like her, and to be rather lonely. "Let us go walking again soon," she finished.

"Oh, yes," agreed Constance, and the two girls separated happily.

Nine

The two weeks before Jonathan Erland's party passed fairly quickly for Joanna. Between placating Selina and furthering her acquaintance with Constance Williston, she was kept fully occupied; the long warm July days were filled with walks, teas, and long confidential talks. She also saw a good deal of Erland himself, and was thus able to keep up with every fresh development in his scheme. They went riding again, without Sir Rollin this time, and she was liable to find him about the house at any moment, either summoned by her father to discuss his plan for the digging, or searching for her mother to ask advice about some domestic crisis. In the course of time, they evolved an easy, friendly relationship.

Of the Finley party, they saw little. Joanna did encounter Sir Rollin as she walked home from Selina's one afternoon. He was riding his black horse across the fields and stopped to greet her briefly. But he seemed put out by something and soon rode on. The Finleys themselves remained at home, totally engrossed, so rumor had it, in renovations. When the neighborhood talk was not of the coming entertainment at Erland Abbey, from which no invitations had issued for years, it was of the amazing changes taking place at the Finley residence. Adrienne's search for a hermit had begun, with disastrous consequences when old Mr. Jenkins was approached, and the small circle of society thereabouts was getting no end of enjoyment from observing her setbacks. Georgiana Grant insisted that it was as good as a play. Everyone looked forward to seeing Adrienne at the picnic, and perhaps picking up a bit more knowledge of her plans.

The day Erland had chosen dawned cool and clear. The guests were invited for two, and by a quarter past the hour, the Rowntree party was in the carriage and riding along toward the Abbey. Mr. Rowntree looked impatient; only the promise that he might wander in the ruins and plan the next step of his project had lured him out of his study. His wife sat beside him in the chaise, murmuring calming replies to his complaints and smiling at her two oldest children who sat across. Joanna, fresh and pretty in crisp white muslin with blue ribbons and a straw hat, smiled back. And she gave her older brother a sidewise glance to see if he shared the joke. Paying no attention, of course, he had chin in hand, staring out the window. With a small shake of her head, Joanna turned to look out the other side. She would never understand Gerald whom she had fully expected to refuse to come to this picnic, but had shown no signs of that. In fact, he had been visiting them far more often than usual this summer, and she was wondering whether he had finally become bored with his studying.

When they turned in through the Abbey gates and started down the avenue, Joanna leaned out to see who was before them. She saw at once that someone had been trimming the trees beside the lane, and the park looked tidier than it had in previous years. She saw the Townsend family alighting from their carriage in front of the house, and there was another vehicle just driving around to the stables. So they were not the first.

Jonathan Erland was there to greet them when they pulled up before the front door. He handed her mother down first, then Joanna. As the men followed, he gestured toward the door. "It's easiest to walk through the hall, I think," he said.

They stepped inside. Here, changes were less evident. The long corridor that went from the door to the library in the rear of the house was perhaps a little cleaner, and when they reached the library itself, Joanna thought it seemed cozier and more lived-in than before. But the Abbey remained a dark gloomy house, filled with worn outmoded furnishings and an overabundance of dust.

When they stepped through the French doors at the back of the house, and onto the terrace, however, this impression disappeared. Joanna could not restrain a pleased exclamation. The flagged terrace had been set up for luncheon, with small tables here and there and the wide stone balustrade serving as buffet. Several young people from the village stood waiting to serve. From the chairs, there was a fine view of the old abbey's ruins, which spread down a slight incline behind the house.

To the left, an area had been set up for archery and other games, and to the right, by the ornamental pool, an awning had been erected for those who found the sun too hot. The shabbiness of the flower beds, the broken fountain, and even the slight musty smell emanating from the house behind were overshadowed by these amenities.

Joanna turned to find Erland smiling down at her. "You approve?" he asked.

"Oh, yes indeed. I never imagined it could look so fine."

He looked around them. "Well, it may not be fine, but it's certainly a vast improvement." Hearing another carriage approaching the door, he added, "Excuse me," and walked back into the house.

Joanna started off to look at everything. The tables had obviously been gathered from various corners of the house, but Erland had had them covered with white linen and decorated with small bunches of flowers. There were a few scattered chairs under the awning, which was pleasantly cool. She was just peering into the pond, trying to see to the bottom through the murky water, when Selina hurried to join her.

"Isn't it wonderful?" she exclaimed, excitement blazing in her pale blue eyes. Selina had been in raptures ever since her mother had given in to her pleas to be allowed to come to this party. "Isn't everything perfect? Did you see the cunning targets? And the loo counters? I can hardly believe I am here!"

Smiling, Joanna agreed and the two girls walked around the area again, so that Selina might see everything close up, then went back to the terrace, where the host was beginning to marshal the group for lunch. The Willistons had arrived, as had several young men from Oxford and three other neighborhood families. Only the Finleys had not come, but sounds from the hall indicated that they were even now here, so Erland was placing his guests about the tables.

Joanna found herself sitting with Jack Townsend, Constance, and Gerald, hardly the table she would have chosen. As he seated her, Erland apologized softly. "I would have put you at my own table but I must be polite to the older ladies. Will you take a stroll with me later?"

"When you have put me beside my odious brother?" she asked playfully. "I don't think I will."

He laughed. "No, no, you mustn't hold it against me. Recall my total inexperience at this sort of thing."

"Well, I shall see."

He smiled and turned away.

Luncheon was good. There was cold meat and cheese, accompanied by fresh bread and butter and an assortment of pickles and relishes. Tall glasses of lemonade and mugs of ale were offered to the ladies and gentlemen, and for dessert, they were served luscious freshly sliced peaches, floating in sweet juice, and cakes of all kinds. Erland received a great many compliments on his choices, to which he responded with easy good humor.

Joanna enjoyed the meal, but not the conversation that accompanied it. Jack Townsend prosed on nearly the entire time about a horse he had bought and

Gerald explained some boring poem to Constance, who persisted in looking enthralled until Joanna felt quite out of charity with her. She was very glad when dessert came and she could look forward to getting up and talking to someone else. She had just finished her peaches when a sharp exclamation behind her made her turn.

Selina was standing up, brushing futilely with her napkin at a large sticky stain on the front of her pink gown. "Oh, dear! Oh, dear!" she was crying helplessly.

Mrs. Grant got up and went to her.

"I've spilled it; I've spilled it all over my new dress," said Selina to her mother, and the girl burst into tears.

Mrs. Grant put an arm around her shoulders and led Selina toward the house. Joanna flushed a little, in sympathy for her friend, especially when she noticed Sir Rollin Denby exchange a smile with his sister. "Oh, poor Selina," she heard Constance say.

Wondering whether she should go and try to help clean the dress, Joanna rose uncertainly. Perhaps Selina would rather be left with her mother? Before she could decide, Sir Rollin came up to her.

"Are you also finished, Miss Rowntree?" he asked. "The young lady's *contretemps* seems to have officially ended luncheon. Would you care to stroll a little? You can explain all of this to me, I'm sure." He waved a hand to indicate the park.

"I—I was just going to Selina," murmured Joanna, remembering his mocking smile and resenting it for her friend's sake.

"I am sure she would rather you didn't," replied the man smoothly. "One doesn't care for an audience at such moments, you know."

"Well . . ."

"Really." He offered his arm. Joanna did not know what else to do but take it, so she did, and they walked down the three shallow steps that separated the terrace from the lawn.

"This place is certainly in need of extensive repairs,"

said Sir Rollin when they had passed the broken fountain and some untidy flower beds. "These gardens haven't been properly tended in years."

Joanna nodded. "Mr. Thomas Erland neglected everything."

"Adrienne is in ecstasies." He turned to look behind them and saw his sister talking animatedly to Jonathan Erland, one hand resting on his arm as she made a point. "I daresay, she is telling poor Erland what should be done to set his place to rights, all according to Repton and the latest fashion, of course."

His mocking tone was so obvious that Joanna did not know quite how to answer. "Your sister is making a great many alterations in her new home," she said finally.

Sir Rollin threw back his head and laughed heartily. "A decided understatement, Miss Rowntree. My sister has gone completely mad on the subject. There is no innovation so bizarre but she must have it. If it were not for the noise and inconvenience of having workmen about the house, I should be tolerably well amused here by Adrienne's freaks."

There was a short pause as Joanna searched for a suitable reply. "I suppose our small neighborhood must seem very dull to you after London," she ventured at last.

"You suppose correctly." Sir Rollin laughed again, harshly. "You should count yourself lucky, Miss Rowntree, to have traveled so little. It allows you to be content." Deep lines appeared beside his mouth, and looking up at him, Joanna felt almost frightened for a moment. Then, he laughed again. "But where are my manners?" he said mockingly. "I believe I should have said that any neighborhood containing such charming company could not be dull. What is that, Miss Rowntree?"

Following his pointing finger, Joanna replied with some relief, "The old cloister." She was confused by the man's manner. But for the rest of their walk, he continued to ask unexceptionable questions about the ruins around them, and she gradually began to feel more at ease.

At one point, they came upon her father and a group of the other guests, standing beside a freshly dug hole. "You can see here the base of the wall," her father was saying. "The foundations are of stone, and there are three crosses carved here." He traced them with his hand. Joanna saw that his coat was mussed and one sleeve muddied. She flushed.

"Instructive," murmured Sir Rollin as he guided her away from the group. "Such dedication."

Her flush deepened.

When they reached the terrace once more, Selina had returned, and Joanna went over to commiserate with her over her accident. Selina was extremely embarrassed and much subdued, and seemed determined to stay beside her mother for the rest of the afternoon. Joanna sat with them for a while, then went to speak to some of the other guests.

As she walked across the terrace, Joanna saw Constance strolling on Gerald's arm, and she smiled. They were so engrossed in talk that she did not believe they were conscious of anyone else. Her mother sat under the awning with the older ladies. Sir Rollin had joined Jack Townsend, the Finleys, and the rest of the young people at the other end of the terrace, and after some hesitation, Joanna started toward them. Jonathan Erland was urging them all to try a round of archery.

He had persuaded Jack, who was seconding his efforts manfully. But none of the others seemed inclined to agree. Adrienne was saying, "Oh, Mr. Erland, you must excuse me, I fear. I have no skill at games."

But her brother said, "My dear Adrienne, how can you say so? You know that you are a deadly marksman." He smiled sardonically as she glared at him.

"Splendid," cried Jack Townsend. "You must lead off, ma'am, though I daresay, Sophie can give you a good match." Sophie blushed prettily as he continued, "Come, I will back her against you."

"Ah, a wager," murmured Sir Rollin.

"Come along," said Jack again, and he began shepherding the unenthusiastic group toward the targets set up below.

Joanna lingered for a moment, watching them descend the steps and start to examine the archery equipment.

"You don't care for the sport?" asked Jonathan Erland behind her.

Joanna shrugged. "It is not so much that—"

"As it is the company," he finished for her. "I understand your view." He looked down at the others with a grimace. "I should have left them all to their own devices; but I suppose I really must continue to play the host." He started to move away. "You needn't come if you don't like it."

"Oh, well," began Joanna, but she was interrupted by a crash from the house behind. "Good heavens, what was that?" she exclaimed.

"I don't know." Erland started for the French door that led into the library. Joanna followed, curious. None of the other guests appeared to have heard the noise.

When she stepped into the room, Joanna was astonished to see her brother Frederick standing beside the desk, ruefully eyeing a large book, which had obviously fallen to the floor a moment before. "Frederick, whatever are you doing here?" cried the girl. "You were not invited."

"Pooh," retorted Frederick. He looked both defiant and embarrassed.

Joanna noticed that several of the desk drawers had been pulled out and the top looked very untidy. "What have you been doing?" she said again, horrified.

"Nothing," answered Frederick unconvincingly. He crumpled a paper he held in his hand. "I didn't see why everyone should be asked but me. I came over to see the fun. But I can tell when I'm not wanted." He turned as if to go to the door, but as he moved, he caught a foot on the fallen book and fell headlong onto the carpet. The paper he had been clutching floated away and landed before Joanna.

She stooped quickly and picked it up.

"Are you all right?" asked Erland, going to the boy and helping him into the desk chair.

"Yes," said Frederick sullenly. He put his chin on his hand and sighed disgustedly. "If only I hadn't been so stupid as to knock over that book," he murmured.

"What's this?" exclaimed Erland, bending over the desk. "I believe there's a secret drawer."

Frederick sighed again. "The panel turns by a spring." He looked down, shook his head with annoyance, and began to kick the leg of the desk.

Joanna made a sharp sound, and Erland turned to look at her. "This is yours," she said, holding out the paper. "It is from your uncle."

As the man walked toward her to take it, Frederick burst out, "It isn't fair. I found it! Why should I have to give it up? *He* never looked for it."

"Oh, do be quiet, Frederick," said Joanna sharply. "In a moment, I shall call Mama, and we will see what *she* has to say about your being here." She turned her eyes back to Erland, who was reading and looking more and more astonished. He finished and met Joanna's eyes, shaking his head.

"This is incredible," he said.

Joanna nodded. She had read it, too.

"Well, I think the treasure should be half mine," put in Frederick. "I found the clue, after all." Joanna glared at him, and he subsided.

Erland was still bemused. "It is my uncle's hand," he said, staring at the paper. "I can't deny that, but surely it is some sort of joke. He cannot have meant this."

"He was a queer old man," ventured Joanna.

Erland frowned. "Yes, but to leave his fortune, if there is indeed such a thing, in this way?" He looked down again and read the letter aloud:

*So, nephew, you have found this letter at last? I
wonder how long it took you to find the drawer? Are
you still a young man? Or old as I am now? That
would be amusing. I should like to see it. But I
shan't, of course.*

*You know I have always encouraged enterprise
in you. A man should be able to make his own way
in the world without the help of his elders. I did.
You've done well enough for yourself, and I don't
mind leaving the Abbey to you. You'll do better
than that worthless son of mine would have. But I
leave you one last test. You'll have the place, but not
the money, unless you can find it for yourself. It's
here; make no mistake. More than you ever imagined, I fancy. But I'll not make it too easy. If you
remember your family traditions, you will find it.
Otherwise, let it stay where it is until someone does.*

Erland blinked. "Can he have been mad?"

"Doubtless," replied a voice from the door, and all
of them whirled to discover Sir Rollin Denby on the
threshold. "I beg your pardon," he added. "I find archery insufferable."

There was a silence.

Finally, Frederick burst out, "What does it mean,
'traditions'? Do you know?" He leaned forward eagerly.

But Erland shook his head. "I haven't the least
idea." He frowned. "In fact, I am convinced this must be
rubbish, my uncle's idea of a joke."

"Well, he *was* a great miser," said Joanna uncertainly.

Erland's frown deepened as he tapped the letter with
one finger.

"And a fortune is worth some hunting," added Sir
Rollin meditatively. They all turned to look at him again.
"Ah, if you will excuse me; I fear I intrude." He bowed
slightly and left the room.

Erland watched him walk across the lawn.

"What are you going to *do?*" questioned Frederick.

"I haven't the least notion," answered Erland. "Nothing, I suppose."

Frederick snorted. "Well, if that's not the stupidest thing I've ever heard. You must search for it. Don't you want a treasure? I'll help you."

The man's eyes rested on Joanna for a moment; she was frowning at her brother. "Oh, I should like a fortune," he said, "very much."

"Well, then, we must look for it." Frederick got up and walked over to Erland. He peered at the document again. "Have you some famous family traditions?"

"What?" Erland looked down at the top of Frederick's head. "Traditions?" He considered. "I can think of none."

"But there must be *something*. Why would he have said it?"

The man nodded. "Yes—that is true. My uncle was not given to idle remarks. Perhaps it does mean something."

"Well, of course it does," exclaimed the boy contemptuously.

"I must think about it." Jonathan's eyes began to twinkle.

"I dare swear you should and I'll help you." Frederick scanned the shelves above them. "Some of these musty old books might help."

"Frederick, you will come with me to Mama this minute," interrupted Joanna, outraged at her brother's nonchalance after his inexcusable behavior. "That is, after you apologize to Mr. Erland for breaking into his desk."

Her brother gaped at her. "Apologize for finding the clue to the treasure? Don't be a ninny, Joanna."

Erland laughed. "He has a point."

"How can you encourage him?"

He spread his hands. "It appears I need the help."

"Capital!" cried Frederick.

"But, you know," the man added, "I think that the fewer people who know of this the better. It is a great pity that Sir Rollin happened to come in. I shall ask him to keep it quiet." He did not look particularly happy about this prospect. "And if you do not mind, I shall ask the same of both of you."

"I shan't tell," replied Frederick stoutly, "word of honor. But Joanna will. Girls always gab."

Joanna put her hands on her hips. "Do they indeed? Well, I can keep a secret as well as anyone, but that will not stop me from taking you to Mama." And with this, she grasped her brother's arm above the elbow and hustled him out onto the terrace. His protests could be heard for some time.

Erland remained in the library for several minutes, deep in thought. When he finally returned to his guests, he scanned the scene carefully, not entirely surprised to see that Sir Rollin Denby had joined the group listening to Mr. Rowntree expound.

Ten

The day following Mr. Erland's picnic was naturally devoted to visiting and discussing it. The entire neighborhood, it seemed, was either receiving visits or making them. Joanna and her mother had the Grants in the morning, Selina still full of mortification over her clumsiness, and Joanna got a note from Constance asking her to tea at the vicarage. But these events were overshadowed by the afternoon call of Sir Rollin Denby and his sister.

The Rowntrees had seen little of Adrienne since her arrival. After her early call and their evening party, she had more or less ignored them. Thus, Joanna and her mother were surprised when a maid came to tell them that Adrienne and her brother were below.

"Just Mrs. Finley and Sir Rollin?" asked Mrs. Rowntree. "Is not Peter with them?"

"Only the two, ma'am."

Mrs. Rowntree looked at her daughter, who shrugged. "Well, send them up, Mary." The maid went out. "What can they want, I wonder?" murmured Mrs. Rowntree.

This was no more clear when their guests walked in. Adrienne was very splendid in a morning dress of amber cloth, trimmed with French braid. And the modishness of her brother's long-tailed coat and buff pantaloons was unsurpassed. But the callers seemed to have nothing particular to say. Adrienne sat down beside Mrs. Rowntree and began to chat languidly about the picnic. "So charming," she drawled. "And that house!"

Sir Rollin arranged himself beside Joanna, one arm flung along the back of the sofa, and said, "And so, have you recovered from the excitements of yesterday, Miss Rowntree?"

"Excitements?"

He raised his eyebrows. "Don't you call them that? I confess that finding a clue to a treasure strikes me as exciting."

Joanna looked toward her mother with some alarm. She had done as Jonathan Erland asked and mentioned the discovery to no one.

Sir Rollin smiled. "They are not listening. Have no fear, I shall not reveal the great secret."

His voice held such mockery that Joanna flushed. "Mr. Erland wishes to keep the discovery quiet for the present."

"Very wise of him, no doubt. I daresay, he would be plagued with treasure hunters if it came out. What does he plan to do?"

This last question was sharp, but in her flutter, Joanna did not notice. "I don't know. It is so hard to believe that there is really a buried treasure. It seems so odd."

"Does Erland think it is buried?" asked Denby quickly.

Joanna raised startled eyes to his face.

He smiled down at her. "You see how the idea excites even my curiosity. It is an irresistible concept. I am so glad that there is at least one friend with whom I can discuss it." He looked deep into Joanna's eyes.

The thought of being Sir Rollin's confidante thrilled her. She smiled tremulously at him, then dropped her eyes. His gaze was overpowering. She turned to look the other way and was nonplussed to find that Adrienne was staring at her, a hard unfriendly look in her eyes. Joanna looked down again quickly.

"My dear Miss Rowntree," said Adrienne in a cold brittle voice, "I have just been telling your mother about our newest addition to the house. The grotto is nearly finished."

"Is it?" asked Joanna. "How splendid."

"Yes, but I am quite put out with Mr. Erland. He has stolen a march on me with his picnic. I meant to give one in our park when the work there was finished."

"Well, I am sure everyone would enjoy another," said the girl. "They all seemed to have such fun."

Adrienne tittered. "Repeat an entertainment. Indeed not."

"Adrienne means to dazzle the neighborhood with some unknown treat," put in Sir Rollin mockingly. He met his sister's smoldering eyes with calm amusement.

"We are certainly experiencing a social whirl," said Mrs. Rowntree. "I cannot remember so active a summer in this neighborhood."

Adrienne chose to take this as a compliment to herself, and her expression softened. "I believe that one can be almost as well amused in the country as in London," she replied graciously. "If things are arranged properly, of course."

"We rely upon you to do so, my dear," drawled Sir Rollin, and Adrienne looked nettled again.

How could brother and sister talk to each other so, wondered Joanna? Sir Rollin seemed to be almost goading her. And the looks she gave him were venomous. She glanced from one to the other uneasily. She and Gerald might be very different sorts, but he would never speak so to her.

"Have you been riding again, Miss Rowntree?" asked Sir Rollin, breaking her train of thought.

"Not for several days," answered Joanna. "The afternoons have been so warm."

"But you must ride in the morning in July, of

course. Will you do me the honor of riding with me, perhaps tomorrow morning? I go out every day, but I confess that I am bored with my own company."

"Oh. Oh, yes." Joanna looked toward her mother, but though Mrs. Rowntree did not seem pleased, she said nothing.

"Splendid. I shall come by about ten then."

Joanna nodded.

A muffled exclamation from Adrienne made them all turn to her. "I had nearly forgotten," she said. "We have an important errand in Longton. We must be going." Sir Rollin smiled.

The ladies escorted their callers out to the landing and watched them walk down the stairs. Mrs. Rowntree returned to the drawing room immediately, but something made Joanna linger by the doorway. A scrap of conversation drifted up from the front door below.

"I can't imagine why you insisted on coming here today," Adrienne said to her brother. "We were mistaken; there will be no trouble from this quarter. And it's a dead bore visiting these bumpkins."

"Is it?" murmured the gentleman.

"It is indeed, as you have been continually saying." Adrienne's voice sharpened. "And I hope you do not think to set up that insipid child as your next flirt, Rollin. In the first place, it will not do, and in the second, it would drive me quite mad having her about. What a ninnyhammer! You should go to Brighton. You have nearly fixed your interest with Susan Chudley, and you should cement the bargain as soon as may be."

Joanna could not hear what Sir Rollin said to this, but his sister's reply came floating up from the front lawn.

"Not marry Susan? You must be mad! I warn you, Rollin, if you whistle this fortune down the wind, you cannot rely on me to keep you. Sometimes I think you want to ruin yourself."

Again, Sir Rollin's reply was an inarticulate murmur. But Joanna moved to the hall window in time to see

Adrienne snatch her arm away from him and hurry to their barouche alone. Sir Rollin was laughing as he followed her.

Joanna was still thinking about this incident as she walked toward the vicarage at four. A host of new thoughts had been called up by her inadvertent eavesdropping, and she was not at all sorry to have overheard. Was Sir Rollin going to flirt with her? Was that why he did not go to Brighton and Miss Susan Chudley? The thought that the magnificent Sir Rollin Denby might make her the object of his attentions caused a flutter in Joanna's breast.

And the notion that she had been expected to "make trouble" for Adrienne was also unsettling. It was clear now that the Denbys had known of her attachment to Peter. Joanna blushed as she thought of that. Then, her complexion returned to normal when she remembered what Adrienne had called her. A ninnyhammer, was she? An insipid child? She would show that horrid woman that she was no such thing. Perhaps she would make her brother fall in love with her, and forget the rich Miss Chudley. Joanna toyed with the picture of Sir Rollin smitten with love for her. A small smile played about her mouth.

These thoughts were interrupted by a shout from behind her, and Joanna turned to see a horseman coming across the fields. It was Peter, riding fast. In a moment, he had pulled up beside her. "Hullo, Joanna," he said a little breathlessly.

"Peter." It was less a greeting than a question.

"I hoped to catch you today. I know you often walk here. I haven't had the chance before."

Joanna frowned up at him.

Peter looked self-conscious. "That sounds odd, perhaps. I won't try to explain. I've been, ah, busy lately."

"Yes, with all the work on your house," replied Joanna. She felt awkward with Peter for the first time in her life and hoped to steer the conversation onto commonplace topics.

But Peter said only, "Yes," and sat on his horse looking down at her.

Joanna shifted from one foot to the other. She did not know what to say. Peter, the easy companion of her childhood, seemed almost a stranger suddenly. Yet, there was such embarrassment attached to his presence as would never have been associated with a stranger. Joanna looked up at him uneasily. Why did he not say something? Her brows drew together. Peter looked pale, and his light blue eyes held an unaccustomed hunted expression. The untidiness of his blond curls and the carelessness of his riding dress were highly uncharacteristic of the man who had been the neighborhood dandy since he was sixteen.

"Where are you going?" he blurted suddenly.

"To the vicarage, for tea."

He nodded. Then, with a quick movement, he dismounted and looped his reins over his arm. "I'll walk with you a bit."

Joanna was disconcerted. "Oh, you needn't; that is, it isn't far. And I am late; I must hurry."

Peter was looking at the ground. "That's all right. I won't keep you. But I want to speak to you, Joanna."

There was nothing to be said to this, so they started off side-by-side. Peter said nothing more for a while. He seemed to be having difficulty with whatever it was he wanted to say.

Finally, when they were nearing the vicarage lane, he said, "Joanna, I meant to write to you. I really did. And I know I should have, but, well, what with one thing and another, I didn't. I wanted to apologize to you for that. To tell you I'm sorry."

"It's all right," murmured the girl, looking at the path.

"No, it isn't. I behaved badly, and I know it. But things happened so quickly, you see, and I . . . well, that's beside the point. I am sorry. I wanted you to know that. It's what I tried to tell you at your mother's party." Joanna started to speak, but he shook his head. "You needn't say anything. That's all of it; I must get back."

"I wish you happy, Peter," blurted Joanna.

He had started to remount his horse, but now he turned back. "You're a first-rate person, Joanna. I wish you the same. And I hope you . . . never mind." He swung up onto his horse. "I'm not such a coxcomb as to say that I'm sorry I hurt you. I'll just say again that I'm sorry." And he turned his mount and rode off.

Joanna watched with wide eyes as he left. Peter had sounded so subdued and, not unhappy precisely, but pensive. He had not been at all this way in the past. What had been happening to make him seem so much older, she wondered?

Turning down the lane toward the vicarage, she continued to consider the conversation. She was not upset exactly, but she was preoccupied. She nearly walked past the Willistons' garden gate and had to turn and retrace her steps to go in. Constance was there, reading, and she rose as soon as she saw Joanna. "Hello. You are just in time. I was about to get up."

Joanna returned her greeting absently, and the two girls entered the house. The family was just sitting down to tea, and they joined them when Joanna had taken off her things. Conversation was lively during the meal; the young Willistons always had a great deal to say. But Joanna took little part in it. Twice, a remark addressed to her had to be repeated, and she lost the train of the talk even oftener.

When she and Constance went upstairs afterward, Constance asked bluntly, "What is the matter, Joanna?"

The younger girl looked at her. She wasn't sure she should tell anyone about Peter's apology. "What do you mean?"

Constance shrugged. "I do not mean to pry, and you needn't tell me. But I can see that you have something on your mind. You've hardly said a word since you arrived."

Joanna thought for a moment. She knew that Constance was trustworthy. And it would be comforting to talk over her experience with an understanding friend. Coming to a decision, she told the other girl the whole.

Constance was not surprised. "What he said was very proper. You deserved an apology. He might have done better just to write you in the first place, but as he did not, this was next best."

"It was so odd," said Joanna.

"It must have been." The older girl looked at Joanna shyly. "I hope it was not too unpleasant. Your feelings for Peter . . ." At a loss for a way to finish, she stopped.

Understanding what she would say, Joanna nodded. "I have been thinking a good deal lately," she replied. "And I do not think I ever really understood my feelings for him. We were always together, you see, and everyone had spoken of our marrying for so long that I simply took it for granted that I loved him." She frowned. "And I did. But I begin to see that it was not the sort of love one feels for one's husband."

"He was like a brother, perhaps," offered Constance. "I remember how you and he always played together."

"Yes," agreed Joanna, "I suppose he was. Gerald was always too busy for me, and Frederick was only a baby. Peter was more like my brother than they were." Joanna smiled. "I was very foolish, I suppose. It was so pleasant being with Peter, I thought it would be just as nice being married to him. But I think now that marriage is not at all the same thing."

Constance returned her smile. "I believe you are right. One wants quite a different sort of man for that." She flushed. "Not different from Peter, I mean, but one about whom one feels differently." She shook her head. "I am getting all muddled."

"No, I know what you mean."

The two girls' eyes met, and they smiled again.

"So," added Joanna, "it has not been so hard to see Peter as I imagined it would be. And I feel as if I had learned a great deal in the last few weeks. I feel years older."

Constance laughed. "Practically thirty."

"Did I sound so affected?" laughed Joanna. "Not thirty. Perhaps nineteen. Or even twenty."

They laughed together.

"But all I want for Peter now is for him to be happy. I hope he is." Joanna's expression showed some doubt.

Constance nodded, having nothing to say to this.

Joanna took a breath. "Well, let us think no more about it now. Tell me, did you enjoy Mr. Erland's picnic? Everyone is talking about it today."

"They are indeed. The Townsends were here this morning. I had a lovely time. Did you?"

Joanna nodded. She considered telling Constance about finding the treasure note, then decided not to. She had promised Jonathan Erland that she would tell no one.

"I enjoyed myself immensely. Gerald took me all around the ruins and showed me the work they have been doing there. It is fascinating." Constance smiled mischievously. "Have you heard that Mr. Templeton has been taking instruction in the use of a shovel."

This diverted Joanna from her thoughts. "Instruction?"

Constance nodded, still smiling. "Yes. He has engaged a college gardener to show him the way of it."

"No. You made that up to roast me. He can't have."

"But he has. And he is coming along very well, according to the last reports. He hopes to be able to join the digging quite soon."

Joanna burst out laughing.

"Gerald says that it is an edifying sight, watching Templeton go at it in the flower beds below his chambers. Last Tuesday, he worked so hard he blistered his hands and had to have them wrapped in cotton and ointment by the housekeeper."

Joanna laughed harder.

"He has said that when he masters the shovel, he means to go on to the trowel," finished Constance.

"Stop, stop," gasped Joanna. "It is all a hum, I know, but I cannot stand any more."

"It is not a hum," retorted Constance. "Gerald told me the whole; he has seen it." She grinned. "I have never been so amused as when he described the flower beds."

"Indeed not." Joanna was trying to imagine her solemn brother telling such a story. "I wish Gerald might amuse *me* so. He never tells funny stories at home."

Constance flushed a little. "Well, but I am sure, that is, he may not realize . . ."

Joanna smiled at her now. "He may not find the company so agreeable, I think."

The older girl's flush deepened. "Oh, I don't . . ."

"Well, I do. It is obvious Gerald likes you, Constance."

Constance raised anxious eyes to Joanna's. "Do you think so? Truly?"

"Yes. And I am very glad of it, though how anyone can like Gerald I do not see." She shrugged.

"But he is so brilliant, so knowledgeable, and with that so kind; I do not see how . . ."

"Enough!" cried Joanna. "Let us leave it that I am very glad." She looked at her friend teasingly.

Constance flushed again, smiled, and looked down. "Of course, there is nothing in it. Sometimes, I think he likes me a little, but then, I am not sure. It is all uncertain."

"Well, I have never seen Gerald so interested in anyone. And he has been visiting us much more often lately, you know."

"Has he?"

The shy eagerness in Constance's tone made Joanna smile again. "He has. You needn't worry, Constance—I shall help you all I can. I should like it above all things to have you for my sister."

The older girl's eyes filled. "Thank you. But you will not do anything . . ."

"I shall be perfectly discreet."

This made them both laugh.

"How odd it is," continued Joanna, "to be thinking of Gerald in such a way. I cannot imagine wanting to marry someone like him."

Constance grinned. "But we have already seen how one feels about brothers, have we not?"

Joanna laughed again. "We have. Do you feel the same about yours?"

"Absolutely. They are impossible creatures."

"How lucky that we needn't consider them," Joanna laughed. "Oh, Constance, it is such fun talking with you. I have not laughed so much in weeks."

The other girl's smile faded. "Indeed, Joanna, I am so glad to have a friend in you. When I came back from school . . ." She paused.

Joanna flushed a little. She did not like to think of her earlier treatment of Constance.

"Well, I am just so happy to be friends," added Constance in a rush.

"And I," agreed Joanna.

They exchanged a smile.

"Come," said Constance, "let us go and sit in the garden for a while. It is cooler there." And the two girls walked downstairs together, very pleased with their new, closer relationship.

Eleven

Sir Rollin arrived at the stroke of ten the next morning. Joanna, dressed and ready for riding, drew a breath when he took her hand to greet her, remembering the conversation she had overheard the previous day. She briefly raised her large dark eyes to his, and he smiled down into them more warmly than he had ever done before. Joanna blinked and looked down again.

Her mare was brought round, and Sir Rollin lifted her into the saddle. His groom fell in behind them as they trotted down the lane in front of the house. The sun was warm, but not yet hot, and a light breeze stirred the leaves of the oak trees beside them. "A fine day," said Denby.

"Isn't it?" she agreed.

"And you are looking ravishing, Miss Rowntree." The man's hazel eyes sparkled as he surveyed her. "I must say that rose pink becomes you admirably."

Joanna looked at him sidewise. "You didn't say so the last time we rode together," she ventured.

"Did I not? Yet, I'm sure I meant to. I know I thought it. Perhaps I was tongue-tied by your beauty."

The girl puzzled over this for a moment, then dimpled. "I don't think you ever are."

Sir Rollin laughed. "Do you not?"

Joanna looked over at him, a little breathless. She

had never before had an opportunity to flirt, and she found it very exciting. Sir Rollin, as always, looked complete to a shade. His buckskins and top boots were flawless, and his olive green coat stretched across his wide shoulders without a wrinkle. Joanna followed the intricate folds of his neckcloth with something akin to awe. She knew from Peter's early efforts just how hard it was to tie such a complex design. With a happy sigh, she told herself that she was flirting with a true nonpareil.

Sir Rollin's smile broadened a little. "Shall we have a gallop?" he asked. They had by now come to some open country.

"Oh, yes," answered Joanna. She spurred her horse, and they leapt forward. With the breeze in her face, she threw back her head and laughed. All the unsettling things that had happened in the past few weeks seemed to drop out of her mind, and she felt she hadn't a worry in the world.

They finally pulled up two fields away. Joanna was breathing faster, her cheeks flushed nearly the color of her habit and her dark eyes shining.

"You ride very well," said Sir Rollin as he reined in beside her. "Do you hunt?"

"A little but I don't often get the chance. If we take the road here, we can go around by Longton." Joanna thought of the acquaintances she might see in the village. It would be splendid to bow to them while riding beside Sir Rollin.

"No, let us go that way," replied Sir Rollin, pointing in the opposite direction. "I haven't ridden along this part of the road."

Slightly disappointed, but agreeable, Joanna turned her mare. They crossed another field and entered a lane. As they rode, Sir Rollin chatted easily. He was more attentive than before, saying nothing that might make Joanna uneasy or puzzle her, and was clearly exerting his not inconsiderable charm. He talked of hunting in Leicestershire and told an amusing story of his discomfiture over a five-barred gate, then shifted to riding in Hyde Park and some of the follies committed there in the name of fashion. He soon had Joanna laughing and enthralled.

After about twenty minutes, they came out near the back boundary of the Abbey park. "Ah," said Denby, "we are at Erland's. I didn't realize that this lane led here. Shall we go and see how your father's investigations are getting on?"

Joanna frowned; she had no desire to see her father just now. "I'm not certain Papa is here today," she said.

"Oh, yes. Look there." Denby pointed with his riding crop to a cluster of men standing in the ruins. And before Joanna could speak again, he had started toward them. She followed perforce.

The group consisted of her father and brothers, Jonathan Erland, Templeton, and another student Joanna did not know. Her father held a bit of muddy crockery and was turning it this way and that and musing aloud. "Possibly a chalice, or a reliquary. Yes. I like the idea of a reliquary. You see this curving portion here."

Templeton gazed at him with awe-filled eyes. "Yes, sir," he murmured.

Gerald moved restlessly. "You know, Father," he said, "it seems to be nothing more than glazed clay. Surely a reliquary would be more ornamented?"

"Perhaps." Mr. Rowntree held the fragment up to the light and squinted at it.

"Dash it if it doesn't look just like my cousin's chamber pot," muttered the other student.

Templeton whirled to glare at him. "Clodpole," he began.

But Mr. Rowntree interrupted him, exclaiming, "That's it! That's precisely what it looks like. You have a keen eye, Carstairs. A chamber pot. Very interesting. Mark it down, Gerald. A chamber pot here in the cell. Perhaps one in each. We shall see."

Carstairs looked nonplussed, and there was a stifled sound from Sir Rollin. But when Joanna turned to look at him, his face showed only impassive interest. As Gerald bent to a large square of parchment spread out on a piece of flagstone, Denby spoke. "Good day. Are you mapping the ruins, then?"

Mr. Rowntree started and turned. "Ah, Joanna. And, er, ah, yes. Good day. I didn't hear you come up."

"You are mapping the old abbey?" repeated Sir Rollin.

"Yes. Yes indeed. All of our findings will be recorded." Rowntree indicated the paper on which Gerald had finished making a note. A large rectangle was drawn on it, and several areas had been filled in with smaller enclosures and notations. Rowntree gestured to the left. "There, you see, is the refectory. We have established that." He pointed to a spot on the map. "It is here. Then the cloister is here, and the chapel there. We have been digging in the monk's cells this morning." He straightened. "One must have method in these things."

"Indeed." Sir Rollin was surveying the map closely. "Have you found any underground chambers, or anything of that nature?"

Joanna's father frowned. "You mean the church crypt? No. Though that is a very useful idea. An underground chamber might remain intact, even today." He bent to the map again. "It should be about here, I suppose, if there is a crypt." He put a finger on the parchment. Sir Rollin watched closely. "Yes, indeed. A splendid idea. We shall try it, perhaps tomorrow. You have a quick mind, Mr. ah, yes. What do you think, Templeton?"

"By all means."

Jonathan Erland frowned slightly. He had not looked happy since Joanna and Sir Rollin rode up, and now he eyed Denby warily.

"Perhaps I might join you?" asked Denby.

Mr. Rowntree rubbed his hands together. "Of course, of course. Whenever you like. Another head is always welcome. Why not now?"

Sir Rollin indicated Joanna. "Your daughter has

kindly consented to ride with me today. I cannot abandon her so rudely."

"I could escort Miss Rowntree home," offered Erland, "if you wish to stay here."

Denby smiled slightly. "Not at all. I could not give up our ride. But if I may come tomorrow?"

"Of course," replied Mr. Rowntree. "Joanna, you might come, too. Meant to ask you; Erland was just reminding me."

Joanna was astonished. Her father had never asked her to join in his scientific pursuits. "I?" she stammered.

Her father nodded. "You could help Gerald with the notes and drawings. You always had a very fine hand."

This compliment reduced Joanna to gaping silence.

"Why not, Miss Rowntree?" put in Erland. "We may find something interesting, you know."

Sir Rollin smiled. "We mustn't bore Miss Rowntree. If she does not wish to dig . . ."

Joanna found her tongue. "Oh, but I do. I mean, I should love to help. I'll come tomorrow, first thing—and I can draw the map. I've had hundreds of drawing lessons." She stopped, out of breath.

Erland smiled, as did Gerald.

"Splendid," said Mr. Rowntree. "We shall see you tomorrow then." And he turned back to his pottery fragment, immediately forgetting that Joanna and her escort were there.

"Shall we go on?" asked Denby after a moment. Joanna started and agreed. They said their farewells and turned their horses' heads away from the ruins. Erland watched them until they were out of sight around a bend.

"A novelty," said Sir Rollin when they reached the lane once more. "It is fascinating. I have never encountered anything just like your father's enterprise. Frankly, I am somewhat bored in my sister's house. She talks of nothing but alterations and grottoes, and one cannot be out with charming companions every hour of the day." He smiled at Joanna as he said this.

She flushed a little. "Indeed, it is a quiet neighborhood, though we have had more entertainments this summer than usual. But you must wish for Brighton and your friends."

Sir Rollin's mouth twisted. "I have not come to that yet," he murmured.

Remembering what she had heard his sister say, Joanna blushed in earnest. Was Denby referring to Miss Susan Chudley? At least, he could have no idea that she understood him. But she thrilled a little to think that he did not want to go to Brighton after all.

"It's growing hot," said Sir Rollin then. "Shall we turn back?"

Joanna nodded, and they headed toward the lane again, riding in silence until Denby said, "Erland takes an interest in the excavations, it appears."

She nodded again.

"I wonder why?"

Surprised, the girl considered. "Well, it *is* his land, after all. He will want to know what they find."

"Indeed. And they may unearth something quite extraordinary, I suppose."

"In that jumble?"

Sir Rollin looked at her. "One never knows."

"Well, I doubt it. The ruins have been there for hundreds of years, and no one has found anything valuable in all that time."

"I daresay you are right."

Sir Rollin dropped the subject, deftly turning the conversation to lighter topics. They arrived back at Joanna's house well before luncheon, but he refused her polite invitation to come in, saying he wished to get his horse into the stable before the heat of the day. He helped Joanna dismount and waited politely as she walked up the steps to the hall, raising a hand when she turned in the doorway. "Goodbye, Miss Rowntree. I am in your debt. A charming ride. I hope we may repeat it. And I shall see you tomorrow."

Joanna smiled and nodded as the door was shut behind her and the man mounted his black once more. She stood with her back to the door panels for a moment, smiling dreamily. What if Sir Rollin *should* fall in love with her, she mused? What an extraordinary thing that would be. She was embroidering on this theme when the digging party came in, and they were all called to luncheon.

After the meal, Joanna went to the drawing room with a book, but the story did not hold her attention for long, and in a few minutes she was indulging in pleasant daydreams once again. Thus, she frowned when her brother Frederick came bouncing into the room and sat down opposite.

"Hullo, Joanna," he said. "Do you want to go treasure hunting at the Abbey this afternoon?"

"Treasure hunting? What do you mean? The digging? I thought Papa was staying home this afternoon."

"He is. It's not digging. It's something else." Frederick looked conspiratorial.

"What are you up to?"

"Nothing!"

Joanna frowned at him. "Well, I have better things to do than crawl about the ruins with you, and . . ."

"I told him you would not wish to come," interrupted her brother, with evidence of satisfaction. He started to turn away.

"Told who?"

"Mr. Erland. He said I must ask you, but I told him girls have no interest in such things." Frederick grimaced. "The silly things you do instead of having fun."

Joanna was frowning. "Mr. Erland wanted me to come?"

Her brother considered, his round face wrinkling. "Well, I don't know that. He was being polite, I guess, since you were there when we found the letter."

"But he did *ask* you to come? This is not some scheme of your own to look through his house again?"

Frederick looked indignant. "Of course, he asked me. You heard me promise Mama that I would not go there again without an invitation. What do you think me?"

Joanna hastily begged pardon. "And so you are really going to look for a treasure?" she added. "Mr. Erland thinks there is one?"

Her brother shook his head wearily. "What have I been telling you? Girls! They never understand anything." He raised a hand and spoke with exaggerated simplicity. "Mr. Erland asked me back today to search for the treasure. So he must believe there is one. I'm going. He said I should see if you wished to come along."

"You know, I think I will," said Joanna, ignoring his tone. As she thought again of finding that letter, she became rather intrigued.

Frederick seemed surprised and not wholly pleased. "We shall probably be crawling about in the attics and basements," he warned. "It will be dusty, and I daresay there may be spiders."

His sister smiled. "Then I must change my dress, mustn't I?"

Defeated, Frederick turned toward the stairs. "I mean to leave right away," he said over his shoulder. "And I shan't wait for you. Father said I could use the gig."

Startled, Joanna said, "Did you tell Father about the treasure?"

The boy made a rude noise. "Do you take me for a nodcock? Besides, we promised not to tell, remember? Though I daresay you have. Girls are such tattleboxes. And if you have told Selina Grant, the whole neighborhood will know it within a day."

"I have told no one," replied Joanna with cold dignity. She picked up her skirts and started toward the stairs. "I shall be ready in five minutes."

Unimpressed, Frederick retorted, "See that you are." He thrust his hands into his pockets and strolled out, whistling.

They pulled up before the Abbey at two, in the midst of an argument over Frederick's handling of the ribbons. Joanna insisted that he went too fast and had nearly overturned them at the gate. Her brother was as certain that it had been no such thing. He believed himself to be a top sawyer.

They were still disputing the fact when Jonathan Erland came out of the front door to greet them, and the man smiled as he put up a hand to help Joanna down. Seeing this, the girl snapped, "I daresay it seems funny to you, but we were nearly tumbled out at the turn. We might have been hurt or killed all because of Frederick's care-for-nobody driving."

"Pooh," said Frederick.

Joanna tossed back her somewhat disheveled curls and walked into the house haughtily.

Erland suppressed another smile as Frederick jumped down. A groom came around the corner of the house and took charge of the gig, and they followed Joanna into the house.

"Come into the library," said Erland when they joined her. "I want to show you something."

They found the library in some disarray. Books had been taken down and replaced carelessly, or not at all. The desk was nearly covered with piles of dusty old volumes. "Sit over here," suggested the host, directing them to chairs near the window and the afternoon sunshine.

When they were seated, he pulled out his uncle's letter once more. "I have been thinking about this," he said, addressing himself chiefly to Joanna. "At first, I thought it must be some sort of joke, but the more I considered my uncle and the kind of man he was, the more I became convinced that it could be true. It is just the sort of mad scheme that would have amused him."

Thinking of old Mr. Erland, Joanna nodded.

"Well, and so I began to wonder what to do. I thought of showing this to the lawyers and perhaps hiring some workmen to search, but that does not seem right.

There may be nothing to find after all, and I would look quite a fool in that case." He smiled.

"We don't want a lot of strangers pushing in anyway," said Frederick. "Ten-to-one, if the treasure were found, one of them would make off with it."

"There is also that possibility," agreed Erland, though his smile broadened. "Then I remembered the wording of the letter. My uncle said that if I remembered the traditions of the family, I would find his fortune. That brought me to this." He gestured toward the piles of books. "I have gone through the library. These are the books having to do with the family and their history. Unfortunately, I am not familiar with them. It was never thought necessary. I was to make my way in Canada, and Maurice was to inherit."

"There are so many," exclaimed Joanna, somewhat daunted by the heavy musty tomes.

"There are indeed," said Erland wryly. "And most of them as dry as they look, I fear. That is why I have asked for your help."

She raised startled eyes to his face.

"I thought you and Frederick might help me go through them. I don't want word of this to spread, but since you know already, I thought you might be willing to help me." His gray eyes held Joanna's dark ones.

"You may be sure we will," cried Frederick. He jumped up and went to the desk, picking up a huge old leather-bound volume and taking it to a chair. "Let us waste no time." He opened the book energetically and a cloud of dust puffed out; he began to cough as it settled over his face and coat.

Joanna and Erland laughed. "Will you help me?" said the man, looking at Joanna once more.

"Yes," she replied, getting up in her turn. "I should like it above all things."

Two hours later, all three of them were very dusty and discouraged. Each sat in a straight chair, surrounded by a small pile of books. Erland had paused to wipe his brow with a kerchief, grimacing when it came away black. Joanna was looking frowningly over a small volume full of cramped handwriting. Frederick dropped another disgustedly. "Another book of recipes," he exclaimed. "That makes six! Did these old Erlands think of nothing but food? And some of them are beastly." He picked up the book again. "Here, boiled garlic; would you eat that? I promise you I shouldn't."

"Well, I have another account book," said Joanna. "One of your ancestors kept careful records when he made the grand tour," she told Erland. "It is interesting, really. Here is the list of monies spent in Paris. What can this mean I wonder? 'Spent fifty guineas at Mrs. Lavalle's House on Monday and Friday.' It can't be a boarding house; that's much too expensive."

Erland raised his eyebrows and held out a hand. "Let me see."

"Oh, who cares for that," said Frederick, uninterested. "It can't be the clue." He surveyed the piles of books dejectedly. "We shall never find it among all these."

Erland closed the small volume and laid it aside behind him. "Don't be discouraged. We have eliminated those after all." He gestured toward a large pile in the corner. "But it is clear that we won't do it all in one day. I suggest we abandon the task for now and call for some tea, or perhaps some lemonade. It's hot."

Joanna agreed.

"You aren't giving up?" cried Frederick.

"Only temporarily."

"It is too bad. All this work and nothing to show." Frederick got up and went over to the desk. "I have never seen a duller collection of books." He gave the tallest pile a disgusted shove, and it slowly began to tumble over.

"Frederick!" cried Joanna.

"I didn't mean to knock them off," retorted her brother, as the ancient volumes hit heavily one by one. The last, a thick tome, fell end on, and the cracked leather back gave way entirely, splitting the book down the spine.

"Oh dear," said Joanna, running to pick it up.

"You've ruined it." She tried to fit the halves together again, without success, but as she lifted one of the sides, three thick parchments fell out and floated to the floor. "Oh," she continued, "the pages are coming loose."

"It doesn't matter," said Erland, retrieving one and bringing it to her. As he held it out, however, he paused. "This paper doesn't look the same," he said. He compared them more closely. "No, these aren't pages of that book." He opened the parchment. "It's a chart of some kind."

"Let me see," cried Frederick. He pushed under Erland's elbow to look at the paper. "It looks like a plan of the house."

"I think it is." Erland went to pick up the other two sheets. "And this one is the grounds. The third is odd, it looks older." He raised his eyes. "We may have found something here."

"Hooray!" said Frederick. "I found the clue."

Erland smiled. "You do seem to have a definite talent for treasure hunting," he agreed.

"Let's see it."

But the man folded the papers again and turned away. "Later we will examine them in detail. Now, I think we need a wash and a rest. Let us see if we can persuade Mrs. Smith to make lemonade. Come, lend your argumentative powers to mine."

After much protest, Frederick agreed. And Joanna was very glad after she caught a glimpse of herself in the dark mirror in the corner. "Oh my," she said. There was a smudge of dust on her nose, and several down her primrose muslin gown. Her curls were still tumbled from the drive over, and her hands were filthy.

"Yes, I think we could all do with a wash. I shall send Mrs. Smith to show you the way. Come along, Frederick."

Grumbling, the boy followed him down the corridor.

Later, in somewhat better frame, the three of them pored over the charts. But Joanna could make nothing of the crisscrossing lines and many crabbed notations along them. Frederick's frown made it clear that he saw little more.

"I think these may require long study," said Erland finally, "before they yield any important facts."

"Dull stuff," repiled Frederick. "Let us search the house instead."

The man smiled. "We may do so in time. But I should like to look over these first. It might be a great help."

Frederick made a face.

"As I see it," continued Erland with a laugh, "the treasure, if there is indeed such a thing, must be either in the house or in the ruins. There is no place else connected with family traditions." He gestured. "Unless my family had a lamentable habit of burying things in the lawns."

Joanna laughed. "Surely not."

"As you say. So, I wish to go over these plans looking for possible hiding places."

"That will take forever," complained Frederick.

"It will take some time at any rate. I'm sorry."

Frederick subsided into morose silence, while Joanna and Erland smiled at one another over his head. "You will find it," she said.

"Your confidence encourages me." His eyes were warm.

As they drove home, later that afternoon, Joanna was thoughtful. Her brother chattered on and on about the treasure, what a fine chap Erland was for letting them help look for it, and what he meant to do with the share that Erland would surely give him. Joanna listened with half an ear. She was thinking about Erland also, but not in the same terms. She was considering how likeable he was in spite of his lack of polish and the airs and graces she had always thought indispensible in a man. She contrasted him in her mind with Sir Rollin Denby, whom she had seen this same day. It was really much easier to talk to Mr. Erland, and more fun, too. He did not make her feel terribly young and blundering, nor did he laugh at her.

Instead, they had laughed together several times this afternoon, over some of the absurdities in the old books. Joanna was beginning to wonder if there had not been more in what Constance had said than she had realized at the time. Not that Mr. Erland would ever outshine Sir Rollin, she added to herself. The latter would always be the more exciting and dazzling companion. But their new neighbor might turn out to be an easier friend, more like a brother perhaps. Joanna wrinkled her nose. Yet another brother!

When they got home at five, the family was having tea in the drawing room and Frederick and Joanna joined them. Their mother looked surprised when she heard where they had been, and she frowned at their disheveled appearance, but she made no objection. Mr. Rowntree was engrossed in telling his wife of the morning's digging. Gerald was preparing to ride back to Oxford, and Joanna was amazed when he stopped to sit beside her before he went out.

"I wanted to speak with you, Joanna," he said.

She looked at him; here was a new start.

Gerald looked at his hands. "It is rather awkward— I don't know quite how to begin."

Joanna frowned, still more amazed. Then, a thought came to her. Did Gerald want to talk of Constance?

But he blurted, "It is that man Denby."

"Sir Rollin?"

Gerald nodded, looking down again. "The thing is, Joanna, one of the fellows with us this morning lives in London and knows of Denby. It appears, that is, it is pretty well known that he is, a, well, an ugly customer."

Joanna's surprise and amusement at seeing her self-absorbed brother grope for words gave way to a spark of resentment. "And so?" she replied.

"Dash it, Joanna, you must see what I'm driving at. I'm trying to drop a word in your ear, a warning, you know. Denby's just not, well, the sort of man you should go about with."

"Do you mean he is a rake?" said Joanna baldly, hoping to shock him into silence. What right had Gerald, who had practically ignored her for years, to dictate whom she should see?

But Gerald looked relieved. "That's it. Carstairs says it's well known. Mothers keep their girls away from him. He's been involved in all sorts of havey-cavey turnups. Seems to care for nothing and nobody, including himself."

With a small smile, Joanna permitted herself to wonder if this were still true. "You're telling me to stay away from him?" she asked belligerently.

"Oh, I haven't any right to do that," said her brother hastily. He seemed quite embarrassed by his unaccustomed venture into her affairs. "But Papa won't notice, you know, and Mother may not have heard about him, so I thought I'd just speak to you. You're a sensible little puss when you want to be, Joanna. You'll know what to do."

Though she was still angry with him for his interference, such praise from Gerald silenced Joanna. "Th–thank you," she murmured at last.

"Right." He stood. "I've got to go." He took his leave of the family and strode out, already forgetting Sir Rollin and Joanna.

The girl sat still for several minutes. She had no intention of paying any heed to Gerald's strictures, but she was amazed that he had bothered to make them. And Gerald, *Gerald* had called her a sensible little puss! Where would it end?

Twelve

When Joanna came down to breakfast the following day, she found her father very upset.

"Boys!" he was saying, in outraged accents, to her mother. "That is what Erland thinks, and I suppose he is right. It is intolerable, Emma. How can one approach a problem scientifically if one is subject to such interference. Boys indeed! Would that I knew who it was; I should show them interference."

"Most vexatious," murmured Mrs. Rowntree.

"What is it?" asked Joanna. "Has something happened?"

"Something?" sputtered her father. "I should say it has. Someone got into the ruins of the abbey last night, after we had gone. Just at the church, where we were to work today. A whole wall damaged, nearly falling down! Erland heard the crash from the house last night, and he frightened the rascals off when he came out to see what was toward. But this is intolerable. I cannot work with such intrusions."

"Well, well, George," put in Mrs. Rowntree, "you have ensured that it will not happen again."

A look of satisfaction crossed Mr. Rowntree's face, and he laughed shortly. "I have that. Young Carstairs' mastiff will see that there are no more trespassers, boys or not."

During this conversation, a suspicion had been growing in Joanna's mind, and when at this moment the door opened and her brother Frederick came in, she turned to glare at him angrily. Frederick returned her look with bland surprise in his round blue eyes.

They sat down to baked eggs without further conversation. And though her father occasionally grumbled under his breath during the meal, no more was said about the abbey. As soon as she was finished, Joanna got up and went out. But instead of going upstairs, she waited in the corridor until Frederick appeared, then pounced on him.

"Frederick, you went to the abbey ruins last night, didn't you? And after your promise to Mama. You should be ashamed!"

Her brother frowned. "I don't know what you're talking about. Are you touched in your upper works, Joanna?"

The girl repeated what her father had said. "It must have been you, Frederick. You are always exploring those ruins. And who else could it be?"

His frown deeper, Frederick replied, "I do not know, but you may be sure I mean to find out. If Johnny Townsend is sneaking about trying to get the treasure without me, I shall thrash him soundly."

The conviction in his voice gave Joanna pause. "It really wasn't you?" she asked, still suspicious.

"I have said it wasn't, have I not? Why should I skulk about in the dark when Erland is letting me help him search? A pretty fool you must think me."

His sister let this sink in. "But who could it have been then?" she said again, in a different tone.

Frederick grimaced. "We shall see." The light in his eyes boded ill for any neighborhood boy who had the temerity to intrude on his ground.

Joanna had no more time to puzzle over this mystery, for her father was ready to set out for the Abbey, and today, she was to accompany him. As she hurried up to her bedroom to gather her drawing materials, she felt a quiver of excitement. The prospect of sketching their finds was exciting, and the idea that she might really aid her father in his work made her glow. She had never been able to do that before.

Jonathan Erland, Templeton, and Carstairs were all on the scene when they arrived. They were standing near a toppled wall in the ruins and surveying it carefully. Carstairs held the collar of a large, fierce-looking dog.

"Good morning," cried Mr. Rowntree when they came up to them. "Is this the place the fools spoiled? We ought to call in a constable. It is disgraceful that anyone would interfere with scientific work in this way." He came over to look. "Why, someone has been digging here!"

Erland nodded. "That is what made the wall topple, I think. They began to dig too close and undermined it."

"Yes, yes, I see." Mr. Rowntree walked around the hole. "It just shows what fools they were. A ridiculous place to excavate—not at all safe. We shall start here when we unearth the crypt." He indicated a space further from the fallen wall."

"Brilliant!" cried Templeton. "You always know just what must be done, sir."

Though her father paid no attention to this, Joanna looked at the youth curiously. She had not really noticed Templeton and Carstairs before this, but now that she would be working with them every day, she began to wonder what sort of gentlemen they were. Templeton was slender, very dark and intense, and he watched her father's every move with the light of hero worship in his eyes. He had never spoken to Joanna, and she wondered now if he ever would. He did not seem to see that she had come along today.

Turning to look at Carstairs, Joanna found that that young man was already gazing at her. When their eyes met, he flushed slightly and mumbled a greeting. Carstairs was a bit plump, with brown hair and ingenuous blue eyes. He looked cheerful and comfort-loving and not at all the sort Joanna would have expected to be interested in her father's project. Smiling in response, Joanna walked toward him. But Frederick was before her. "Say, that's a lovely mastiff," he told Carstairs. "Yours?"

"Yes." Carstairs glanced down, then looked up again to return Joanna's smile. "His name's Valiant. I've had him only a few months."

Frederick knelt beside the animal, eliciting a warning growl.

"Be careful," said Carstairs. "He's not more than half trained, and he can't seem to get used to strangers. Makes no end of trouble at the college."

"Are you allowed to keep a dog?" asked Joanna, surprised.

The young man grinned. "Well, strictly speaking, no. That's why I have to train him as soon as possible. And that's why I'm glad to leave him here to guard the Abbey for a while. Someone told the bagwig about Valiant, and he's on the lookout."

"I'll wager he's a splendid watchdog," said Frederick from his knees. "Aren't you, boy?" He ruffled the dog's ears affectionately, a caress which the animal suffered with only a baring of teeth.

At this moment, Gerald came striding across the lawn. He was a bit later than usual, so he was hurrying, and he had already picked up one of shovels from the shed and was carrying it jauntily over one shoulder. Valiant took instant exception to this unaccustomed sight. Barking fiercely, he lunged toward Gerald, and such was Carstairs' surprise that he let go of the dog's collar, setting him free to charge.

"Look out," called Joanna. All of the others turned to see what was the matter.

Startled, Gerald watched the mastiff approach. He seemed uncertain about what to do. But finally, at the last minute, Valiant's bared teeth and deep growls convinced Gerald that he was in earnest, and he held up the shovel before him in defense.

"Valiant!" cried Carstairs. "Down, sir, down!" He started to run after the dog.

Confused by this command, but still deeply suspicious of the shovel, Valiant turned slightly aside. His great jaws snapped at the shovel, but he did not offer to renew the attack, and in a moment, Carstairs had his collar once more and was apologizing volubly to Gerald. For a short while, all was confusion, but finally Gerald had been told the story of the night's incursion and Valiant, his presence explained, had been taken off to the stables to rest for his evening labors.

"A very satisfactory animal," said Mr. Rowntree as he was led away. "No one will get past him to interfere with our work." He rubbed his hands together. "And now, let us get to it. We have wasted enough time already this morning."

It soon became obvious to Joanna that Jonathan Erland and Gerald did most of the real work on this project. Frederick, quickly bored by mere digging, disappeared on his own explorations after a very few minutes. Templeton made no move to lend a hand, but stood talking and listening to Mr. Rowntree. Carstairs occasionally tried to help, but he so clearly did not enjoy it that one of the others soon returned. And Joanna's father, though more than willing to take a shovel, seemed to hamper more than he helped when he did. Joanna herself found a reasonably comfortable flat rock and sat down to watch until she should be called upon to sketch something or perform some other service.

Erland and Gerald dug; Mr. Rowntree peered at their excavation and gave directions; the sun rose higher in the sky, and the day grew hot. With a muttered excuse, Carstairs went off to "see about Valiant." And Joanna began to be bored. She had thought that they would find exciting ancient objects quite often and that she would be asked to draw them. But after two hours, nothing of the sort had happened. They were finishing the unearthing of a long wall, started several days ago, before moving on to the chapel foundations, and there seemed to be nothing of interest to be found in this hole. Joanna's head began to droop. The heat was making her drowsy. Thus, she did not hear the footsteps approaching from behind her and started violently when Sir Rollin Denby said, "Good morning."

As she jerked around to face him, he added, "Did I frighten you? I'm sorry."

Joanna blinked up at the tall immaculate figure. In his fashionable morning dress, Sir Rollin looked incongruous surrounded by ruins. But he did not seem to notice; he was blandly poised, as ever. Joanna stood up. "G–good morning," she said.

"I am late, I fear. You are all such early risers." He looked toward Erland and Gerald, now hip deep in the excavation. "And such diligence—I am impressed."

He didn't sound impressed. Joanna murmured something indistinct.

"They have not moved their work?" asked Denby. "I understood that they were to begin on the church today, but perhaps I am mistaken?"

"Papa wanted to finish here first," answered Joanna. "Then they will move."

"Ah. Your father is laudably methodical. He completes what he starts no matter how, ah, tedious." The man looked from under lowered eyelids at the widening trench.

Joanna swallowed. Sir Rollin looked bored. She searched for something to say. "Someone broke into the ruins last night," she blurted finally.

Denby raised his eyebrows. "Broke in?" he repeated, looking around.

"Well, not precisely that. They are quite open, of course. But someone disturbed them." And Joanna went on to tell him the whole story. "So Mr. Carstairs' mastiff will be on guard from now on," she finished.

Sir Rollin was frowning over her head, but when she stopped speaking, he looked down. "Indeed. Erland feels that his rocks must be guarded then? Perhaps he hopes his treasure is here?"

Joanna looked around apprehensively, but no one was listening to them. "Oh, it was my father's idea, I think," she replied. "But Mr. Erland thinks the money must be either in the house or in the ruins. Those are the only two possible places."

"Does he indeed?" The man looked over to Erland, who straightened at that moment and paused to wipe his brow. As he lowered his kerchief, he turned his gaze in their direction, but after a brief glance, he resumed digging.

"Yes," continued Joanna, pleased to have some interesting information to impart. "We found some charts of the house and grounds; he is studying those."

"Charts?" asked Denby sharply.

Joanna nodded, a little surprised by his vehemence.

Meeting her wide brown eyes, Sir Rollin smiled. "Fascinating. But Miss Rowntree, I particularly wanted to speak to you today. I enjoyed our ride so much, and I wanted to tell you so."

Joanna's color rose. "Thank you." She dropped her eyes.

"In fact, I dared hope we might repeat it soon. I thought of getting up a party to ride into Oxford next week. We might ask Miss Williston, and perhaps Mr. Townsend, to join us. I had a sudden desire to see my old college after ten years."

"It . . . it sounds delightful," replied Joanna.

"Splendid. I shall see what I can arrange for, say, Tuesday next. We will set out early, in this heat. Do you think nine would be too soon?"

"Oh, no."

"Nine it is then." He smiled down at her. "Of course, you have seen Oxford countless times, but I hope our party may be pleasant enough that you won't be bored."

"I'm sure I won't be."

He smiled again. "It is settled then. And now, perhaps we should make some move to look at the digging.

Though I should much prefer talking with you, it is perhaps rude not to speak to your father." He offered his arm, and Joanna took it with a little thrill. No other gentleman of her acquaintance would have done such a thing for a walk of a few yards.

They worked on until eleven, exposing more and more of the old wall. Finally, Mr. Rowntree judged that enough was visible, and he asked Joanna to make a careful sketch of the whole. She sat down before it and got out her pencils and pad, determined to do a perfect job on this first commission. Erland and Gerald went for water, and Sir Rollin took his leave soon after, looking very bored by the proceedings. A few minutes later, Frederick returned from wherever he had been, his clothes very wrinkled and dusty, and came to crouch down beside Joanna. "I've been all over the ruins," he told her, "and I could not find any signs of who it might have been last night. No footprints or anything."

Concentrating on her sketch, Joanna murmured, "Well, the ground is very hard."

"I know. It is too bad there hasn't been a good rain lately." Frederick flopped to lie at her side in the grass. "And you know what else, Joanna—I was looking for places where someone else might have dug, and there weren't any."

"What do you mean?"

"Well, if old man Erland buried his money out here, there would have to be some sign. He couldn't have done it more than a year or two ago, could he? I mean, he'd want his money above ground while he was alive. So I should be able to find the place, if he dug. But I can't. So I think the treasure's in the house. It has to be."

"Why does it have to be?" asked someone behind them, and Jonathan Erland came to sit beside Frederick.

The boy repeated his tale.

"Yes, I see," agreed Erland when he finished. "You may be right. Of course, my uncle might have covered the spot with some of these stones." He gestured toward the piles of rocks surrounding them.

"I thought of that. I looked under the smaller piles, figuring he could not have moved the big ones. There was nothing there but grass, and one snake."

"Hmmm." Erland looked around thoughtfully.

"We have to search the house," urged Frederick. "It must be there. Did you find anything on those old charts?"

"No, not yet."

"Well, we must just start in then. What about the attics?"

The man groaned. "Have you *seen* the attics in this old barrack? They are huge, and crammed with every sort of rubbish. It would take weeks to go through it all."

"I'm ready," said Frederick, looking wholly undaunted by this prospect.

"Not now," said Joanna. "It is nearly time for luncheon. Look, Father is getting ready to go home."

Frederick started to protest, but Erland added, "And I am worn out with digging. You must give me time to rest, Frederick."

"Pooh," responded the boy. "We shall never find it at this rate."

"Well, I am not ruling out the attics," said Erland, "though I cannot believe that my uncle would have hidden anything in that mare's nest. But there are other places as well. The basements, for example. I believe they are extensive. We must make a plan before we plunge in."

Frederick looked mulish. "Oh, very well," he muttered.

"Frederick, Joanna, we are going," called Mr. Rowntree.

Joanna added one more line to her drawing, then began to pack up her things.

"I'll tell you what, Frederick," added Erland. "You may help me plan this afternoon. Your father is otherwise engaged and won't be coming back today, so we can search together."

The boy's eyes lit. "Oh, first-rate. I'll come right after luncheon."

"You are welcome, too, Miss Joanna," offered the man hopefully.

"I'm not sure," she said, continuing to pack up. "I must see if Mama wants me."

Erland looked down. "Of course."

Mr. Rowntree called again, and they walked over to join him. In a very few minutes, they were driving back toward home, Joanna's father full of the progress they had made that morning.

When they entered the house, Joanna found Selina awaiting her in the drawing room. "Wherever have you been?" asked the younger girl. "I came to see you, and your mother asked me to stay to lunch." She surveyed Joanna's smudged face and dusty gown with wide eyes.

"Hullo Selina," replied Joanna without much enthusiasm. She didn't feel like chatting. She had been looking forward to washing her face in cool water and changing her dress. "I must go up and make myself tidy."

"I'll come with you," said Selina comfortably.

Joanna turned and started toward the stairs without further comment. She knew it was no good telling Selina that she did not want company.

"Where have you been?" asked the visitor again as they walked up the stairs together. "You are positively sticky with dust, Joanna. I have never seen you so. Were you out walking in this heat?" Selina's voice sharpened on this last question.

"I have been at the Abbey, helping at my father's digging."

Selina gaped. "Whatever for?"

"He asked me to, and I wanted to help." Joanna hurried on before Selina could frame another question. "And I am excessively hot and dirty and feeling quite out of sorts, Selina." They had reached Joanna's bedroom by this time, and she went over to the washstand and poured some water from the pitcher into the basin. It was barely cool, but she began to splash her face.

Selina shrugged and plumped down on the bed.

"Well, I suppose you are, if you have been digging. But Joanna, I came today to tell you the most prodigious news!"

Joanna was patting her face with a towel, and her voice was muffled by its folds. "What?"

"The oddest thing. Or I shouldn't say odd, but ... sad, or ... oh ... I don't know."

"What?" repeated Joanna, a bit impatiently.

Selina clasped her hands together and opened her pale blue eyes very wide. "I saw Peter yesterday," she said in thrilling accents.

Joanna raised her eyebrows, putting down the towel and going to her wardrobe to get out a fresh gown. "Well, and how is that news? He lives in the neighborhood after all? We must see him frequently."

Selina leaned forward. "Yes, but Joanna, he was alone and so was I. I was walking across the field to the Townsends', you know, and he came up with me on horseback."

"And the two of you chatted? You have known each other all your lives, Selina."

"Joanna," said the other girl reproachfully. "Of course I know that. Why won't you listen to me?"

"Well, I am listening, but I cannot see anything wonderful in what you have said so far."

Selina looked hurt.

"I am sorry," continued Joanna in answer to her look. "I told you I was out of sorts. What do you wish to tell me?"

Only partly mollified, Selina replied, "I wanted to tell you that we talked of *you*, Peter and I." She looked up triumphantly.

"Oh, dear," said Joanna.

"It was the most romantic thing imaginable," Selina went on. "Of course, he has made a mistake; I knew that from the beginning."

"He said so?" Joanna was aghast. How could her friend have embarrassed her this way?

"He didn't have to say it. I knew."

Exasperated, but relieved, Joanna turned to pull a fresh gown from her wardrobe. "Nonsense, Selina."

"It is not. I could tell by his tone. He knows, of course, that I have your fullest confidence. It was so affecting, Joanna. Had you heard the way he spoke your name!"

"Well, I have heard it," snapped the other girl, struggling to button the back of her gown. "I saw Peter myself not long ago."

Selina stared. "You didn't tell me!"

"There was nothing to tell. We spoke briefly, I wished him happy— That is all."

The younger girl leaned forward. "He was holding back and didn't trust himself. But he still loves you, Joanna. I know it!"

Joanna stared at her, appalled.

"He does," repeated Selina defensively, beginning to quail under the anger in her friend's eye.

"Have you said anything of this kind to *anyone* else?" demanded Joanna.

"No, no, of course not. It is only between ourselves . . ."

"Good. You must promise not to do so. And you must understand that all is at an end between Peter and me. Please do not talk of me to him."

"But Joanna . . ."

"It makes me shudder to consider what you might have said. You must never, never do so again."

"But I didn't . . ."

"Don't you see, Selina, how very, very improper it would be if the things you said just now were true? They are not, of course, but everyone does not know that. If Peter did love me, which he does *not,* how dreadful it would be!"

Selina seemed much struck. "I thought it was romantic."

"It is not at all. Think how uncomfortable it would

be, living in the same neighborhood and seeing him constantly."

"Yes." Selina was amazed.

"So I hope you will forget this idea, as I have forgotten my unfortunate *engagement* to Peter. It was nothing but a childish misunderstanding, and it is over. I see now that Peter was never the sort of man I could truly admire. Now that I am out, and have met other gentlemen, I see what a mistake I nearly made."

Selina gazed at her, awestruck. "What other gentlemen?"

Joanna lowered her eyes. "Why, all sorts. Sir Rollin Denby, for example. He is completely different. So assured, so much the man of fashion." She began to comb out her curls before the mirror. "I am going riding with him again next week."

"Joanna! With *him?* You shouldn't," cried Selina, scandalized.

"Nonsense," replied the other girl, still annoyed.

"But he is, you know, what I told you."

"Malicious gossip, Selina. I don't wish to hear any more. I've been riding with him already, with only a groom, and he was perfectly polite and amusing."

"You did? You have?" exclaimed Selina. She looked at the other accusingly. "I didn't know."

"Well, I forgot to mention it. You see how harmless it was." Joanna looked down. She had not told Selina because she wished to avoid just such a conversation as this.

"But Joanna, two riding parties. He is *flirting* with you!"

"Nonsense. I daresay he is bored here in the country and wants some amusing outing. You are making a great work over nothing."

"But Joanna . . ."

"Selina please! Come, we must go down to lunch."

The younger girl paused, looking anxious and uncertain, then turned away. "I hardly know you now, Joanna," she murmured, her voice breaking slightly. "You are so changed."

"I am not, Selina."

"You are. You used to tell me *everything* and to, to feel just as I did on every subject. *Now,* you care nothing for what I think, and you are . . . oh, I do not know, you are different."

Somewhat taken aback, Joanna considered this. "Well, now that I am out, I suppose I *am* a little changed."

"You are wholly changed," wailed Selina, looking at her friend with tragic eyes.

Impatiently, Joanna turned and began to walk downstairs again. "I think you are making too much of a very trifling thing."

Selina sniffed once, then hurried to catch up. "Well, I am sorry, Joanna. I did not mean to push in where I am not wanted, I'm sure." When there was no answer to this, she added, "I *was* trying to help."

"I know," said Joanna. She kept her eyes on the stair carpet.

Selina peered down into her face anxiously. "You are not angry?"

"No, no. I believe I must be out of sorts still."

"I didn't mean to . . ."

"It's all *right,* Selina. Let us talk no more about it."

The younger girl fell silent, and they walked into the dining room together.

Thirteen

The heat persisted into the following week, slowing their digging and even stopping it on two occasions. Moreover, they had little success to lighten the burden of temperature. Mr. Rowntree's estimate of the chapel's location appeared to be slightly off, and they dug deep holes in several places without striking any evidence of it. Erland and Gerald were discouraged, and the former had shown Rowntree the charts they had discovered in hopes of pinpointing the proper spot. Joanna's father, delighted with these documents, had returned to his study to pore over them and make notes.

On the day set for the riding party, Joanna stood before her wardrobe uncertainly in the early morning. She did not think she could wear her pink velvet habit in this hot weather, yet her only other riding dress was an old and shabby pale blue cloth. She had had that habit since she was fifteen, and it was not at all the thing for a ride with Sir Rollin Denby.

She went to the window, looked out, then sighed. It was a perfect day, cloudless and still. But even now, only an hour after dawn, the air was warm. It would be hot again, and she would stifle in velvet. Resignedly, she took the blue habit from the hook and began to put it on. She had had it pressed, foreseeing this unfortunate contingency, so it looked as well as a three-year-old riding habit, well used, could look.

She ate her breakfast abstractedly, thinking of a lovely peach-colored riding dress she had seen in a fashion plate last week. Sir Rollin would think her a country dowd in her blue; he would probably be sorry he had asked her to go riding.

"Do be careful not to get overtired today, Joanna," said Mrs. Rowntree.

The girl started. "What?"

Her mother repeated her admonition.

"Oh, oh yes."

Mrs. Rowntree watched her daughter narrowly for a moment, started to speak, then changed her mind. "You go at nine?" she asked blandly.

"Yes. It is almost time, in fact." Joanna rose. "I must have Sybil brought round."

Her mother watched her hurry from the room. "If I only knew just what I should do," she murmured.

"Eh? What's that?" Mr. Rowntree peered out from behind his newspaper and looked at his wife questioningly.

"Nothing, dear. I was merely thinking aloud."

The man went back to his reading, and Mrs. Rowntree stared out at the back garden.

Sir Rollin arrived betimes, bringing with him Constance Williston and Jack Townsend, and the party started off toward Oxford immediately. Without appearing to maneuver in any way, Sir Rollin placed himself beside Joanna, leaving Constance and Jack to amuse each other. Constance's face showed a distinct lack of appreciation as young Townsend enthusiastically began to describe a new hunter he had purchased only the day before.

"And so, Miss Rowntree," said Sir Rollin.

"And so?"

"Yes."

Joanna smiled. "What do you mean?"

"Why nothing. It was a mere feint, said to gain me time to recover from the dazzlement of your joining us."

"Pooh," said Joanna.

He raised his eyebrows. "You don't care for compliments?"

"Not that sort."

He considered. "Not that sort," he repeated musingly. "What sort do you like?"

Joanna had expected him to ask what sort she meant, and she was a little taken aback by this question.

When she didn't speak at once, he added, "I can see what you mean, of course. It was a conventional compliment, perhaps a bit fulsome." He considered again. "Yes, decidedly fulsome. I really put very little thought into it. But you must tell me what sort you do like if I am to mend my ways."

Joanna burst out laughing. "What a complete hand you are."

"I? But haven't you just told me you dislike my style of compliment?"

"I don't think I could say anthing to put you out."

"Is this your aim? I am desolated. But if it is what you wish, I shall endeavor to be put out by the next remark you make."

"You are too absurd."

Sir Rollin's eyebrows came together; he appeared to concentrate. Then, a chagrined expression crossed his face. "There," he said.

"What is it?"

"I was put out. Couldn't you tell?" He looked down. "I suppose I haven't the way of it."

Joanna laughed again. "You must practice."

"Oh, no. I should much rather not. But you haven't answered my question."

"Which?"

"About the sort of compliments you like."

"Oh." Joanna flushed a little. She found Sir Rollin's conversation very novel and invigorating, but she did not quite know how to reply to this. "Well, I like sincere compliments."

"Was I not sincere?"

"It is difficult to tell with you." Joanna hurried on before he could speak. "And I like truthful ones as well. And no one could think I looked dazzling in this old habit."

Denby surveyed her appreciatively, taking in her sparkling dark eyes, flushed cheeks, and slender erect form. "Could they not?"

Joanna's flush deepened slightly. "No, not dazzling."

"Ah, perhaps I should have said charming."

The girl looked down. She had gone rather beyond her depth.

"I shall remember," continued Sir Rollin. And to Joanna's relief, he turned the subject. "You have visited Oxford many times, I imagine, Miss Rowntree?"

Joanna agreed that she had.

"It has been years since I was there. In fact, I daresay I haven't set foot in the place above twice since I came down. I declare I shall go to look at my old college." He laughed.

"Which is it?" asked Joanna, a little puzzled. Her father visited the colleges all the time.

"Christ Church. The house."

"Oh, my father was at Magdalen. So is Gerald."

Reaching the town, they turned their horses onto the Broad and trotted by Clarendon Building and the Divinity School. Constance and Jack came up with them, Constance looking determined to join their conversation. "Shall we go up into the cupola of the Sheldonian?" she asked. "I love to look out over the roofs."

"Later," murmured Sir Rollin with a careless wave of his hand. "I want to go down to Christ Church first of all. How amusing this is."

Constance looked affronted and said nothing more.

They rode on past the Sheldonian Theatre to the corner of the Broad. Sir Rollin lazily remarked on places he remembered. "Blackwells. I was in there once or twice, I believe. Shall we? But no, books are hardly a proper diversion for a riding party." He turned his horse, and they went on, passing High Street and Bear Lane. Denby paused suddenly. "The Bear," he exclaimed. "How long is it since I thought of it? Let us leave our horses there and continue on foot. It is a paltry inn, but dear to my heart."

There were no protests, so the group turned into Bear Lane and rode along to the pub. The man there took their horses with some reluctance, but Sir Rollin ignored him and hurried the party through one quadrangle and into Tom Quad of Christ Church. He stopped in the center. It was the long vacation, so few students were about. Only those like Gerald, who were working for some special purpose, lingered.

"Charming, charming," murmured Sir Rollin as he looked around the Quad. The others stood about behind him. Suddenly, he laughed rather mockingly. "Let us stroll about town," he added.

And so, they did. They walked back up through Oriel and All Souls, looked at the Radcliffe Camera and the Bodleian, and ended up on Broad Street again. Throughout, Sir Rollin's mood seemed odd. At moments, he appeared to be enjoying himself, but most of the time his comments were sarcastic. He paid no attention to anyone else's wishes in the matter of sights, but went just where he pleased and stayed as long as he was diverted. Constance's mouth began to tighten, and Joanna was puzzled.

As they came out on the Broad once more, Constance said determinedly, "I should like to go up in the Sheldonian now." The look in her eye seemed to challenge Sir Rollin to deny her, but he made no move to do so.

They walked down to the theatre, looked at the inside, and got the caretaker to let them into the stairs for the cupola. In a few moments, all were on top, looking out over the spires of Oxford. Constance was very pleased. She hurried to an opening and began to point out various landmarks to Jack. "See, there is the Magdalen tower," she said. Jack muttered some reply as Joanna walked over to another aperture. She had been here before, but not often, and she loved the view from the top of the building. The roofs of Oxford were spread out below them, each seeming more fanciful than the last. Here, one was ornamented with grotesque figures and gargoyles; there, slender carved spires pointed to the heavens. And perhaps the best part was the diversity. Each small building or college quad had its own distinct style. Some of the garden enclosures, with bright flowers in the sun, were also visible.

They stayed for some time, all but Sir Rollin enjoying the view and trying to pick out the buildings they knew. Denby leaned in one corner, listening to their talk with an amused expression, but contributing nothing. His interest in Oxford seemed to have been exhausted.

It was nearly one before they descended again, and the streets below were getting quite hot. A breeze in the cupola had obscured the growing heat of the day.

"Time for refreshment, I think," said Denby. "Shall we go back to The Bear? They used to serve tolerable cold meat."

No one objected, and they retreated in the direction they had come, more quickly and with less indirection. By the time they reached the little inn, Joanna was very hot indeed and very ready to go inside and relax.

They had a light luncheon of cold meat and fruit, with large pitchers of lemonade and ale to cool them after their walk. Conversation came chiefly from Constance, who knew a great deal about the town's history. Seeing the others had little to say, she shared her knowledge.

By the time they left the inn, it was midafternoon and sultry. They had decided to sit in one of the shady gardens for a while before riding home, but when they came into the lane once more, Jack Townsend noticed a bank of clouds on the horizon. "Thunderstorm," he said positively, and so they ordered their horses at once, having no wish to be caught in a downpour.

In less than a quarter of an hour, they were riding up Catte Street on their way out of the town. They went quickly and said little, one or the other glancing back from time-to-time to see whether the clouds were much closer. They had passed the corner of Catte and Broad and were riding by Trinity Garden, when Joanna heard someone call her name. She turned and saw Gerald standing on the pavement waving to her. She pulled up, and he came over, but she said only, "Hello, Gerald. I didn't think to see you. We have been looking about Oxford, but now we are hurrying home. There is a storm approaching."

Gerald held her bridle. "There is indeed. You will be lucky to make it to the house before it breaks."

"Well, let me go then," retorted Joanna.

"Yes, of course."

At this moment, the rest of the party came up. Gerald started a little when Constance spoke to him.

"Let go," said Joanna again, more sharply.

Gerald stared at her like one in a trance, then stepped back hastily. "Of course," he said again.

"I will see you Thursday," Joanna called back over her shoulder, not wishing to be uncivil to her brother.

Gerald waved vaguely, his eyes following their group as it trotted down the road away from him.

When they left the town, they stepped up the pace. Dark clouds covered a good part of the sky now, and there was no question that it would soon rain. Sir Rollin seemed particularly averse to the idea of a wetting. On his more powerful mount, he gradually moved to the head of the group, and then pulled away a bit until he was leading by several lengths. The others kept generally together.

When they were about half way home, they heard the ominous roll of thunder behind them. The clouds had obscured all but a line on the opposite horizon, and the storm was very near. Joanna saw one or two large drops spatter the dust on the road.

"It's beginning," Denby called back over his shoulder. "We had best gallop from here or we shall be thoroughly wet." Without waiting to see if the others agreed, he spurred his big black and pulled ahead.

Jack Townsend frowned a little, but he agreed. "He's right. Are you set for a run?"

Joanna nodded, and Constance added, "I suppose we must." Constance was a fair rider, but she did not hunt and preferred a more sedate pace.

The three of them urged their mounts to a gallop. Though the horses were a little tired, they seemed as eager as their riders to reach a dry haven before the storm burst. As they hurtled along, they occasionally glimpsed Sir Rollin ahead of them. His powerful horse pulled further and further away as they rode.

They had covered another quarter of the distance, when Constance suddenly cried out. Joanna turned quickly to see that her horse had stumbled in the road and was trying desperately to recover its stride. "Hold his head up," cried Jack Townsend, and Constance valiantly tried to do so, but her mount's imbalance was too great, and in another moment, both she and the horse were down in the middle of the lane.

Joanna had already pulled up, and now she jumped down, holding her horse's bridle and running toward Constance. But although she had been quick, Jack was before her, leaping from his mount even before it stopped. He reached Constance first. He took her arm and leaned over her.

"I'm all right," said Constance shakily, "only bruised. How foolish of me."

"Wasn't your fault," answered Jack laconically, "bad rut just there."

Joanna came up, and Jack left Constance to her as he went to the latter's struggling horse. He got it up and began running his hands down its legs.

Joanna put an arm around Constance to help her up. The girl started to stand, but when she put her left foot on the ground, she cried out again and would have fallen if Joanna had not supported her. "Oh, my ankle," said Constance. "I must have come down on it."

Jack looked up. "Can you walk?"

162

Constance tried, leaning on Joanna's arm. "Ow! No. Oh, I am sorry."

"Nonsense," put in Joanna. "It was not your fault at all. It might have happened to anyone."

The other girl smiled wryly. "But it did not, did it? You all three ride better than I."

Jack came to their side. "Well, you will have to ride my horse," he said. "Yours has a badly strained shoulder; shouldn't be ridden." He looked about for his gray, and at that moment, they all realized that Jack's horse was gone. He had not held it when he leaped off.

As they gazed helplessly up and down the road, trying to see it somewhere near, the storm broke violently over their heads, huge drops of rain pelting them backed by a stiff wind.

"Damn!" exclaimed Jack, not bothering to excuse himself.

As one, they turned their backs to the wind and rain, using the two horses as a shield. Already, they were soaked through. "Constance can ride with me," gasped Joanna, the cold water making her breathless.

"It looks as if she will have to," agreed Jack. "I can lead her horse home."

"Oh, no," cried Constance. "You mustn't."

The young man shrugged. "Well, I must walk in any case, since I was so foolish as to let go of the reins. Thunderbolt is my newest horse; he won't know to come back. And if I am walking, I may as well lead yours." A flash of lightning and clap of thunder followed one another very closely. The girls jumped.

"Sir Rollin will see that we are gone and come back," said Joanna. "Then you can ride with him."

They all looked down the road; they could see nothing but rain. Jack looked doubtful.

"Of course," replied Constance, but she sounded unsure.

"Well, you must go along," Jack said finally. He lifted Constance onto Joanna's horse, she helping all she

163

could with her right foot. Then, he helped Joanna get up behind her and gave Joanna the reins. "You will have to go slowly," he added. "The mud will be slippery, and your horse is overburdened. Take care."

"We will," answered Joanna. The two girls looked down at him.

"Go on."

"Leaving you here . . ." began Constance.

But Jack made an impatient gesture. "It will do no good for all of us to stand about in the storm. Go on."

Joanna tightened the reins. "We will send Sir Rollin to you when we come up with him," she said. "He is probably searching for us now."

"Do," replied Jack. He picked up the trailing reins of Constance's horse and started forward. The animal limped slowly along.

"Well, goodbye," said Joanna.

"Yes, yes. Go on."

Joanna touched the mare's flanks, and they started off. Their pace was barely above a fast walk, but they left Jack behind even so. Both girls huddled against the storm, bending their heads and trusting the horse to keep on the road.

Though the remaining distance was not long, it seemed so. Constance said little, and Joanna was certain that her ankle pained her. The wind drove the rain into their backs, and it dripped down their collars clammily. Before long, both were shivering. The air was much cooler than it had been earlier.

They reached the vicarage without seeing anyone on the road. Joanna wondered briefly what had become of Sir Rollin, but she was too grateful to see the house looming ahead to do more than that. She pulled up in front of it and carefully slid to the ground, turning to brace Constance as she did likewise. Then, with Constance leaning heavily on her arm, they walked slowly up the two steps and into the front hall. The door, thankfully, was not locked.

As soon as they were safely in, Constance sank onto a chair. "Oh, I am cold," she said.

Joanna shut the door. "I will find your mother." But she was not required to go looking, for at that moment, attracted by the noise of the door, the butler came into the hall. He exclaimed when he saw the dripping girls and began ringing bells and snapping orders at once.

Twenty minutes later, Constance and Joanna sat in the former's bedroom before a crackling fire. Their drenched habits had been taken away to be dried, and both wore dressing gowns, Joanna's borrowed. Mrs. Williston was examining her daughter's ankle, while Joanna stared out at the darkening day. "Oh, I hope they have found Jack," she said, for the third time.

"I'm sure they must have," replied Mrs. Williston soothingly. "Well, I do not think it is broken, Constance. But it is a nasty sprain, I believe. We will have the doctor."

"Oh, I feel so foolish," said Constance.

"There is one of the grooms with your mare," cried Joanna from the window. "They must have found him. But where is he?"

"I daresay he went to his own house," said the older woman. "It is hardly a step."

"Yes, of course." Joanna came and sat before the fire. "I am so glad he is not still out walking in this rain. I suppose the note I sent to my mother has arrived also."

"Certainly." Mrs. Williston got up. "And if the rain has not stopped after dinner, we will send you home in a closed carriage, just as we told her." She glanced out the window. "I don't believe it will stop." With this, she went out.

Constance leaned her head on the back of the chair she sat in and sighed. "Does your ankle hurt you?" asked Joanna sympathetically.

"Only a little. But I feel strangely tired."

"Yes, I am tired, too. It was a long day." She rose and went to the window again. "Whatever can have

165

become of Sir Rollin? I hope he did not lose his way in the storm."

Constance grimaced. "I imagine that he rather got home dry and safe. At the pace he was going, he should have."

"Oh, no. He must have looked for us."

Constance raised her eyebrows, then shrugged.

"Constance! He would have. No one could have left us in that storm."

The other girl shrugged again.

"Well, I know he would have. I hope he did not blunder down some lane and lose his way. He does not know the neighborhood." Joanna looked out at the driving rain once again. "I suppose it's no use sending someone to look for him."

Constance frowned, started to speak, then changed her mind. "He must have found his way home by now," she answered drily. "It is nearly six."

"Yes, I suppose so."

Constance looked at her for a moment, then with a tiny shake of her head, abandoned the subject.

Fourteen

The only member of Joanna' family who was excited by the story of her adventure was Frederick. Her mother, after ascertaining that Joanna had taken no hurt from the mishap, dismissed it, though her mouth tightened when she heard the part Denby had played. Mr. Rowntree scarcely seemed to listen when she recounted the events of the day, but Frederick was charmed and asked innumerable questions. The following morning he was up early and off to the Townsends to see his particular friend Johnny Townsend and to hear more about Jack's part in it.

Joanna spent a very quiet morning, rising late, doing a little sewing, and reading. Though she felt quite well, the exertions of the previous day urged quiet. The sky remained overcast, and it rained lightly from time to time, but the air was cooler than it had been for weeks. There was no digging because of the damp.

When Frederick returned about eleven, he came directly to the drawing room to find Joanna. She sat there alone, reading a novel. "Jack Townsend has taken a severe chill," said Frederick as soon as he walked through the door. "He's in bed." The boy seemed to relish the idea.

"Oh, no," exclaimed Joanna, putting her book aside. "I must go to see how he does."

"Can't," answered her brother smugly. "No one is to see him."

Joanna frowned. "Well, I shall send a note then." She rose and went to the writing desk in the corner.

"Johnny says he's coughing and wheezing like a buzzard," added Frederick. Joanna ignored him and began to write. "He walked the whole way home leading that mare," added the boy. His sister bent her head. Frederick shrugged and walked over to the window. It was raining harder now, and he watched the droplets run down the panes until Joanna finished her note and sealed it. When she had taken it out to a footman and returned, Frederick came to sit beside her on the sofa and lean forward confidentially. "You know what else I found out today?" he asked. "Something much more important."

"Oh, Frederick, do leave me alone," said Joanna crossly.

He sat back, offended. "Well, perhaps I shall. And perhaps I shan't tell you the news about the treasure."

Joanna turned back to him. "What news?"

Her brother rose, jammed his hands in his pockets, and strolled to the window again. "Can't say. I'm to leave you alone." He looked out once more and began to whistle an irritating high-pitched tune.

Joanna grimaced. "I'm sorry, Frederick. What is it?"

The boy turned eagerly, his blue eyes lighting. "I've found out that there were no 'boys' nosing around the abbey ruins, that's what. I've asked everyone and their friends too. Not one of them went over there that night."

Joanna looked disgusted. "Is that all? I daresay they are afraid to tell you they were there. That is not news, Frederick."

"Is it not? Well, I am not such a gapeseed as you think me. I did not ask them outright. I was very careful. There were no boys."

"What difference can it make?"

Frederick looked amazed. "What difference? Don't you see? If it wasn't the boys, it must have been someone else."

"And so? I don't see . . ."

"Dunce!" exploded Frederick. He leaned toward her again. "There must be someone else searching for the treasure. Don't you see that? And we must find it first."

"You are imagining things. You always do. Perhaps it was a tramp or a gypsy looking for shelter for the night."

"Digging?" answered her brother incredulously.

"Oh . . . well . . ."

Frederick put his hands on his hips and looked down at her disgustedly. "You are the stupidest thing, Joanna. What if he finds the treasure first? He will go off with it, and we shall never see a penny."

"There is no *he*. You have imagined the whole."

Her brother turned away. "All right. We shall see. But I mean to keep a watch. And I am going to the Abbey this afternoon to tell Mr. Erland what I have found out. *He* will see how important it is."

"Has he invited you?"

"I am always welcome. He said so."

"That is a polite nothing, Frederick. You go over there too often. He must be heartily sick of it by now."

"He is *not!* You think you know everything, Joanna, but you are quite out there."

Joanna frowned. She could not believe that Mr. Erland welcomed the constant visits of a schoolboy. "I shall go with you," she said. She would see for herself.

"You? Why?"

"Haven't I helped in the treasure hunt?"

"Not lately you haven't. You've been too busy digging with Father and riding all over the countryside with dandies." Frederick took several mincing steps and made a mock bow.

Joanna laughed. "How horrid you are. But I mean to go with you just the same."

169

Frederick laughed, too, his good spirits restored by this show of interest. "All right. But I shall leave at two sharp. Mind you are ready. You'll see, Joanna. We'll find the treasure all right and tight."

Joanna wisely made no reply to this, and after warning her again not to be late, Frederick bounced out of the room.

They took the gig to Erland Abbey. The rain had nearly stopped, but both wore cloaks well pulled up around them to keep off stray droplets and mud. Joanna had insisted they send a note before them, so they found Jonathan Erland at home and waiting.

He seemed glad, even excited, to see them. "I believe I have found something," he said as they walked down the hall to the library.

"Not the treasure?" cried Frederick, deeply chagrined.

"No, not that. But a clue perhaps."

"Ah, I have found out something too."

When they had sat down, Frederick poured out his story. "So you see," he finished, "there must be someone else looking for the treasure. We must take care."

Erland nodded a bit dubiously. "It is possible, though it might have been something else, or perhaps only some sensation seeker."

Frederick started to protest, but Joanna was ahead of him. "That is what I said. It is ridiculous to imagine that someone else would come to dig at the abbey. Who would it be? One of the neighbors? Nonsense."

"Yes," replied Erland slowly. He seemed as uncertain of her assertion as of Frederick's.

The boy snorted. "Well if that is not the stupidest thing. There are heaps of people who might have heard of it. In Oxford perhaps. One of Father's students. I wager that Sir Rollin Denby told everyone."

"He did not," retorted Joanna hotly before Erland could speak. "He would not do such a thing."

Frederick snorted again.

Erland was looking at Joanna, an anxious expression in his gray eyes. There was a momentary pause. Frederick had turned away, and Joanna was frowning at him. Erland cleared his throat briefly, then said, "Well, well, it is all over, you know. And no one has trespassed again. Let me tell you what I have found. It may mean that anyone can dig as much as he wishes without disturbing us in the least."

Frederick turned back immediately. "What is it?" Joanna, too, looked interested.

Erland opened a drawer of his desk and took out the charts they had found some days ago. "I have been going over these with your father," he said. Frederick made an inarticulate noise. "Without, of course, telling him of our search. He has much more knowledge of historical documents than I, and he has been a great help." Erland unfolded one of the sheets. "We have concluded, from some of the markings here and the probable dates of the notations that some of my ancestors may have been Jacobites."

Joanna gazed at him blankly.

Her brother frowned, waited for something more and then said, "What has that to do with anything? I daresay they may have been, but what have Jacobites to do with the treasure?"

"You know who they were?" asked Erland.

Frederick looked superior. "Of course. They wanted the Pretenders for king, the Stuarts. It was all hundreds of years ago." His smugness wavered a bit. "Or a long time ago at least."

"It was," agreed the man solemnly, only the twinkle in his eyes showing what he thought of the young Rowntrees' reception of his news. "But the important thing is that there were several plots and rebellions over the question. And many times, men had to be hidden from the authorities for long periods of time. The oldest of these charts suggests, very obliquely, that Erland Abbey was one such hiding place."

Joanna was frowning. "You mean," she said slowly, "that there is some sort of secret room?"

"I think so. It may be that this is the family tradition my uncle wished me to remember."

"A secret chamber," murmured Frederick, immense gratification evident in his voice. "First-rate. Where is it?"

Erland smiled. "That is the problem. If there is such a room, it is the obvious hiding place for the money. But the charts are by no means clear about the location. Come and look."

Frederick and Joanna jumped up and came over to the desk.

"You see that here," said Erland, pointing, "there are several unusual lines on the chart, on the side of the house nearest the ruins. Your father thinks these indicate some sort of built-in hiding place there, but we cannot make out exactly where. The instructions are purposely misleading. They were breaking the law, you understand, and had to be careful. The chamber might be anywhere in that wing."

There was a short silence as the three of them thought of the huge old house and all the nooks and crannies it contained. Searching even one wing would be a monumental task.

"Well, we must simply look everywhere," said Frederick. His expression was complacent. "I am ready."

Erland laughed. "Indeed, I see you are. But it would be better to form some plan of action first."

"Pooh. I say, start at once." Frederick suited his actions to his words. "I shall get a lantern. I daresay some of the rooms are dark." He ran out of the room.

Erland laughed again. "He is full of enthusiasm."

But Joanna was frowning. "Too full. He is abominably rude, though he doesn't mean it."

"I know it."

"You must not let him plague you to death."

"He does not. Quite the contrary. I enjoy having some lively company in this gloomy barrack."

Joanna looked at him. "You don't like living here?"

"It isn't that." Jonathan looked about the room. "I'm fond of the old place, right enough. But it needs so many repairs I cannot make. That galls me and depresses my spirits occasionally."

"Well, but you will when you find your uncle's fortune."

He smiled wryly. "Do you truly believe there is a fortune, Miss Joanna?"

Her eyes widened. "Don't you?"

"I don't know. I wish it, of course, for many reasons, but I cannot quite bring myself to believe it."

"Frederick believes it," offered Joanna, not knowing quite what to say. Erland looked tired and dispirited.

He smiled. "Indeed he does. If anyone can find a treasure, he can."

"You will. I know you will," said Joanna impulsively.

Erland looked directly into her eyes followed by a long moment of silence. For some reason, Joanna found she was holding her breath. "Do you think so?" he said finally, allowing her to breathe again. "It *is* important to me."

"You could repair the Abbey," she agreed.

"Yes—and I could think of marriage, a family, as I cannot now." He watched her. "I never did think about such things until I came to this neighborhood. But now I do, often."

A sudden thought came to Joanna, making her move involuntarily. Erland saw it and gave a bitter little laugh. "It is all ridiculous, of course. A treasure." His tone was derisive. "I don't really suppose that there is such a thing. But I will grasp at any straw."

The look in his eyes made Joanna get to her feet. She felt a little breathless again, and her emotions were uncertain. Though Erland had not said anything directly, the look in his eyes and the way he spoke suggested that he felt some special interest in her. She was startled, confused, and certain that she did not wish to continue this conversation.

173

"No," said the man sharply as she turned away. Joanna looked at him nervously. "I mean, I did not intend to say anything. I know I cannot yet . . . that is, I have no right . . . oh gods, what a tangle."

The moment was horridly embarrassing. Joanna found that she was incapable of movement, and she wondered wildly what she should do. She wanted to get away, but she couldn't seem to begin.

Erland recovered first. "Miss Rowntree, I must and do apologize," he began. But he was interrupted by a sudden noisy clanging from the lower regions of the house, followed by the sound of voices raised in angry dispute.

"What is it?" exclaimed the girl automatically.

"Let us see." They hurried out of the room together, both looking relieved.

Following their ears, they went down a corridor and descended a narrow set of stairs, the noises increasing in volume as they went. They came out in the kitchen, to be greeted by the sight of Frederick running past, head down, arms pumping. Hot on his heels was the housekeeper, Mrs. Smith; she was brandishing a broom and scolding continuously. "Lanterns, is it?" they heard her mutter. "Lanterns, and then oil, and then perhaps a bit of bread and butter or a slice of cake. Cake! As if I kept such nonsense in my kitchen. And the next thing you know, the minute I turn my back, the milk pail on the scullery floor and all the cream ruined. Trying to reach the shelf, is it? I'll show him shelf. Boys! Won't have 'em in here. Worse than rats."

Throughout this monologue, Mrs. Smith chased Frederick with the broom, once managing to strike him glancingly. At last, the boy saw the two of them in the doorway and hastily ducked behind Erland. "She's mad," he gasped, and without another look behind dashed up the stairs and disappeared.

Mrs. Smith also noticed her employer. She lowered the broom and made no move to follow Frederick. But

174

the look in her eye was daunting. *"Mr.* Erland!" she said before the others could speak. "I will not have boys in my kitchen. It's not what I'm used to, and it's not what I'll stand." The tone in which she said the word *boys* implied that she would indeed have preferred an infestation of rats to Frederick's visit. "He's pushed over the pan where the cream was rising, and it's spoilt. There'll be no milk for your breakfast. Such things never happened in the Master's time." She crossed her arms and looked at him. Mrs. Smith had never gotten out of the habit of calling Thomas Erland "the Master." To her, he remained so even though dead, while his young nephew was *Mr.* Erland.

"Oh, I am so sorry," stammered Joanna.

But Erland made a quick gesture to silence her and turned to Mrs. Smith with raised brows. "The milk was an accident, I'm sure, Mrs. Smith. Frederick will apologize. You make too much of a trivial incident. And you must become accustomed to having my friends in the house."

"I'll not have boys, and I'll not do for boys," answered the woman implacably.

Erland looked even haughtier. "You will be polite to all of my guests, I hope, or we shall fall out."

Mrs. Smith struggled for words. Finally, she muttered, "Extra butter, a joint twice a week, dust the corners, air the hangings, and now—now BOYS!" Her tone was progressively outraged as she spoke. "I *won't* have it," she exclaimed at the end. "Things were never so under the Master."

"My uncle, regrettably, is dead, Mrs. Smith," replied Erland cooly.

Mrs. Smith was fumbling with the strings of her apron. At last, she got it untied and flung it down at his feet. "You may do what you will," she snapped, infuriated, "but I'll not stay to see it. I give my notice this minute." And with this parting shot, she stamped off.

They stood silently, listening to her heavy footsteps

175

die away. Erland was turned a little away from Joanna; she could not see his face, but he appeared to be laboring under some agitation. "Oh, I am sorry," she said. "It was all Frederick's doing. He is entirely at fault. I shall scold him roundly."

Erland turned, and Joanna saw to her surprise that he was laughing.

"Scold him?" he said. "More likely I shall reward him handsomely. He has rid me of the worst housekeeper in the county. I have puzzled and puzzled how to make her leave, and he did it in three minutes. Where is he? I must thank him." He turned and began to climb the stairs.

It was so absurd that Joanna had to laugh also. "You are roasting me," she said as they climbed. "I know you did not care for Mrs. Smith, but you cannot be pleased to be without a housekeeper."

"Can I not? I am more than pleased to be without Mrs. Smith. I daresay *I* am a better cook than she ever was."

Joanna laughed again.

"You don't believe me? But I have many times cooked a meal on the trail. I am a fine cook. Ah, here he is." They had reached the hall by this time, and Frederick peered out at them from behind the staircase.

When he saw who it was, he came out, his expression sullen. "I did not mean to knock over the milk," he said. "And I am sorry. I tried to tell her so. The oil for the lantern was sitting just above it. Rum place to keep oil, I thought. And I slipped when I reached for it. She had no reason to chase me that way."

"Frederick, my lad," said Erland, putting an arm over the boy's shoulders, "there is no need to apologize. Mrs. Smith has left me, and I was never happier about anything in my life."

Frederick looked up at him suspiciously. "You're bamming me."

"I'm not."

Frederick looked at Joanna, who was still smiling

176

slightly, then back at Erland. "Heigh ho!" he cried then. "We can search all we like now." And he ran back down the stairs for the lantern, followed by the laughter of both the others.

Fifteen

They did not actually search that day. Joanna insisted that it was time they went home, and Frederick was brought around by the promise that he might poke about all he liked tomorrow. Joanna was eager to leave; after the excitement of Mrs. Smith's departure faded, the embarrassment of the previous minutes in the library returned, and she did not want to stay at the Abbey. Erland seemed to concur.

As they drove home in the gig, Joanna was too preoccupied even to deliver the customary strictures on Frederick's neck-or-nothing driving. Her emotions were in turmoil: on the one hand, it was exciting and flattering to be clearly the object of a man's regard; on the other, she was embarrassed and uneasy, because she was fairly certain that she did not return it. The thing that confused her even more was that she was not *entirely* certain. Before Erland had spoken to her, she would have unhesitatingly said that she cared for him only as a pleasant friend. But in that awkward moment in his study, she had been forced to consider him in another light, and with that, something had changed. She did not know just what. And now, all she wished for was the solitude of her own chamber and time to think.

This wish was not to be granted. When Frederick pulled up the gig before the door, it was immediately clear that they had callers. "Ugh," said the boy. "I shall take the horses around to the stables. You may do the pretty in the drawing room. You like that."

Joanna sighed, but she said nothing as she got down. Frederick took the gig away, and she started for the door. The sooner she went in, the sooner it would be over and she could retreat to her room.

In the drawing room, she found an ill-assorted group. Her mother sat on the sofa chatting desultorily with Sir Rollin Denby, and opposite them, Selina Grant and Constance Williston were making stiff conversation in two armchairs. Everyone looked relieved when Joanna walked in.

Sir Rollin rose and bowed slightly. "I called to see how you got on after our mishap," he said, "and I was fortunate in finding Miss Williston here. I meant to go on to the Rectory, of course."

From the corner of her eye, Joanna saw Constance grimace, and she hurried to say, "How kind. It was too bad, was it not? Did you get a wetting also?"

"I did indeed." Sir Rollin smiled wryly. "In fact, I cut a pretty figure altogether. Not only was I caught out in the storm, I lost my way in the lanes and had to ask directions. The cottager I spoke with made it clear he thought me mad."

Joanna laughed. "I knew it was something like that." She was glad to hear Sir Rollin's story. Too many people had seemed to think that he had simply left them. She could not resist throwing Constance a speaking glance.

"Ah, did you think I had abandoned you?" asked the man, his voice amused.

"Of course not." Joanna looked across at Sir Rollin. As usual, he was the picture of a fashionable Londoner. She found herself comparing his careless elegance with Jonathan Erland's equally careless dishevelment. There could be no question that Sir Rollin shone in contrast. He looked up suddenly, his sparkling hazel eyes meeting Joanna's darker ones, and smiled. Joanna's heart beat a little faster.

"Come and sit here," he said, pointedly drawing her

a little away from the others. It was not quite polite, but Joanna could not resist sitting down beside him. He seemed to hold her with his eyes. "There was so much I meant to say to you on our ride," continued Denby, "and then I got caught up in seeing the town and said none of them. Can you forgive me?" He laughed down at her.

"Of . . . of course," stammered Joanna. Then, realizing this was an inane response, she began, "I mean . . ."

"No, no, let it go at forgiveness. Don't let us go on about my cloddishness." Joanna thought that Sir Rollin could never be cloddish, whatever happened. "I am so glad you took no hurt," he continued smoothly. "I really cut a poor figure, stumbling through the mud and wet. I wish I could have rescued you all. Miss Williston mentioned that she took a fall."

Joanna nodded, recounting the story of their homecoming. "Luckily, the injury to her ankle was less serious than we feared. She can walk on it already."

He nodded, paused a moment, then asked, "And how is your digging getting on? I have not been able to look in these past few days."

"It is not going too well. We cannot seem to find the church, though Papa was sure he knew where it was. However, Mr. Erland has given him the chart of the ruins. I daresay he will find it soon."

"Ah yes, those mysterious charts. I had meant to ask you more about them. You were so clever in finding them. Have they been of help?"

Joanna nodded. "Mr. Erland thinks one of them shows a secret chamber. His family were Jacobites." Proud of her knowledge, Joanna sat up a little straighter. So he thought her clever?

"Fascinating. And I daresay these, er, Jacobites hid their friends in the secret room?"

Joanna nodded again, a little disappointed at his quickness. She had thought to make a real story of it.

"You astonish me. And have you found this chamber?"

"No, that is the vexing part. The chart is unclear

about where it is. Mr. Erland showed us some marking on the side of the house near the ruins, but I could make nothing of them. No one could."

"A pity. Perhaps your father could be of help?"

"He has looked at them already. I think he is more interested in the other chart, the one of the ruins themselves."

"Ah, to be sure. But Erland thinks that his uncle's fortune is hidden in this secret room, I suppose?"

His tone was so avid that Joanna raised her eyes to his.

He smiled. "You must forgive me. Erland's treasure hunt is providing almost the only excitement I have found in this neighborhood. Were it not for that, I should be unutterably bored." He moved to lay his hand over hers on the sofa cushion. "That, and one other thing, of course." His eyes held hers once again.

Joanna flushed and looked down.

"My greatest pleasure," added the man, "has been to discuss this fascinating event with *you*. It is such a piquant combination—a treasure in a secret chamber and a ravishing fellow searcher."

"Th-thank you," stammered Joanna.

"And Erland does think the treasure is really there?"

"In the secret room? Yes."

"Ah." With this, Denby turned back to look about the room. Both the younger visitors were staring at the couple in the corner, and in a moment he had caught Constance's eye. "Your friends seem a bit put out," said Sir Rollin. "Perhaps, unfortunately, we should rejoin them."

"Oh," replied Joanna, disappointed but a little guilty also, "oh, yes."

They rose and went back to the group before the fireplace. Selina was openly staring at them, her pale blue eyes wide. Constance had looked away, but her mouth was tight. Mrs. Rowntree, with better control, kept her expression bland.

"Have you heard that Jack Townsend has caught a

severe chill?" asked Constance determinedly when they sat down again. "He is really ill."

Pulled back to the present, Joanna was all sympathy. "Oh, yes. I am so sorry. I sent him a note, though I don't suppose he cares for that. When one is feeling sick, the last thing one wants is to read."

"Poor Jack," said Selina, in an effort to join in their conversation. But her remark served rather to end it, as there seemed nothing to do but nod agreement. A silence descended on the room.

After a moment, Sir Rollin spoke again. "I have come for another purpose today as well. My sister is finally ready to stage her gala as the house is nearly finished. When she heard I meant to come here, she gave me this to deliver." He handed an envelope to Mrs. Rowntree. "The invitation. And there is one for Mrs. Williston as well. Will she think me an oaf if I send it with you, Miss Williston?"

"Not at all," answered Constance colorlessly, holding out her hand for the missive. Her face and tone did not agree with her words.

Sir Rollin merely smiled. "Make my apologies to her, please." This done, he rose. "And now, I fear, I must take my leave. I have overstayed in any case, hoping to speak to you, Miss Joanna."

Joanna looked down, murmuring something inarticulate. Mrs. Rowntree rose and saw their guest out.

When he was gone, she turned to the three girls. "Selina, Constance, you will excuse me, I know. I must speak to Cook, and I have delayed over-long already." And she left the room also.

Silence fell. For perhaps the first time in her life, Joanna wished fervently that her friends would leave her. She was still in a turmoil, even more after seeing Sir Rollin. But neither of the others showed any sign of going. Indeed, they eyed each other as if determined to stay. At last, Constance ventured, "You are completely recovered, Joanna?"

"Oh, yes, I am perfectly fine. And your ankle?"

"It is nearly healed, I always mend quickly."

"Joanna is very delicate," put in Selina positively. Joanna stared at her. "But one can see, Miss Williston, that you have an extremely robust constitution. I daresay you were a great strapping baby, too."

Joanna's eyes widened further. Constance's lips jerked. "Actually, I was not," she replied. "It is unaccountable."

"I myself am greatly subject to chills," Selina continued. "I feel prodigiously for Jack. There is nothing more unpleasant than being ill in the summer. In the winter, one doesn't care, of course; it is so dreary. But in the summer, one wants to be out."

"Very true," murmured Constance.

"So Mrs. Finley is to entertain at last," blurted Joanna. "I must say I am curious to see the house."

This diversion was partly successful. Selina tittered, "Oh, yes. The housekeeper says she hardly knows the place, so much is changed. And not for the better."

"Mrs. Finley certainly has some peculiar ideas," agreed Constance. "I wonder, did she find a hermit?"

Joanna shrugged, but Selina was better informed. "She did. I don't know who, but it is a man from the charity hospital in Oxford, they say. She had such trouble over the thing." Selina giggled again. "They say old Mr. Powers had quite a bit to say when he was asked. He nearly threw them out of his cottage. How I wish I might have seen it!"

Both the other girls smiled, and they all contemplated this picture in silence for a moment. Then Selina added, "The house is very fashionable now, though. There is a billard room and a croquet lawn."

"Well, I prefer the old style," said Constance.

This judgment, though not directed at her, made Selina recall her earlier hostility. "Of course," she said, "you are fond of all kinds of ancient things." She turned to Joanna and asked with seeming innocence, "By the by, I have not seen Gerald this age, Joanna. When is he to visit?"

Constance flushed and looked at the floor. Surprised at Selina's unsuspected perspicacity, Joanna said, "Have you not? He was here only last week." She rose before anyone could reply. "Heavens, it is almost tea time. I really must go upstairs and leave my bonnet."

Constance took her cue and rose also, shooting a grateful look in Joanna's direction. Selina got up reluctantly. "Shall I see you tomorrow, Selina?" Joanna asked. She could tell the other girl was not going to leave without some definite engagement. "We might go walking." She had not been out with Selina in days, and she felt guilty over this.

Selina's face cleared. "Oh, yes. Unless it rains. But I shall walk over in any case." After this, she was quite ready to depart and quickly put on her bonnet and shawl.

Constance squeezed Joanna's hand as she took her leave, though they made no plans. And in a few moments, Joanna was alone. She gave a long sigh and started up the stairs. Finally, she could have some time to herself. In her room, she sank into the armchair by the window and stared out blankly. So many thoughts revolved in her mind at once that she hardly knew what she felt.

For several days, Joanna felt disinclined to go out. She saw Selina for their walk and went to church on Sunday, but otherwise, she stayed home. So much had happened in the last few weeks, she felt she needed time to assimilate it all. She did not go to the Abbey with her father, even after they finally discovered the corner of the old church near the end of the week. She promised him that she would come to sketch it very soon, but made no move to do so.

She was a little surprised to see nothing of Sir Rollin Denby during these days. He had been so attentive at their last meeting that she had expected him to call again. But he did not. She had no word of him at all. After a time, she decided that he had been drafted to help with his sister's coming entertainment, but she still wondered at his silence.

Jonathan Erland was also absent. But his did not

surprise Joanna in the least. She thought he had been as embarrassed as she at their last encounter. She did not know what she would say to him the next time they met, and was glad he did not visit them, even staying away from one of her father's Thursday night gatherings. Frederick twice urged her to go with him to the Abbey. He and Erland were having a capital time, he said, searching for the secret room. But Joanna refused. She must first understand her feelings about this man very clearly.

Joanna could not marry him, of course. He was not at all the sort of man she had always meant to marry—a man of fashion. But she found that for some reason she was reluctant to tell him this. It was wrong to allow him to hope, she realized, but every time she imagined telling him the truth, something inside her balked. Joanna told herself that she did not wish to hurt his feelings, but she was not completely satisfied with this explanation.

Inevitably, Sir Rollin Denby entered these meditations also. What if it were he who had spoken of marriage, Joanna wondered more than once? What would her reaction have been then? The very questions made her shiver with excitement. To think of being married to Sir Rollin! His wife would surely be the very height of fashion, surrounded by a whirl of gaiety in London. Beside Sir Rollin, Jonathan Erland was clearly . . . but at this point, Joanna always stopped. Mr. Erland was clearly what? When she had first seen him and his countrified appearance, she had put him down as a bumpkin. But now, she no longer thought of him so. When she tried to judge the two men against one another, she found she could not. They seemed in such different categories.

Joanna began to feel very young and inexperienced. She had hardly realized how complicated life could be when one was forced to make one's own decisions. She could not run to her mother this time, as she had with so many other problems. Her mother would never understand. She would say that Jonathan Erland had been irresponsible, to have spoken so in his circumstances, and Joanna had the feeling that her mother disliked Sir Rollin enough to try to discourage her daughter's growing interest in him. All was left to her, and Joanna felt increasingly burdened by the situation.

It was for this reason that she stayed at home and kept to herself. Some decision seemed to be required of her. But as the days passed, none came.

Sixteen

The day of the Finleys' gala arrived before Joanna had satisfactorily resolved these problems. As she prepared for the event, she frowned. Both Sir Rollin and Erland would of course be present. What would she say to Erland? And what would Denby say to her? It was both exciting and daunting to wonder such things.

The party was set for eleven. They were fortunate in the weather: the clouds and rain of the last several days had departed, and the day was sunny but not too hot. When Joanna came down to the drawing room, looking brightly pretty in white muslin sprinkled with tiny yellow flowers and a straw hat, only her mother awaited her. Mrs. Rowntree smiled approvingly when she saw her daughter. "Your father has absolutely refused to attend the party, Joanna. I fear there have been too many invitations this summer. We shall have to go alone. You look lovely, dear."

"Should we stay home?" asked Joanna doubtfully. The idea was not entirely unpleasant. If she did not see the gentlemen, she would not have to worry about what to say to them.

"Oh, no. It is a neighborhood party. And after all, there is no reason why we should not go out without your father. We shall do so continually in London next season. And Gerald is coming up from Oxford; we shall meet him there."

189

They said little in the carriage on the way. Joanna was deep in thought, and her mother appeared to be enjoying the scenery, though she looked sharply at her daughter more than once. The changes Adrienne had made in the Finley estate were apparent even before they reached the house. The avenue leading up to it, which had been lined with ancient oaks, was now completely bare. Though Joanna had more than once complained about these trees, saying that their overhanging branches made the lane gloomy and dark, she was horrified. The open vista up to the house looked appallingly bleak to her. And when they had pulled up before the door and been ushered in by a haughty London butler, her feelings were even more intense. The entrance hall had been freshly painted peach, and she recognized none of the furniture. The old front parlor was gone; walls had been removed to turn it into a billiard room, and the green table looked like an alien intruder. Even the library on the other side of the hall seemed different, though Joanna could not say just how.

They were escorted through the house, and Adrienne greeted them effusively on the back terrace. Joanna let her mother answer for them both as she stared incredulously at the gardens. This formerly familiar place was utterly different now. She recognized nothing. The old arbor, so cool and secret in summer and full of hanging grapes later in the year, was gone, as were the homely beds of daisies and lavender. In their place was a rose garden, a wilderness, and near the back of the property, the famous grotto. It was all quite fashionable, but somehow Joanna could not like it.

"You are admiring the gardens, I see," cooed Adrienne. Peter had come up to greet them, and she took his arm possessively. "It was a great work, but I admit I am prodigiously pleased. Did you see the billiard room? We hope to try it today, though my brother has already christened it, so to speak." She tittered.

Mrs. Rowntree murmured something vaguely complimentary, and they moved off to allow another guest to be welcomed. Joanna stared about like a sleepwalker. "It certainly is changed," said her mother. "The roses are lovely." She sounded unconvinced.

"Changed?" exclaimed Joanna. "I should say so. It is ruined."

"Quietly, my dear. It is natural that they should wish to refurbish the place, to make it their own."

"I suppose so. But I do not like it."

"Well," responded Mrs. Rowntree good-naturedly, "I am not certain I do either, but it is hardly necessary that we do, is it? Ah, there are the Grants."

They walked across the lawn to where Mrs. Grant and Selina stood talking to some other neighbors. Selina immediately took Joanna's arm and pulled her away. "Isn't it hideous?" she whispered. "To think we played in this garden so often. And now I declare I do not know one corner of it. And the house! The new hangings in the drawing room are ugly, and I heard Mr. Townsend say that the billiard room is nothing but pretension."

This echoing of her own thoughts gave Joanna pause. Selina sounded very ill-natured. "I suppose they want their own things around them," she replied.

"I cannot imagine why," tittered Selina. "Their own things seem to be quite horrid."

"Selina!"

"It is the truth."

"People like different things," offered Joanna.

"Do you mean to say that you like this garden now?" Selina was outraged. "And the house?"

"No," replied Joanna slowly.

"Well, there you are then." Selina looked smugly pleased. She eyed the terrace and the crowd complacently. "Oh look, there is Jack Townsend. I am so glad to see him. They didn't know whether he would come today; he must be better. Let us go and say hello."

They walked across to the group of young people around Jack and were soon immersed in the conversation. Adrienne had invited every family within ten miles, and they saw neighbors that they encountered only once or twice a year. A general effort to catch up on the news and become reacquainted occupied the group for some time.

Because of it, Joanna did not even see Jonathan Erland arrive, and she hadn't a moment to wonder where Sir Rollin might be. It had seemed a little odd that he was not there to greet them along with his sister, but now this was forgotten in the general chatter.

By noon, everyone had arrived, and soon after the hour, Adrienne stood up on the terrace and called out, "Everyone. Please listen, everyone!"

It took a moment for her to get the crowd's attention; they were enjoying their talk too much. But finally silence fell, and she spoke again.

"I have a surprise. Everyone please follow Peter and me, and you shall see it." Adrienne took Peter's arm and walked down the terrace steps onto the lawn. The two of them started out across the grass toward the wilderness at the back of the garden.

"What can it be?" wondered Selina as the rest of them followed. But no one answered her.

The whole crowd strolled down to the copse, finding a path there which wound through it. Adrienne and Peter stayed a little ahead. "Isn't it amazing," said Constance Williston, who had joined Joanna and Selina a moment before, "that they could make all this in so short a time? Where can they have found these trees?"

Joanna opened her mouth to agree, but at that moment they emerged from the thick growth, and instead of speaking, she merely gaped. The center of the wilderness was a clearing, planted with the smoothest grass. And in the middle stood a tiny greek temple, complete with dome and pillars, and as fresh and new as could be. Tables had been set out around it. Clearly, lunch was to be served out here. And Sir Rollin Denby stood on one of its steps, smiling sardonically at the party and looking darkly handsome.

"Oh, my!" said Constance.

There were murmurs of astonishment all around. Some of the guests were surprised and impressed, and others appeared to be amused. Glimpsing her brother's face, Joanna knew that at least one was outraged.

"Here is our surprise," called Adrienne gaily. "And now Mr. Erland must admit that even though he got in before me with his picnic, I have triumphed."

From the other side of the group, Erland replied, "I admit myself utterly outdone." Craning her neck a little, Joanna saw him. He was smiling good-naturedly and looked immensely amused.

Adrienne made a grandiose gesture. "Let there be music and revelry," she cried. And to everyone's further astonishment, music began. Heads turned in concert to see a four-piece orchestra seated in the trees not far away. Adrienne laughed. "We are to be just like the Greeks," she added. "We shall feast in the glade."

Constance made a stifled noise, and Joanna saw Gerald frown fiercely. She caught his eye, and he came swiftly over to them. "That woman knows no more of Greece than an insect," he hissed. "It is outrageous."

Constance was restraining a smile. "It is," she agreed. "But a little funny, too. Where can she have got the idea?"

Gerald looked at her. "Do you think it funny?" He frowned thoughtfully.

"Come Joanna," said Selina, pulling at the other girl's arm. "Let us go look at the temple."

Joanna let herself be taken away, leaving Constance and Gerald together. She and Selina went up to the little building. It was raised three steps off the ground and oval-shaped. As Selina ran her hand along one of the pillars, Sir Rollin came down the steps. It seemed at first as if he might walk right past them, so Joanna said, "Hello."

He turned his head, raised one eyebrow, and nodded a careless greeting. Joanna was puzzled. "You waited here?" she added inanely.

"I could not resist watching everyone's reaction to my sister's folly."

"Folly?" echoed Joanna involuntarily. This seemed harsh.

"That is what they are called, my little innocent." He looked around. "If you will excuse me now . . ."

Joanna's cheeks reddened. He seemed completely uninterested in talking with her. Had she done something to offend him? But how? She had not seen him in days.

"Look Joanna," called Selina, "there is a mosaic in the floor."

With some relief, Joanna turned to examine the temple. There was indeed a mosaic, made of chips of different colored stones.

"What is it, Sir Rollin?" called Selina.

The man, who had been turning to go, came over to them with obvious impatience. "It is Daphne, being turned into a tree to escape the attentions of Apollo. My sister chose the subject." The mockery in his voice was cutting, and it made Joanna intensely uncomfortable. She could not tell if it was directed only at his sister, or if he was mocking them as well.

"A tree?" answered Selina. "How very odd."

"You are not a student of the classics, I see," responded Sir Rollin.

Selina gaped at him, but before she could speak, her mother was heard calling her to be introduced to a distant neighbor. The girl hesitated, then with one uneasy look at Joanna, scurried away.

A silence fell. Adrienne Finley was guiding most of the guests around the edge of the glade, showing off her creation. The rest stood near the orchestra, chatting and commenting on the music. For the moment, Joanna and Sir Rollin were alone, partially screened from the others by the pillars of the little temple.

He moved slightly, as if to walk away, and Joanna took her courage in both hands and said, "Sir Rollin?"

"Yes?" he replied without interest, turning back to her.

"May I speak to you?"

He raised his eyebrows. "You are speaking to me."

"Oh, what is the matter?" she blurted out. "Have I done something to offend you?"

These questions came out more loudly than she intended. Denby glanced around to see if they had been overheard, while Joanna blushed scarlet. But no one was paying them any heed. Adrienne had her audience on the far side of the space now, showing them a hidden path. And the others had moved to join her. Sir Rollin strode up the three steps and stood very close to Joanna. She gazed up at him nervously; he was surveying her much as her father did one of his abstruse scientific problems, a slight frown wrinkling his brow.

"Offended me?" he said finally. "How should you offend me, Miss Rowntree?"

"I . . . I don't know."

He glanced around them again and moved a bit further into the shadow of one of the pillars, drawing Joanna with him. They stood even closer now, and Joanna felt very awkward. She gazed at his tie pin, which was only three inches from her eyes, and wondered what to do.

"Beauty never offends me," continued the man, bending his head. She felt his breath on her cheek and trembled a little. His voice sounded odd, almost as if he were amused by something, but she could not meet his eye.

Suddenly, she felt his arm slide around her waist, and she was pulled against his chest. For a moment, she was so startled she couldn't move. Sir Rollin put a finger under her chin, raised her face to his, and kissed her expertly.

Recovering her wits, Joanna pulled away. "Sir Rollin!" She backed up a few steps. "Someone will see!"

He smiled. "Ah, you would prefer to continue when they can't perhaps?"

She stared at him, wide-eyed. Her emotions were in such tumult that she could scarcely frame a reply. Did he really mean what he had said? Was this some sort of unconventional proposal? Meeting his dancing hazel eyes, she knew that it was not. Sir Rollin was not thinking of marriage at this moment. The red in her cheeks deepened. "No, I do not," she said.

"Turning missish all at once? What a pity. When you know you enjoyed it as much as I."

Putting her hands to her flaming cheeks, Joanna stared at him. Her mind was chaos. But one thing stood out clearly—he was wrong. She had *not* enjoyed the kiss, not at all. And this fact was as confusing to her as any of the rest. She had thought that she wanted Sir Rollin to fall in love with her. She had excitedly imagined how it would be to be his wife. But now it appeared that she had been mistaken again. When he had held her, she had felt only worry that someone would see them, and a strong desire to escape.

She started to tell him so, but just then, Adrienne announced lunch and Selina began calling Joanna to join her group. "We must find seats together, Joanna," she cried. "Come along." The younger girl moved quickly to secure a table for six.

"Oh, no," murmured Joanna. She did not see how she could face the others just now.

"Courage," said Sir Rollin, and the mockery was clear in his voice once again. "May I?" He offered his arm.

Though she didn't wish to, after a moment Joanna took it. She was too shaken to walk proudly off across the grass, as she wished with all her heart to do. And the important thing now was to get control of her emotions; there were hours to get through before she could go home.

Selina had gathered Jack Townsend and Jonathan Erland to her table, along with one of her female friends from the neighborhood. When Joanna and Sir Rollin came up, she said, "There, we are six. Let us sit down before someone tries to part us."

Sir Rollin looked chagrined, but he could not now escape without being extremely rude. Jonathan Erland smiled warmly at Joanna and held a chair for her, which she dropped into at once. She was too preoccupied even to remember that she had been nervous about seeing him again.

With poor grace, Sir Rollin took the remaining chair on her other side, and everyone sat down.

Selina was overjoyed with her position between Jack and Jonathan Erland. She bounced in her chair as the servants began to bring around the food, and showed every sign of ominous overexcitement. Joanna was alarmed to see her accept a glass of champagne when one of the waiters offered it, and she tried to catch her friend's eye without success. Her own concerns receded a little as she wondered how she might hint that Selina should curb her spirits. Should she mention her mishap at Erland's picnic? No, that would be unkind.

"I have not even spoken to you yet," said Jonathan Erland then. "How do you do?"

His easy pleasant voice somehow filled Joanna with a vast relief. She could not have said just why, but suddenly her problems seemed much less significant. She smiled up at him in gratitude. "I am all right."

Her tone made him look closely at her, but he said only, "Your father is not here today?"

Joanna's smile broadened. "No. He could not bear the idea of another party."

Erland smiled. "Ah. I shall see him tomorrow at the ruins then."

"You have found something?" asked Denby sharply, leaning forward around Joanna.

Erland looked at him blandly. "What do you mean?"

Denby drew back. "Nothing, nothing."

"I say!" exclaimed Jack Townsend suddenly. "What the deuce was that?"

Everyone looked up, startled. Jack had spoken very loudly. They followed the direction of his gaze, but there was nothing there except trees.

"I saw a face staring out at us," said Jack. "Frightening thing. It seemed all surrounded by hair." He turned back a bit sheepishly and looked at his champagne glass. "Can't have imagined it."

"Not at all, Townsend," said Sir Rollin. "That was my sister's hermit."

Jack goggled at him. "Beg pardon?"

"Hadn't you heard? Adrienne hired a hermit."

"H—hired?" Jack was obviously out of his depth. He looked helplessly around the table.

"Oh, how I wish I had seen him!" exclaimed Selina.

"You'll see him," answered Denby drily. "He has instructions to show himself about the edges of the clearing every few minutes. Must be quite tedious for the poor fellow."

"I should say so," said Jonathan Erland. He sounded much more sincere than Denby.

"B—but all that hair," said Jack.

"Oh, yes, he has been growing it for weeks. Adrienne is so pleased."

The tone of Sir Rollin's voice made Joanna wince. And at that moment, Adrienne herself came up. "Is everyone enjoying himself?" she asked. "Can I have anything brought for you?"

"We are getting on splendidly, my dear," answered her brother. "Townsend has seen your hermit, and I have been telling everyone about him." The mockery was so clear that Adrienne flushed.

"Indeed? Well, I hope Mr. Townsend was not startled. I wanted it to be a surprise, but I know he hasn't been well. Have you completely recovered from your wetting, Mr. Townsend?"

Jack signified that he had.

"I'm so glad. That was a nasty storm. Rollin was very lucky to reach home before the rain really began." And with one sharp triumphant look at her brother, Adrienne moved on to the next table.

Joanna looked at Sir Rollin, then away. He had

distinctly told her that he had been caught out in the storm.

The man said nothing and looked sublimely unaware that there was anything to be said.

At that moment, Selina screeched, "Oh, I saw him; I saw him!" She swept out an arm extravagantly. "I saw the hermit, over there!" Unfortunately, her arm caught her full glass of champagne and knocked it flying across the table. The liquid hit Jonathan Erland's shoulder, smacked wetly across Joanna's face, and ended up squarely in Sir Rollin Denby's lap. All of them pulled back, startled.

"Oohhh," breathed Selina. "Oh, I beg your pardon."

Joanna put a hand to her wet cheek.

"Oh, how clumsy I am," moaned Selina. "How could I be so careless? I declare I did not see that glass at all."

"It's nothing," replied Jonathan Erland. He pulled a large handkerchief from his pocket and offered it to Joanna. "A drop merely. We'll have it off in a trice." He paid no attention to his damp coat and shoulder.

Joanna wiped her cheek gratefully, and started to reassure Selina, but before she could speak, Sir Rollin Denby was on his feet. "A drop!" he said cuttingly. "Hardly." His waistcoat and pantaloons were drenched. "Your ineptitude is only exceeded by your plainness, Miss Grant." And with this, he turned and stalked away.

"Oh, dear," said the other girl at the table. "How rude."

"It certainly was," agreed Jack Townsend. "I've half a mind to go after him and bring him to book." He frowned, but made no attempt to rise.

"Oh, no," said Selina. "You mustn't. I was abominably clumsy." She sounded near tears.

Erland took his handkerchief from Joanna's limp hand and began to wipe his coat. "Might have happened to anyone," he said. "With that hermit about, I shall be surprised if we don't see a good many spills today."

"Yes, indeed," said Jack eagerly. "I dashed near knocked over my glass when I saw him. Gave me quite a start."

"Yes," agreed Joanna. "It was hardly your fault, Selina. And no harm was done. I am not even wet."

'But Mr. Erland is," murmured Selina, all her high spirits crushed. "And . . . and Sir Rollin. Oh, I thought I should sink when he . . ."

"Don't think of it," said Erland. "He was upset for a moment. I daresay he will apologize later." He said this heartily, but without much conviction.

"Not him," protested Jack Townsend. Then, catching Erland's eye, he added, "Or, that is, yes, of course. It's nothing but a trifle, Selina. Bound to get over it."

"Look there," said Erland. "We are to have ices. Mrs. Finley has certainly outdone me all along the line."

This attempt to divert everyone's attention was partly successful. And when Joanna added, "There must be four or five kinds," Selina brightened perceptibly.

"I'll go snatch us some from that fellow there," said Jack, indicating a waiter with a large tray. "It'll take him forever to get to us."

This notion was applauded, and Erland offered his help. By the time they returned, laden, Joanna had so soothed Selina that she could laugh at the gentlemen's antics in serving the ices. And the group's enjoyment in eating two, or in some cases three, each was hardly clouded. The meal ended in merriment with Erland describing his efforts to get ices in Canada, one day when his nostalgic longing for them was acute, and his utter failure to do so.

The company rose from the table by two-thirty. Sir Rollin did not reappear, and no one seemed to miss him. Adrienne had not planned any games for the afternoon; rather, she called all the young people together and tried to get them to dance to the strains of the small orchestra. But at midafternoon it was rather warm, and her guests showed more inclination for strolling about the gardens chatting and flirting. After a time, she gave up with an annoyed shrug and left them to it.

Selina went to speak to her mother, to pour out the tale of her further disgrace, and Joanna was left with Jonathan Erland, who offered his arm and suggested a walk. Only now did Joanna remember her embarrassment, and she was a little reluctant to go. But Erland had been so gallant over lunch that she could not refuse.

As soon as they were away from the others, she expressed her gratitude. "You were so kind to Selina. Thank you!"

He shrugged, smiling. "I really did no more than say the truth. It wasn't any great tragedy, after all."

"No, but it was awkward for poor Selina. And Sir Rollin . . ." Joanna paused. She did not want to talk about Sir Rollin. His behavior all day had been inexcusable, and she was still too upset herself to consider it.

"Ah, well," answered Erland lightly, "if my clothes were as elegant as his, I daresay I should be angrier when they were wetted. I wonder if he's coming back? He must have changed by now."

Joanna said nothing, and after a moment, Erland changed the subject, to her relief.

They walked through the wilderness to the other side and strolled around its edge, admiring some beds of flowers that backed up to the wall of the park. Then, as they rounded a corner, they came abruptly upon Constance Williston and Gerald, sitting on a rustic bench, and, Joanna was certain, holding hands, though they moved quickly apart when they saw the newcomers.

"Hello," said Gerald. "We had to get away from that monstrous temple. So we, we came out here." He smiled a little sheepishly.

"Do you call it monstrous?" asked Erland, also smiling.

Gerald's eyes kindled. "What else? How could they *build* a Greek temple? It is . . . it is . . . blasphemous!"

"Oh, no," exclaimed Constance.

"Well, no, not exactly that, but very near. I can't stand to look at it."

"And you needn't," finished Constance calmly. "You may look at the flowers instead." She gestured toward the wall.

"Yes." Gerald turned to his sister. "Joanna did you know that Constance, Miss Williston, knows all about flowers? She had just been telling me."

Joanna nodded and smiled. Constance flushed a little, but looked remarkably happy.

"Well, it is dashed fascinating."

"We won't interrupt your discussion in that case," put in Erland. "We were going to look at the side garden."

"Yes," agreed Joanna, still smiling. "We will see you later."

They walked on. After a while, Erland said, "That will be a fine match, I think."

Joanna looked up at him, surprised. "Did you notice it? I think you're right. It's the greatest thing. I never thought Gerald would marry."

"He's very lucky. I should think they will suit admirably."

"Oh, yes. Constance is interested in all his boring ideas."

He laughed.

"I didn't mean . . ." began Joanna.

"I know," said Erland. "I know exactly."

Joanna cocked her head, a bit doubtful, but she felt again that same warm relief she had experienced when sitting down to luncheon. Mr. Erland really was a good friend.

At that moment, they came out into the side garden, finding some of the other guests there, and their private conversation came to an end.

The rest of the afternoon passed swiftly. Sir Rollin did not reappear, and there were no new disasters. Mrs. Rowntree called for their carriage at four, and Joanna climbed up without regret. She had much to think of and was very ready to go home. Gerald went back to tea with the Willistons, and as they drove off, Mrs. Rowntree said, "I am so glad."

"Yes," said Joanna. "I, too." And the two women smiled at one another as their vehicle pulled away from the house.

The men in the group were most unenthusiastically at the spot he indicated. The inside of

Seventeen

When Joanna came down to breakfast the following morning, her father urged her to get her sketchpad and come with him to the Abbey. Today, she agreed, and within half an hour they were on their way. They were accompanied by a complacent Frederick. He had spent every free hour recently in the house or the ruins, and though he had apparently found nothing of note as yet, he was enjoying himself hugely and had struck up a flourishing friendship with Carstairs' mastiff.

They found Carstairs at the Abbey when they arrived. He was talking with Jonathan Erland over tea and toast. Frederick disappeared on his own errands immediately, and the rest started out to the ruins to begin the day's work. Gerald and Templeton arrived from Oxford as Mr. Rowntree was outlining their task. "Today," he was saying, "we shall excavate the church flooring. Now that we have found the corner of the edifice, we know where we are. The pavement is the next step. And once that is cleared, we shall be able to determine whether there is an intact crypt beneath." He gestured toward the expanse of broken rock and grass adjacent to the corner of the church they had already unearthed. "We shall begin at the corner and work outward."

The men in the group, excepting Templeton, looked unenthusiastically at the spot he indicated. The inside of the corner was filled with a heap of broken masonry, which would be difficult to move. Carstairs grimaced.

"Could we not start there?" asked Erland with a smile, pointing to a clear patch a bit to the left. Carstairs turned back to Mr. Rowntree eagerly.

"No, no. Quite off the mark. We must begin at this corner."

Carstairs sagged, and Erland shrugged philosophically. "Well," he replied, "we have no help today, so I suppose you and I had better fetch the shovels, Carstairs."

The other man nodded dolefully, and they went toward the tool shed.

"Do you really think we shall find something here?" asked Templeton excitedly. "We have been working for so long and discovered nothing very singular."

Joanna shook her head, thinking that Templeton at least did very little working.

"You must have patience, John," replied Mr. Rowntree. "That is your besetting sin as a scholar, too little patience. One must be ready to devote years to one's chosen study, with no expectation of revelations."

Templeton frowned, and Gerald exchanged a glance with Joanna. She almost thought he smiled.

Thus encouraged, Joanna moved over to him. "Was your tea at the vicarage pleasant?" she asked. "We thought you might stop at home afterward, but I suppose you went directly back to Oxford."

"Well, as a matter of fact, the Willistons asked me to stay to dinner," answered Gerald. "And it was late when I came away. I had meant to do some work last evening, so I hurried back to my rooms."

"How kind of them," said Joanna innocently. "You must have enjoyed yourself."

"I did."

"I like the Willistons so."

"Yes, they are very pleasant, well-informed people."

"And Constance. I think she is a charming girl,

don't you?" Joanna watched her brother from under her lashes.

"Constance is the most intelligent girl I have ever met," he answered fervently.

A bit taken aback, Joanna was silent. This did not sound very romantic. However, as she considered it further, she realized that this was the sort of thing Gerald *would* say if he liked a girl. He seemed to care nothing for beauty or pretty dresses. And as she thought again, she realized that the fact that Constance was a very striking girl might have something to do with Gerald's opinion after all. She smiled.

Carstairs and Erland returned with the tools, and they, with Gerald, began to move the rocks and pieces of brickwork that lay over the chosen spot. Joanna got out her things and sat down to sketch the corner of brickwork already exposed. It was not yet hot, but the three young men were soon puffing and removing their coats. Mr. Rowntree occasionally lent a hand; he was not so old that he could not move a few stones, he told them jovially. But more often he became engrossed in some line of thought and forgot to pick up another. Templeton stood back and watched, sometimes offering a suggestion. His hands were still too blistered, he said, to be subjected to any chafing.

It was nearly ten before the place was clear. Joanna had finished her drawing and was standing back to watch. Carstairs looked quite done up. His face was red, and he puffed audibly. Thus, it was Gerald who took the other shovel and joined Erland in the actual digging. "You really are a marvel, Erland," he said as they began. "Do you never tire?"

The other man grinned. "Of course. But I have done a bit more of this sort of thing than the rest of you, I suppose. I am accustomed to it."

Gerald heaved a shovelful of dirt into the growing pile. "Well, I wish I were. I find myself blown in ten minutes. Father should have sent me to the colonies with you if he meant me for this kind of labor."

"You'd best not let him hear you say so," laughed Erland. "He might send you yet."

Gerald looked surprised for a moment, then he also laughed. "He might at that, if I would go."

The earth beneath the stones was soft and moist, easier to dig than the gravel they had hit elsewhere in the ruins, and so the hole deepened rapidly. In less than half an hour, it was two feet deep, and Erland's shovel suddenly hit something hard on the far side. Instantly, Mr. Rowntree leapt into the hole with them.

"Ah, here we are," he cried. "Here is something." But when he bent to examine the find, he could tell nothing about it. "Dig further on this side," he told them. "I am certain this is the floor level."

Obligingly, the two younger men enlarged the hole on that side. In minutes, they had exposed a section of old stone. Gerald bent over it. "This looks like flooring," he said.

Mr. Rowntree rubbed his hands together happily. "Yes, indeed. It is just as I thought. Now we shall see something."

Joanna came over to see, and Carstairs got up from the grass. They were all leaning over the hole when a voice spoke behind them. "You have found something significant?" asked Sir Rollin Denby.

Startled, they all turned. Sir Rollin, dressed with his usual somber magnificence, stood behind them, smiling slightly.

"How fortunate for me that I decided to join you this morning," he added. "Do you know I almost rode into Oxford instead?"

The younger people were silent, but Mr. Rowntree nodded vaguely and said, "Ah, yes, Mr.—ah, most fortunate. We have uncovered the floor of the monk's chapel. Interesting."

"The floor of the chapel?" Denby strolled forward and looked at it. "Ah, I see. Fascinating. A Catholic church, I suppose, Erland, since your ancestors were such rabid Jacobites?"

Jonathan Erland looked startled. He glanced sharply at Joanna, then brought his gaze back to Denby. "No doubt," he answered dryly.

Denby smiled.

"Yes, indeed, most interesting," said Mr. Rowntree. "We must uncover more of it, and then Joanna can make one of her neat sketches, recording each detail. Then we can see what lies below."

"You do think there is something beneath?" asked Sir Rollin.

"Oh, yes. That would be only natural, wouldn't it? There should be crypts and perhaps the treasure room."

At this last, Joanna started. She looked at Erland, but he was staring fixedly at Sir Rollin.

"Fascinating," murmured the latter. "You really do progress."

Joanna's father looked pleased. "We do. It is all method and organization, you know. One must be methodical."

"I daresay."

"Let us get on with it then, Gerald, Mr. Erland. Extend the excavation in this direction." Mr. Rowntree pointed. "The church must have been all across here."

"Marvelous," exclaimed Templeton. He gestured widely and began to walk around the hole. "Here, the monks walked, meditated, prayed, while the great Henry sat on the throne and the armada prepared in Spain." He sighed soulfully.

"Well now, Templeton, we haven't established that fact," corrected Mr. Rowntree. "Though I daresay you are right. But let us get on."

Erland and Gerald exchanged a smile, and Gerald bent for another shovelful of earth. "Perhaps you would care to lend a hand, Denby?" asked Erland. "Since you find this discovery so fascinating."

"I shouldn't dream of taking your place on your own property," replied Denby, smoothly. "I leave the discoveries to you."

"Very kind," said Erland, and he, too, bent to dig.

Joanna moved back out of the way. She found she did not at all wish to talk alone with Sir Rollin. She had thought of him a good deal in the hours since his sister's party, and few of her thoughts had been admiring. His behavior yesterday had been abominable. All in all, Joanna was beginning to realize that she had been greatly mistaken in the man's character.

They stood side-by-side, in silence, watching Erland and Gerald strain with the shovels. Once again, Joanna found herself comparing Sir Rollin and Mr. Erland, but this time, the result was rather different.

In half an hour, they had uncovered a large space of pavement. It was all of gray stone, large slabs laid end-to-end. At that point, the gentlemen stood back, and Joanna opened her camp stool and set up her sketching things. She got out charcoal and began to outline the shapes of the stones, very grateful to have something to do.

"How long will you be, Joanna?" asked her father.

"Not long, Papa. Perhaps a quarter of an hour."

"Ah. We shall go back to our previous site and poke about a bit then. You will call us when you have finished?"

"Yes, Papa."

"Splendid. Good girl." Mr. Rowntree turned away and led the group off to another area of ruins. Joanna bent to her sketching.

For a while, there was silence. Joanna concentrated on the pavement, wanting to be as accurate as possible. She became engrossed in her work and heard nothing until a voice just beside her ear said, "Bo!"

She jumped convulsively, her charcoal making a jagged mark on the paper, and whirled. "Frederick! You beast! How could you do that when I was drawing for Papa?"

"Oh, pooh. That's nothing. But I have found a clue!"

"Oh, go away. I must rub this out and finish." She began trying to take off the mark with a gum eraser.

"Don't you understand, I have found something really important. Not these stupid old rocks and things." He bent closer. "A clue to the real treasure," he whispered.

"What do you mean?"

"Shh. I don't want anyone to hear. I've found a place in the cellar where the floor is all scratched and the wall has been worked on."

"Is that all? It's probably just old repairs. I must finish this sketch; they're all waiting. Do leave me alone, Frederick."

Outraged, Frederick turned and stomped away. "To be sure I shall. I shan't tell you anything after this!"

Joanna hardly heard him as she worked to finish her drawing. She carefully added detail until it seemed to her that she had faithfully captured the pavement, then she went to fetch her father. She found Mr. Rowntree watching the young men gather a pile of broken crockery from one of their earlier holes. Sir Rollin stood beside him, and when she came up, he was saying, "You are expert at reading these old plans, are you not? It is most impressive. I believe they are often quite obscure."

"Yes indeed," replied Rowntree, chuckling reminiscently. "The charts Erland found are a good example. A clear plan of the abbey was overlaid with later additions and irrelevant commentary. Why someone had even drawn lines out to the north, toward where the house stands now. Though of course the house was not there. Quite ridiculous. One must know how to reject such later interpolations. There was even some writing, clearly in an eighteenth century hand. How people can deface such a document I do not understand."

"Really?" said Sir Rollin. "What did they write? One cannot imagine."

"Indeed. It was some nonsense like 'here lies the entrance.' Pure hogwash." Mr. Rowntree bent over the hole in front of them. "There is another piece," he said to Gerald. "Do not leave it."

"I have finished, Papa," said Joanna behind them.

Mr. Rowntree turned at once. "Have you? Splendid. Now we can work further on that pavement, perhaps pry a stone loose."

The young men climbed out of the hole, Erland and Gerald looking tired. Gerald wiped sweat from his forehead. "I suggest we lunch first, Father," he said. "Your laborers are worn down to skin and bone and need sustenance."

Mr. Rowntree looked surprised, then concerned. "Of course, of course. You have been working very hard. If we could just . . . but no, there will be time this afternoon. We will adjourn for luncheon." He looked around vaguely. "Did not Frederick come with us today? Where can he have gotten to?"

"I'll wager he's in the stables, visiting Valiant," offered Carstairs. "My mastiff," he added helpfully when Mr. Rowntree continued to look perplexed.

"Ah. Ah, yes," replied the older man. "The dog. He seems to take more interest in that animal than in our researches. We must fetch him."

"I can offer you luncheon here," said Erland, "if you don't mind cold meat and little else. I haven't yet found a new housekeeper."

"No, no, we mustn't trespass on your kindness," said Rowntree. "We will go home and return later in the day."

"I'll fetch Frederick," offered Joanna. Her father nodded.

"I'll help you," added Erland, and he offered her his arm.

Joanna hesitated, then smiled and took it.

"While they are looking," said her father, "we can just take one more glance at this pavement. I believe I saw a fissure larger than the others. It was just at the edge . . ." His voice faded as they drew out of earshot.

"Your father is indefatigable," said Erland as they picked their way across the ruins.

"He is so interested, you see," answered Joanna apologetically.

"Oh, I mean no criticism. I am all admiration. I only wish I were all muscle. My digging is not what it might be."

"You should have help." Distressed, Joanna looked up at him. "You need not . . ."

But Erland held up a hand. "You mistake me. I was not serious. I am enjoying myself immensely."

There was a pause as they negotiated a particularly difficult section of the ruins, stepping over large pieces of stone and piles of rubble. When they at last reached the lawn, Erland said, "Denby is taking quite an interest in our project. It is odd, isn't it? One wouldn't have thought a man like him very interested in science."

Joanna flushed. She was becoming more and more angry with herself for having been taken in by Sir Rollin's careless flirtation. "Yes, it is," she replied curtly.

Erland looked down at her set face. "He is an attractive man, I suppose. You mentioned our discovery about the secret chamber to him?"

Joanna nodded, then, thinking he might be upset over this, added, "He already knew of your uncle's note, so I thought it all right."

The man bent his head. "Of course." He paused, then continued, "You like him?"

Joanna met his gray eyes. "Sir Rollin?" She tried to laugh. "Oh, he is hardly the sort of man one *likes,* is he?"

Erland frowned, unsure of how to take this remark. He watched her face a moment, then shrugged slightly. "Here are the stables."

Joanna was relieved, but also a little annoyed. Why had he given up the conversation so easily? She had an impulse now to tell him what she really thought of Sir Rollin Denby, how she had been utterly disillusioned about him. But it was too late. Erland left her to look through the stables.

"He doesn't seem to be here after all," he said when he returned.

"I didn't think he would be," replied Joanna. "That

is why I wished to come for him myself. I'm afraid he is in the house."

Erland smiled. "Treasure hunting?"

Guiltily, she nodded. "I am sorry. I have told him and told him . . ."

"It doesn't matter. He is welcome to look. I hope he may find something. I have certainly failed to do so. Indeed, I now think . . ." He frowned and stopped.

Joanna looked up, curious, but said nothing. If Erland did not wish to tell her what he thought, she had no right to ask.

He smiled. "I may as well say it. I now think that it is very unlikely there is a treasure. I fear my uncle may have been playing a cruel joke on me."

"Oh, no."

He shrugged. "I have searched the house from top to bottom. My only remaining hope is that it is not *in* the house."

"What do you mean?"

He looked at her, hesitated, then replied, "I should prefer not to say. I am probably quite wrong."

After this, Joanna could only drop the subject. But she wondered if Erland was angry with her because of Sir Rollin. With this thought, she was so shaken that she nearly blurted out an apology, though for what she could not have said.

They went into the house through the library and walked out into the hall. "Where do you think he is?" asked Erland.

"The cellars."

The man groaned. "Of course, he would be. They are like a warren, tiny rooms connected by appallingly dusty narrow passages. We shall be an hour finding him. When I explored the cellars, I was even lost for a time."

Remembering what Frederick had told her earlier, Joanna asked, "Did you search them carefully?"

"As carefully as I could, considering the dust and debris down there. But it did not look as if anyone had disturbed that dust for years." He smiled. "I wish Frederick luck, but I do not think my uncle was ever in the cellars, frankly. And you should not be either. Your gown will be ruined. I'll go after him."

"No, no. He is my brother, and a nuisance as well. I shall find him. You wait here."

"Nonsense. You cannot go down there without a guide."

They came to the cellar door, and Erland reached to a shelf on the left. It was empty. "Fredrick has the lantern," he said. "Wait here. I'll get another."

In a few moments, he returned with a lighted lantern, and they went down the stairs. It was indeed dusty, and got more so when they reached the cellar floor. Joanna held up her skirts and wondered uneasily about spiders and rats. Erland smiled at her expression. "Go back up," he said. "I warned you. I'll find him."

"No," replied Joanna resolutely, "I am perfectly all right."

"As you say."

They walked down one dusty passageway and into another, calling Frederick's name at intervals. The dust stirred by their feet made Joanna cough a little. They peered into small dark rooms, most of which were piled with broken bits of furniture and other castoff household items. "Your family must never throw anything away," said Joanna after a while. They had just seen the iron leg of a suit of armor lying atop a pile of debris.

"Never," answered Erland promptly. "One might need the thing at any moment, you see."

Joanna laughed. "Yes. For example, you might wish to wear armor on one leg."

"Exactly."

"How absurd you are."

He shook his head. "Another failing of the family: my uncle was also absurd, it appears."

Finally, they got a response to their calling, and they saw a faint light ahead. "There he is," said Erland, and Joanna sighed with relief. She was very tired of this dim dusty place.

They came up to the light, finding a tiny room almost completely filled with discarded objects. At first, they could see only slits of illumination through the mess, but then Frederick crawled out from under a table with two broken legs and asked what they wanted.

"It is time to go home for luncheon," answered Joanna. "And you should not crawl about with a lantern, Frederick. You might set a fire." She looked at him. "Not to mention ruining your clothes. You look a perfect shagbag."

Frederick brushed this aside without interest. He seemed eager to go now that they had found him.

"Discover the treasure?" asked Erland lightly as they walked back to the stairs.

Frederick started and frowned at Joanna fiercely. "What do you mean?"

Erland raised his eyebrows. "I thought you were looking."

Frederick turned to look closely at him, then nodded grudgingly. "Well, I was."

"I don't think there's anything to find in this dusty hole."

"Have you looked?" asked the boy quickly.

"I did my best. But I fear I passed by the rooms such as you were in. I couldn't stomach moving all that trash."

Frederick seemed to relax. "Yes, it's a great bother. And never anything behind."

"I thought you said you saw something," put in Joanna.

Her brother glared at her. "No, it wasn't anything after all."

"That's what happened to me as well," said Erland. "Ah, here we are back at the stairs." He held up the lantern to light Joanna's way, and the three of them went back up into the light.

Eighteen

Mr. Rowntree and his crew worked on the pavement again the following day. But though they uncovered even more of it, finding a path to the hoped-for chambers beneath proved more difficult than expected. Mr. Rowntree had predicted that they would come to an opening, a stair or a trapdoor; and they finally did, at the end of the day after much digging. However, the aperture was completely choked with rock and soil, close-packed and hard. Gerald admitted himself daunted at the idea of digging through it, as did Jonathan Erland. And since they were doing most of the work, and Templeton and Carstairs had no desire to change this situation, their wishes prevailed. It was decided that they would try some other means of getting through the floor.

By the following morning, Mr. Rowntree had concluded that their best hope was to pry up one of the paving stones, making their own new entrance. But though they tried all day, they had no success in this. The stones were larger than they appeared, extending down into the earth several feet. And they eventually realized that they would have to find help if they were ever to pry one up. All the mortar would have to be chipped out and some system of ropes and pulleys put in place. They abandoned the task in late afternoon, promising each other to return the following day.

Joanna was tired when she reached home. Though she had done little, she found that standing about watching others work and listening to them argue endlessly about methods was quite as tiring as anything she had ever done. When she reached her bedroom just before tea time, she vowed that she would stay home tomorrow, as Sir Rollin had done today, and think of something besides stone slabs and crypts.

Dinner passed uneventfully: Frederick was unusually silent, but Joanna attributed this to fatigue. He had been out all day, no doubt vigorously searching for the elusive treasure.

After dinner, Joanna sat with her mother in the drawing room, doing some long-neglected sewing and chatting desultorily. But by nine, she was so tired that she excused herself and went up to her room. She read for a while, then tumbled into bed. Paradoxically, once there, she could not sleep. She turned this way and that, finding her pillow hot and uncomfortable. Various recent happenings went through her mind again. Unwillingly, she thought about Sir Rollin Denby. Clearly, if he had been flirting with her, he was done. Once again, Joanna felt angry. But now this emotion was directed exclusively at herself. How could she have been so foolish as to think he loved her? She had been warned often enough about the man. She thought again of the way he had behaved at his sister's party and blushed; that he could think she welcomed his kisses! And the way he had humiliated poor Selina was unforgivable.

Inevitably, this thought brought Jonathan Erland to mind. His response to that accident had been so different, so much kinder. Joanna reconsidered the things Constance had said about the two men. Constance was much more sensible than she, it appeared. She had seen from the beginning what sorts of people they were.

Joanna sighed. Would she never be able to see things correctly? As she grew older, she felt less sure of herself, rather than more so. And at that moment, it seemed to

218

her that she would never be the poised, assured figure she had so longed to be.

She sighed again. Her eyes were getting heavy at last. She snuffed out her reading candle and snuggled down into the covers but just as she was dropping off, someone softly opened her bedroom door.

Joanna started up immediately, crying, "Who is it? Who is there?"

"Shhh," hissed Frederick indignantly. "You'll wake everyone with your screeching. It's me."

"Frederick? What are you doing here?" Joanna reached for the candle on the table beside her bed, but before she could light it, Frederick uncovered a dark lantern he had been holding. The dim light showed that he was fully dressed, but very disheveled. There were smudges of dirt on his clothes and face.

"Don't talk so loud," he said.

"Where have you been? Why are you dressed? It's the middle of the night."

"Quiet, I tell you!"

Lowering her voice, Joanna repeated her first question.

"I've been out, and it's no use scolding, because there's nothing you can do about it."

"I can tell Mother. How did you get out; the doors are all bolted."

Frederick grinned. "I have my own ways of getting in and out. And it's well I do, for tonight I really saw something. Something Father will be glad to hear of."

Curious, Joanna asked, "What?"

"Wouldn't you like to know?"

"Frederick, did you wake me just to be impossible? Because if you did, I shall go back to sleep at once."

Brother and sister glared at one another for a long moment.

"Oh, very well," said Frederick. "I meant all along to tell you. Someone tried to steal the treasure tonight!"

Joanna sat bolt upright. "What?"

The boy looked smug. "I thought that would shake you."

"Tell me what happened at once!"

Frederick grinned. "Not too busy this time? Maybe you want to get your sleep? I shouldn't bother you."

Joanna picked up a pillow and gestured threateningly. "Frederick."

He laughed. "Very well." He leaned forward and lowered his voice even further. "Someone tried to break through that place where you have all been digging. I saw him!"

"In the ruins?"

"Yes." He grimaced. "And I thought all along the treasure was in the house. After I found that place . . ." He stopped abruptly and frowned.

"Let me understand you: someone tried to break through the pavement of the church where we have been digging?"

"I just told you—yes! Someone thinks the treasure is there."

Joanna frowned. "But how could it be? No one had dug there before us."

Frederick started. "That's true. How odd."

"Anyway, how do you know about this? Why were you outside?"

Smiling complacently, the boy went over to Joanna's armchair and sat down. He looked ready to tell a good story. "I couldn't sleep tonight," he began. "Don't know why. So I decided to get up and go over to the Abbey. I do sometimes, to look around when no one else is about."

Joanna started to speak, then thought better of it. Her brother grinned.

"Anyway, when I reached the edge of the ruins, I heard noises. It sounded like rock cracking, and pounding as well. You can imagine that I hurried toward the sound. But Valiant was quicker."

"Valiant? Oh, Mr. Carstairs' dog."

"His mastiff. I heard him start to bark, then I heard

a lot of noise, clattering and that sort of thing, coming from the same direction as before. I legged it, but by the time I reached the place, Valiant was chasing the man off. I saw him running across the lawn; Valiant had his coat tail." The boy laughed. "What a good dog he is."

"But the man got away?"

Frederick's face fell a little. "Yes, he did. He hit at Valiant with something. A riding crop I think. And he got his horse which was hidden outside the wall. When I saw him ride off, I called Valiant back. I didn't want him to be lost chasing a horse. That man would have killed him if he got him well away."

"Oh, Frederick."

"He *would* have. I have not told you what else I found."

"What then?"

"Well, I took Valiant back to his kennel in the stables, to clean off his scratch—that blackguard really slashed him. There at the stable door, I found poisoned meat. It was left for him to eat."

"No! How could you tell?"

The boy looked disgusted. "I looked, of course. I know where Valiant is fed and when. I checked in his bowl; he'd had his supper. This was something quite different, and it was filled with rat poison in the middle. I cut it open to see." He looked at her triumphantly.

"But that's horrible!"

Frederick nodded gleefully.

"Who would do such a thing?"

His glee vanished in an awful scowl. "That's what I want to know. And I mean to find out, too. No thief is going to get the treasure away from me. He made great gouges in the stone. I went to see. He must have had some tool with him."

"Which way did he ride off?"

"I couldn't see." Frederick sighed. "He was beyond the wall, and I was worried about Valiant."

Joanna was considering. "I wonder if Mr. Erland heard?"

"He should have. There was enough noise. But he didn't come out to see. Perhaps it was too far from his room."

"You must tell him tomorrow, as soon as possible."

"I mean to. And Papa, even though I shall get a thundering scold for being out, I suppose."

"And what about that repaired place you told me you found? Have you spoken to Mr. Erland about that?"

Her brother's face assumed a mulish expression. "I told you, I was mistaken."

Joanna frowned at him. "Are you sure?"

Frederick looked down. "That's what I said, isn't it? And besides, what can it matter if the treasure is in the ruins. That place—the one I thought I found—was in the cellar. It couldn't . . ." An idea seemed to come to him then, and he stopped.

"Couldn't what? Frederick, I believe you have found something!"

"Quiet," snapped her brother, "I'm thinking."

"I will not be quiet! You must tell Mr. Erland about anything you have found." She glared at him. "You are not still thinking you can keep the treasure for yourself, are you Frederick? Because you cannot."

"I know *that,*" he answered contemptuously. "I never did think so. Or, at least, only for a moment. I know someone would find me out and make me give it back. But that's not to say that Erland may not reward me if I do find it myself."

"But Frederick, if there is a thief about . . ."

"Then I shall stop him," interrupted the boy fiercely. He grinned. "And I may have thought of a way to do it, too."

"What do you mean?" began Joanna, but her brother was already out of the room.

When Frederick's news was told the following day, the reactions were not quite what he would have wished. His father hardly seemed to hear him, so engrossed was he with one of his charts. Jonathan Erland seemed to think it

222

all a very good joke that someone would want to break into his ruins.

He discounted the poisoned meat story as imaginings, and Frederick was left to bitterly regret that he had pitched the meat into the miller's pond in disgust.

Mrs. Rowntree, naturally, was more concerned about Frederick's nocturnal wanderings than about any elusive thief. She scolded him, but both of them knew that this scolding would have little effect when he wished to get out again. And his mother could not consider the merits of his story properly when she was so worried about him.

Frederick, coming upon his sister in the garden late that afternoon, threw himself onto the grass beside her chair and poured out his grievances. "People are so stupid," he blurted. "No one pays me any heed, and I daresay that fellow will be back and go off with the treasure under our very noses." He glowered darkly. "At least then they will see that I was right."

"You don't think," suggested Joanna, "that Mr. Erland might have been right? Perhaps it was just a curious trespasser, someone who heard about our digging and wanted to see."

Frederick's disgust was transferred to Joanna. "Why didn't he come in the daytime then, when you were all there? And why try to poison Valiant? Or to pound a hole in the stone? A fellow would have to be very curious to do that." He glared. "And if *you* start telling me that I imagined that poison, Joanna, I shall pull your hair. I did no such thing. And besides, anyone can see the marks in the rock. They just refuse to admit they are new. But *I* know! Everyone thinks that because I'm young I must be stupid as well. But I'm not! I know what I saw." He sighed hugely. "I shall never get over having thrown that meat away."

"But if Mr. Erland thinks you are mistaken, perhaps . . ."

"Now that was a queer thing," Frederick put in. "I am not at all certain that he does."

"Does what?"

"Thinks I'm mistaken, of course. He acted strangely."

"What do you mean?"

"Well, when I first told him my story, in his study, he seemed really interested. He asked me all sorts of questions. But then when we went out to see the place in the ruins, and the others came over, he laughed and made a joke of it. It really made me angry." He frowned.

Joanna considered. "Perhaps he does not want everyone talking of it," she suggested.

Frederick looked up, startled. "Huh . . . I didn't think of that." His mouth dropped open. "Or maybe he doesn't want the thief to know that he believes me."

"Well, I don't see . . ."

But her brother jumped up. "I meant to keep a watch on the Abbey and lay this villain by the heels. But perhaps I needn't do it alone after all." He started to turn away.

"Frederick, you know what Mother said. You aren't to go out alone at night."

"Pooh! I shall be careful. And besides, Valiant will be there to help me. Mother doesn't understand how important this is."

"Yes, but . . ."

With a disgusted noise, Frederick added, "Oh, you women are all alike," and he walked off toward the back gate.

When he was gone, Joanna sat still, frowning. Frederick worried her. Though he was often a nuisance and plagued her unmercifully, he was her little brother, and she certainly did not wish to see him hurt. If there was indeed a thief at large, Frederick should be kept out of his way. But how to do this, she had no idea. *She* could not follow him out of windows and over walls. Her frown deepened as she considered this problem. She would have to ask for help.

Nineteen

Their work at the ruins was curtailed the next day. It was Thursday, and Mr. Rowntree had to hurry away to prepare for his Philosophical Society meeting in the evening. Thus, they did not finish chipping away the mortar around the great paving stone they had chosen, and it looked as if it would be another day, at least, before they could try to raise it. Sir Rollin, who had come again to watch, pronounced them abominably slow workers, earnings some indignant looks from Gerald and Erland. But no one else seemed unduly concerned. All were eager to see if anything lay below the pavement, but none were in such a hurry that another day mattered.

When they stopped work in the early afternoon, Gerald went off to the vicarage, murmuring that he had been invited for tea. Joanna watched him go with a smile. They never saw Gerald at the house these days, but she suspected that he spent much more time in the neighborhood than before.

"Is your brother hanging about the vicar's stately daughter?" asked Sir Rollin, who was standing behind her.

Joanna set her lips and said nothing.

"A perfect match in terms of character," Denby added, watching Gerald ride away, "but hardly brilliant. Of course, the little Williston is doing quite well for herself. I suppose your brother will have the estate one day."

Joanna's eyes flashed. "I think Gerald is doing very well indeed. Constance is a wonderful person."

Startled, he looked down at her. Then he smiled sardonically. "Oh, to be sure. I was talking to myself."

Joanna turned and walked away, almost running up against Jonathan Erland as she did so. He had obviously overheard this exchange and was looking at her curiously.

The rest of the party took their leaves soon after, Templeton and Carstairs heading back to Oxford and Denby riding to his sister's house. Joanna's father climbed into the gig, but Joanna, herself, waited for her mare to be brought from the stables. She had ridden over this morning particularly so that she might have a word with Jonathan Erland in private.

"Are you coming, Joanna?" asked Mr. Rowntree, picking up the reins.

"Yes, Papa, in a moment. They are just bringing my horse around."

Rowntree peered about vaguely. "Ah, ah yes. You rode this morning. I had forgotten."

"You go ahead, Papa. I shall catch up."

He nodded and signaled the horse. The gig started slowly off down the lane.

Erland watched it go. "Will he keep it on the road?" he asked. "He does not seem to drive at all."

Joanna smiled slightly. "No, but that horse will go home safely without. She always does."

Erland met her eyes, smiling down at her in a way that somehow made Joanna's heart beat a little faster.

"Mr. Erland," she blurted, "I wanted to speak to you about something. I stayed behind particularly."

Looking gratified, the man replied, "Of course. Will you come in?"

"No, it will only take a moment. The thing is . . ." she hesitated, then rushed on. "I am worried about Frederick."

"Frederick? What's amiss with him?"

"Nothing is amiss exactly. That is, well, he insists

upon watching for the thief he believes he saw. He means to sneak out again and come here, I know he does. And I am worried that he may be hurt."

"Ah."

"He is just a boy, you see, though he thinks himself quite grown up. He does not always understand things."

"Things?"

Joanna frowned. "If Frederick says he found poisoned meat, he did, you know. He does not invent facts, and he is a very acute observer. What it may mean, I can't say, but I am worried."

Erland nodded. "Yes, I can see that you are." He paused, then seemed to come to a decision. "I took his story more seriously than he may imagine. I will have a talk with Frederick."

"Oh good. Did he ever tell you about the disturbed place in the cellar?"

"What?"

"I thought not. He told me he found one, then he said he had not after all. I don't know the truth of the matter."

Erland looked very interested. "I will definitely speak to him."

"I would be so grateful."

He smiled, a bit wryly. "That in itself is sufficient reason."

"You are so kind. You really are. You were good to Selina at the party, and now you are helping me. I don't know how to thank you."

He looked down at her. "Kind, yes." He laughed a little. "Not very dashing, to be kind."

"What?"

"Nothing, Miss Rowntree."

She looked up at him, her dark eyes wide and questioning. She looked so lovely that his hand reached out involuntarily and took one of hers. "You are . . ." he began. But at that moment, a shrill voice from the road beyond called, "Joanna! Joanna!"

For a moment, Joanna could not pull her eyes from

Erland's; then she blinked and turned toward the sound. He dropped her hand and turned also.

Selina Grant was standing up in her mother's barouche, waving a parasol and calling Joanna again. She was alone in the carriage, with only the old coachman on the box, and she was taking advantage of her rare freedom to screech as loud as she pleased. "Joanna!"

"It is Selina," said Joanna unnecessarily.

"It is indeed. You had best go to her before she injures her throat."

Joanna looked up at him sharply, but his smile was without malice. "Yes," she replied, "but first, I must thank you again."

"Not at all. I like Frederick."

"You *are* kind." Joanna went over to her mare, and Erland threw her up. Before she rode away, she looked down at him once more. "I think kindness is one of the most important things there is," she added impulsively. "I never realized it before, but it is true." And with that she trotted off, leaving Erland watching her with a bemused expression.

"Oh, Joanna," exclaimed Selina, when she had come closer to the carriage. "How lucky that I saw you. I was coming back from your house, you know. I called there, but you were out. You are always out lately, always at the ruins with your father. I have hardly seen you this week." She sounded petulantly reproachful, and Joanna sighed a little.

"I am sorry, Selina. You know I am helping Papa."

"Yes, but why? I can't conceive of anything more boring."

"It isn't, you know. I thought I might tire of it, but I have not."

Selina shrugged. "Are you going home now? I shall come with you. Tie your horse onto the carriage and get in with me, so that we can talk."

Slowly, Joanna obeyed. She couldn't help wishing that Selina had not come along at this particular moment.

Selina enlivened the drive back with a constant stream of chatter—chiefly neighborhood gossip. Joanna responded absently, but the other girl did not require more, and she climbed down happily at the Rowntree's front door. "Now we shall have a comfortable coze in the garden, just as we used to," she said.

They went to sit in the arbor, and as soon as they sat down, Selina leaned forward, her pale eyes glimmering. "Now I can tell you," she whispered. "I did not want to do so in the carriage, where John could hear."

"Tell me what?"

Selina licked her lower lip. "Do you know what *she* has done now?" she asked excitedly.

"Who?"

"Adrienne Finley. Do you know what she has done?"

Joanna shook her head.

Selina sat back with a triumphant expression. "She has *sold* Lucy!"

The other girl's eyes widened. "Peter's prize hound?"

Selina nodded, very pleased with the effect of her news.

"But Peter always hunts with her; he says she is the best in his pack. Why, he would not even let anyone else feed her."

"I know, and he's furious over it. He is trying to get her back, but they say that the man who bought her does not wish to give her up." She sniffed. "I do not see why not. I always thought her a disagreeable dog, snuffling around one's ankles so. I never understood why she was allowed in the house. But there is a great to-do over it. I heard that Peter shouted at her, really shouted," she repeated with relish.

"Oh, dear."

"Of course, it serves her right, odious managing woman."

"Selina, you must not say such things."

"But it's true!"

229

"Poor Peter. He really loved that dog, I think. And he hates rows."

Selina shrugged. "Well, he made one this time, they say."

"Where do you hear these things, Selina? I declare you always know everything."

"The Finleys' second housemaid . . ."

"Is a friend of your housekeeper. I should have known."

Selina shrugged again, and there was a pause as Joanna considered Peter's melancholy state. It really was too bad.

As they sat quietly, they heard the back garden gate open and voices approach. "Who can that be?" murmured Selina. She leaned forward and peered around the edge of the arbor. "Why it is Gerald," she continued, in a surprised tone, "and Constance Williston with him. How strange."

At this, Joanna could not resist leaning forward to look also. As she watched, Gerald took Constance's hand and put it to his lips. Constance blushed delightfully.

Selina gasped. "Why I never!"

The couple walked up the path toward them; if they were going to the house, they would pass right by the arbor.

"I have half a mind to . . ." began Selina indignantly. But Joanna motioned her to be silent. Though it was not quite proper, she wanted to hear what Gerald and Constance said.

"Let us go to Mother first," Gerald was saying. "She will be very happy. Father may not even understand our news; he will be so engrossed in something or other. But if Mother comes with us to tell him, he will listen."

"Oh, I hope they will be pleased," murmured Constance.

At this, Gerald stopped. He and Constance stood directly beside the arbor, hardly two feet from where Joanna and Selina sat.

"Pleased?" he exclaimed. "They will be delighted. How could they not?"

"Well, but Gerald, I have no great portion, and I am not . . ."

"You are perfect. You are exactly the wife for me, and my parents are well aware of it, I assure you." Gerald chuckled. "In fact, I shall be very much surprised if my mother does not ask me why I delayed so long over the business."

"You think she suspected?"

"I am sure of it. Come, let us go see."

They walked on, disappearing around a corner of the path. There was a moment's silence.

"Well!" Selina said then. She seemed nearly speechless with surprise and outrage. "Well!"

Joanna was smiling broadly, her eyes just slightly damp. "Isn't it wonderful?"

The other girl swung round to stare at her. "Wonderful?" she tittered. "Well, I suppose you must say so, at least. But I should not like having that great gawking bluestocking in *my* family."

Joanna sat up very straight, her eyes snapping with anger. "You are never to speak of her in that way to me, Selina. Constance is a wonderful person. I like her and respect her, and I am very, very glad that she is to be my sister. Do you understand?"

Selina bridled, then quailed before the look in Joanna's eyes. "Y–yes, yes, of course."

"And if you should *ever* be so mean-spirited as to talk gossip about her, I shall never speak to you again!"

"No, no, I wouldn't. I am sorry, Joanna." Selina, appalled by Joanna's unusual rage, hurried to reassure her friend. "Now that she is to be one of your family, I never would, you know that."

Mollified, Joanna nodded. "You must try to like Constance, Selina. She is really very charming."

Looking as if she thought this unlikely, the other girl agreed. Joanna rose. "I must go in and tell them how glad I am. Will you come?"

"No. No, I think not. I must go. And I do not wish to intrude on a family occasion." Her tone suggested that she was offended, but Joanna paid no heed. She was too excited.

The two girls hurried up the path to the house. Joanna fetched Selina's bonnet and said goodbye, then went in search of the others. They were not in the drawing room, or the morning room, but she finally thought to look in her father's study, and she heard voices there as she approached the door.

"Married?" her father was saying, sounding mystified.

"Yes, dear," responded Mrs. Rowntree, "Gerald and Constance. Isn't it wonderful?"

There was a pause, then her husband murmured, "But when were they married? I have no recollection . . ."

Gerald laughed. "No, Papa, we are going to be married. We came to tell you."

"Oh, going to be? Well, well. Very good thing, too. It's time you married. Splendid."

"Well, Papa, I had to wait until I found the perfect girl for me."

"Yes, yes, to be sure. Very right of you. Miss Williston."

Joanna peeked around the door to see her father looking closely at Constance.

"The Vicar's daughter, yes, of course. Very intelligent girl. *I* remember."

Gerald laughed again. "The highest compliment, Constance. You are received with honors."

Mrs. Rowntree laughed too, as her husband looked bewildered.

Joanna burst into the room. "Oh, I am so glad," she exclaimed. "I am so happy."

They all turned toward her. "What, you have heard already?" asked Gerald jokingly. "The gossips are faster than I imagined."

"I was in the garden. You passed by me."

"Ah."

"I am so glad," repeated Joanna. She went to hug Constance and, after a tiny hesitation, Gerald. "How happy you will be."

Gerald grinned. "We think so, too."

"When will you be married?"

"That is up to Constance."

The other girl blushed a little, but said, "In October, I think. Mama says it will take time to make preparations. And I want you to stand up with me, Joanna."

Her cup now full, Joanna beamed at them. "A bridesmaid! Oh, I have always wanted to be a bridesmaid."

Gerald laughed. "Happy to oblige. No sacrifice is too great for my little sister's happiness."

"Idiot," laughed Joanna. "Oh, how wonderful it all is."

"I propose some sherry," said Mrs. Rowntree, "to celebrate this grand occasion." She went over to ring for Mary. "Our first marriage in the family. I declare I could cry."

Her husband looked at her apprehensively, and Gerald cried, "Oh no, Mama."

"Well, I shan't, but I could. I am so happy." She smiled and went over to put an arm around Constance. "I cannot imagine a finer addition to our family."

Constance smiled tremulously back.

"Indeed, yes," added Mr. Rowntree. "Did not Gerald tell me that you read Latin? You can help us with the glossary of Catullus we hope to prepare."

The group broke into hearty laughter, to Mr. Rowntree's bewilderment, and Mrs. Rowntree led them all up to the drawing room for sherry.

The boy's shoulders slumped. "Mother, I must go.

Twenty

A storm came up that night, and the steady rain that greeted Joanna when she woke the next morning made it obvious that there would be no work at the Abbey for some time. The drizzle had all the signs of one of those English rains that hangs on for days and days, stopping only for short intervals to tempt foolish persons out and then drench them.

But Joanna was not sorry to forego explorations for a while. Recent events had been so exciting that she could think of nothing else. She decided to call on Constance first thing. They had had no real chance to talk the previous day, surrounded as they were by the family, and Joanna wanted to tell her again how very glad she was.

The whole family was at breakfast when Joanna came down, by no means a usual occurrence. Mr. Rowntree was bemoaning the rain, as was Frederick. "We might have finished with that stone today," said the former. "I'm certain that we were almost through the mortar. We might have raised it this very day. But of course, no one will wish to try in this rain."

"Of course not," agreed his wife. "And very right, too. You would all catch your death of cold." She turned to her youngest son. "As will you, Frederick, if you go out. I positively forbid it."

The boy's shoulders slumped. "Mother, I must go.

It's very important. And I don't mean to stay outside more than a few minutes."

"Where are you going? The Townsends?"

"No, well, that is, I . . . not exactly."

"Where then?"

Frederick looked sulky. "Perhaps I will go to the Townsends."

Mrs. Rowntree looked at him, sighed, then turned to her daughter. "What will you do today, Joanna?"

"I thought to call at the vicarage and see Constance."

Her mother nodded. "Yes, I mean to call on Mrs. Williston myself. We can go together."

After breakfast, Mr. Rowntree went grumblingly to his study, and his wife went down to speak to the cook. Frederick rose and started to leave the breakfast room, but Joanna called him back. He came, suspiciously.

"Where are you going today, Frederick?" she asked him. "You did not deceive Mama, you know. It was plain that you are planning some mischief."

"I am *not!*" He looked outraged. "Must I always tell where I am going and when I will be back like a baby?"

"Well, lately you have certainly not encouraged us to trust you—sneaking out in the middle of the night."

"I saw the thief that way!"

"Yes, and you might have been hurt, too. Where are you going today, that you do not wish to tell?"

The boy looked sullen.

"Frederick."

"Oh, very well. I am going to the Abbey." Joanna started to speak, and he added, "Mr. Erland invited me to come."

"He did?"

"Yes, and he said he wanted to have a private conversation with me, just the two of us." Frederick looked smug.

"Ah." Joanna thought gratefully that Erland was keeping his promise to her. "But how will you get there in this rain? Mama and I must have the carriage."

236

"Well, I shall take the gig. Don't worry, I shall wear a heavy cloak."

"I suppose it's all right then, though I can't see why you did not simply tell Mama when she asked you."

Her brother looked mulish. "This is to be a *private* talk. No one else need know of it."

Joanna smiled; there was surely no need to worry if Frederick was with Jonathan Erland. "Very well. Mr. Erland is kind to ask you."

"Oh, kind! I daresay he wants me to tell him more about the intruder." Frederick looked mysterious. "And perhaps other things as well."

"Perhaps. But he *is* kind."

Her brother shrugged.

"Well, I must go and get ready to go out. Do you go soon?"

"Right after you." Her brother grinned.

Joanna laughed and turned toward the stairs.

Half an hour later the ladies of the family were preparing to leave the house. "I daresay we shall get wet," said Mrs. Rowntree when they met in the front hall, "even taking the closed carriage. It is raining harder."

Joanna looked out through the narrow window beside the door. "Yes, it is a storm. But if we run to the carriage, we shall be all right."

Her mother smiled. "You are very happy about Gerald's choice, aren't you Joanna?"

"Oh, yes. I have grown to like Constance so much, and she is interested in all the things Gerald loves." She wrinkled her nose. "It is hard to understand, but she really *is*."

"Indeed," laughed her mother. "There is no accounting for tastes."

Joanna laughed too. "No, but Constance is truly amazing, and they really care for each other. That's the most important thing."

Her face softening, Mrs. Rowntree agreed.

The carriage was brought round, and they hurried through the rain to climb in. On the short drive, they

237

talked about the wedding and what it would be like. Joanna was still excited at the idea of being a bridesmaid.

Their carriage was seen as it pulled up, and the vicarage door was flung open as they ran up the path. Mrs. Williston was there to greet them and help them off with their wet things.

"How glad I am that you came despite the rain," she said. "I was just saying to Arabella that I should call on you today."

Handing her bonnet to a maid, Mrs. Rowntree looked at the other woman. "We had to come, of course, to tell you how happy we all are."

Mrs. Williston smiled. "As are we."

The two women clasped hands a moment, exchanging a speaking glance, then Mrs. Williston swept the whole party off to the morning room, where they found Constance and her sisters sewing.

"Joanna," cried Constance when they came in. She rose to meet them. The two girls embraced briefly, then Joanna stood back. "You look just the same," she said. "How very strange."

"What do you mean?"

Joanna dimpled. "Well, I thought an engaged woman had quite a different look from us poor spinsters."

"Goose," laughed Constance. She looked around. The two older women had gone to sit on the sofa, and they were deep in conversation. "Come, let us go upstairs."

Joanna agreed willingly, and they went up to Constance's bedchamber.

"I am so happy," said Constance, plumping down on the bed as Joanna took the armchair. "I feel as if all my dreams had come true."

The other girl laughed. "It is hard for me to think of Gerald as anyone's dream, but I am happy for you nonetheless."

Constance laughed, too, blushing a bit. "Well, he is. I have admired him since I was a little girl."

Joanna nodded. "Tell me about the wedding," she added, and in a moment, the two girls were lost in the intricacies of gowns, flowers, and wedding breakfasts.

It was nearly lunchtime before Joanna and her mother left the vicarage. They were asked to stay, but Mrs. Rowntree wanted to get home and see that her husband ate something. Their mood on the drive was one of quiet contentment. Everything seemed right with the world during that short space.

When they went in, they discovered Jonathan Erland closeted with Mr. Rowntree. He had been summoned, he told them, to go over the charts of the ruins yet again.

"Well, both of you must stop and come to the table," said Mrs. Rowntree. "Luncheon will be served in five minutes, and I daresay, you need some refreshment after all your work."

Erland came gladly, and Mr. Rowntree somewhat less so, and they were soon seated around the table.

"Where is Frederick?" asked Mrs. Rowntree. "That wretched boy has gone out in the rain even after I forbade him."

"I saw him earlier today," said Erland. "I believe he was going on to the Townsends."

"Well, we shall not wait for him. He may go without lunch." And Mrs. Rowntree signaled Mary to begin serving.

Erland looked at Joanna. With a slight nod of his head, he signaled that he had taken action on the problem of Frederick.

Joanna felt warmed by that idea.

"Saw Finley today," said Mr. Rowntree abruptly. "Oddest thing—young Peter is quite changed."

His wife frowned a little, glancing sideways at Joanna, but she replied, "What do you mean?" Mr. Rowntree so rarely noticed people that any comment he made was received with great interest.

"He looked ten years older," continued the host. "Quite grim about the mouth. I couldn't understand it. Peter was always such a quiet amenable lad."

239

No one had anything to say to this, and after a moment, Mr. Rowntree went on. "Daresay, it's that wife of his."

They all stared at him, stupified. It was the accepted family and neighborhood wisdom that George Rowntree hardly knew one person from another, and that he never noticed anything outside his study. Yet, once in a great while, he would stun them all with a remark like this one, proving that he was capable of noticing a great deal when he had a mind to.

He now noticed their stares. "Stands to reason," he added. "A managing female. But I've got a notion young Peter is about to make a change in that."

The ladies continued to stare. Jonathan Erland's lips twitched. "Do you, sir?" he asked. "What makes you think so?"

"It was the look about his mouth," finished Rowntree wisely, "that always tells." And he returned to his lunch, blissfully ignorant of the sensation he had created in his family.

"Well," said Mrs. Rowntree finally.

Erland smiled.

"She sold his dog," murmured Joanna dazedly.

"What?" replied her mother.

"Peter's wife. She sold Lucy."

"No!"

Joanna nodded solemnly, and Erland broke into laughter. The two women turned to gaze at him.

"I'm sorry," he gasped, putting his napkin to his mouth.

After a moment, Mrs. Rowntree smiled also, and soon, they were all three laughing merrily, to Mr. Rowntree's surprise.

Their guest held up his glass. "Here's to Peter," he offered. "May he prosper in all he tries." They all drank, smiling with varying degrees of amusement and understanding.

Jonathan Erland went home soon after lunch. Mr.

Rowntree retired to his study, and his wife busied herself with household duties. Thus, Joanna was left alone in the drawing room with her sewing and a new novel. She mended three flounces, then turned to the book, but she had barely read four pages before the drawing room door opened cautiously and Frederick peeked around it.

"Frederick!" exclaimed the girl. "Where have you been? You missed your luncheon. Did you eat at the Townsends?"

Seeing no one else in the room, Frederick came in and shut the door. "It don't matter. Cook gave me something just now, but, oh, Joanna, I have found something!"

"Where?" asked his sister, looking him up and down. "In the ditches?" Frederick was indeed very dirty. His clothes were covered with streaks of dust, which the rain had turned to mud in places, and there was even dust in his hair. His nose and cheeks were liberally smudged, and his hands were simply black. As he walked toward her, he left marks on the drawing room carpet.

"Not in the ditches, stupid. At the Abbey."

"The Abbey? I thought you were at the Townsends?"

"I told you I was going to the Abbey."

"I know, but Mr. Erland said . . ."

"Oh." Frederick had the grace to look guilty. "Well, the truth is, I told him I was going there, but I didn't. I went into the cellars."

"What do you mean? The Abbey cellars?"

He nodded. "But Joanna, I have found something really important!"

She felt she should scold him, but she could not resist asking, "What?"

His blue eyes sparkled. "A passage," he whispered, "a secret passage. It is behind the cellar wall where it looked as if someone had been working."

There was a moment of total silence, then Joanna drew in her breath. "A secret passage," she murmured.

Frederick grinned, pleased with the effect of his revelation. "It must lead to that hidden chamber Mr. Erland read of—and to the treasure. There's some stuff to be cleared out yet, then I'll see."

Joanna leaned forward. "Where is it exactly?"

Frederick straightened and smiled derisively. "I shan't tell you *that*, of course. I don't want everyone getting to the treasure before me and taking all the credit. I shall find it first, then show them all."

"But you must tell Mr. Erland. It is his house, after all, and his treasure."

"Yes, I know that. No need to look so pasty-faced about it. I mean to tell him. He was very nice to me this morning. He's not one to scoff at what a person *sees*, at least. But I shall be first to the treasure; it's a matter of . . . of . . . honor."

Joanna frowned. "You should tell him now. He would give you credit for being clever."

"Not likely," answered Frederick skeptically.

"But Frederick, it could be dangerous. You might be hurt."

The boy looked at her sharply. "Thinking of that thief we chased off? He can't get into the house as I can. You needn't worry about him."

Joanna, who had been thinking something of that kind, said, "Well, but this passage, it could be dangerous. It might fall and bury you, and we should never find you again."

He grinned. "Not it. Sound as a bell." He turned away toward the door. "I must go and wash before Mother sees me. I just wanted to let you know."

"But Frederick!"

"Oh, do stop fussing!" was his only reply, and he left the room.

Joanna sat still for some time, a worried frown on her face. It appeared that Mr. Erland's "talk" had had little affect on her brother. And now she did not know what to do. To betray Frederick's confidences about the secret passage seemed wrong, but if he was in danger, and she was afraid he was, she should tell someone immediately. Joanna felt a strong desire to lay this problem, too, on Mr. Erland's shoulders. But should she? She could not decide.

Twenty-one

As it had promised, the rain continued for several days. Mr. Rowntree chafed, but there was no possibility of working in the ruins. Pools of water lay everywhere, and the drizzle was annoyingly steady. This lamentable situation had one good result as far as Joanna was concerned: Mr. Rowntree concluded that Frederick's education had been shamefully neglected in the course of his explorations, and he kept his younger son beside him in his study for much of each day. Thus, Joanna was certain that he had not had the time to slip out to the Abbey and open up his secret passageway.

At the week's end, the Willistons announced a dinner in honor of Constance's engagement to Gerald. And the following Wednesday evening, the four older Rowntrees climbed into the carriage and set off for the vicarage. Gerald's manifest happiness did much to reconcile his father to a social evening among his neighbors.

They arrived first, as arranged beforehand. Gerald went directly to sit beside Constance, and Mr. Rowntree sat down beside the vicar, launching a scholarly discussion almost before their greeting was over. The ladies, thus, were left to Mrs. Williston, and they chatted pleasantly until the other guests began to arrive. The Grants, the Townsends, the Finley party, and Mr. Erland made up the rest of their numbers. All the closest neighbors had been asked, and all came, with the exception of Sir Rollin

Denby, whose excuses were rather stiffly given by his sister. Joanna, watching Adrienne as she spoke, thought she showed signs of strain. Peter was clearly not his usual easy-going self; there were new lines around his mouth.

At dinner, Joanna was placed between Mr. Erland and Jack Townsend, a very satisfactory arrangement from her point of view. She discussed Jack's new hunter during the first part of the meal; or rather, she listened to Jack discuss it, which was all he required in a dinner partner. Then, when the lady on his other side claimed his attention, she turned to Erland. He was looking warmly at her and smiling.

Joanna had pondered the question of whether she ought to tell Erland of Frederick's discovery for nearly a week now. More than once, she had nearly sent him a note. But the fact that Frederick was kept close to home allowed her the time to waver back and forth on the question. Now, however, she had made up her mind. "I have been wanting to talk to you," she told Erland.

His smile did not waver, but his eyebrows went up at the intensity in her voice. "What is it?"

"Frederick. I don't know what to do."

"What has he been at this time?"

Joanna looked around, but no one seemed to be listening to them. She bent a little toward him. "You remember that I told you he had found a place in your cellars that seemed disturbed?"

"Yes. I asked him about it. He said there was nothing there."

"Well, I'm afraid that he . . . he was not telling the whole truth."

Erland smiled. "The whole truth?"

Joanna lowered her voice even further. "He now says that the place concealed a secret passageway in the wall. He thinks he has found your uncle's hiding place, the hidden chamber."

"The money is there?"

"He hasn't cleared out the place yet. I'm sure he

246

hasn't; I have been watching him, and he has not had time."

"But where is it? Why didn't he tell me?"

"I don't know," wailed Joanna, a little too loudly. She started and looked around again. No one had noticed. "He wouldn't tell me where. And he insists upon finding the treasure first, by himself."

The man looked grave. "I don't know that that is wise."

"Of course it isn't wise! He might be hurt. The passage might fall down on him. Or, if there is indeed someone else searching around the Abbey..." Joanna stopped.

"Yes. If there is. I wonder."

Shrugging, Joanna dismissed this unanswerable question. "We must stop him. I cannot always see when he leaves the house; he slips past all of us. He might be at the Abbey now!"

Erland frowned, looked around the table, then met Joanna's eyes again. "I agree that we must do something," he said.

"You must catch him at the Abbey and make him tell you where it is."

Erland smiled again. "A difficult task, or rather two. Finding him, and then persuading him to confide in me."

"You can do *that*."

"Your faith in me is flattering, but hardly justified. Frederick strikes me as a young man who very much knows his own mind."

"Yes, but he would tell you, if you showed him that you knew he had done it all on his own. That is what chafes him, you see. He hates to be treated like a child."

"I will make the effort, certainly. I have been watching for Frederick, as I promised you, but I fear he always eludes me."

Joanna nodded, smiling. "He is really the cleverest boy, much cleverer than Gerald as I remember him. Perhaps he will be a great scholar, too."

Her companion laughed. "Why do I doubt you? Perhaps because Frederick has never shown any interest in books in my presence."

"No, it is the oddest thing. He hasn't any." She considered. "I wonder what he will do?"

"That is easy: he will be a great explorer, spending his days investigating lands never trodden by civilized man."

Joanna laughed delightedly. "And getting horridly dirty. Yes." Her smile faded. "That is all very well, but he is only a boy still. I am very worried about him."

"I know. I will speak to him tomorrow."

"Will you? Oh, that would be splendid."

"We must keep him out of mischief."

"And find the treasure!" added Joanna emphatically, rather to her own surprise.

Erland raised his eyebrows. "Certainly. If there is one and we can. But you are very positive."

Joanna looked up into his level gray eyes, then looked down and swallowed. She couldn't think what had come over her.

He watched the top of her head for a moment, started to speak, and then turned back to his dinner. After a moment, he said, "This rain is annoying, is it not? And we were so close to getting through that pavement."

Gratefully, Joanna discussed their work in the ruins and the weather until Jack Townsend turned back to her once again, and Erland's attention was politely given to the lady on his other side.

After dinner, there was music and more conversation. Mr. Williston opened several bottles of champagne, a rare treat, and the engaged couple was toasted by the party. Joanna found her first taste of champagne a bit disappointing—she had somehow expected that it would taste like lemonade and instead it was quite astringent—but she sipped bravely at the pledges. Selina was even more amenable; she drank two full glasses, waiting until her mother looked elsewhere and then hurriedly asking for more.

She came over to Joanna after the toasts were over. "Isn't this splendid?" she said brightly. "I love champagne!" Her pale complexion was flushed, and her eyes glowed.

Joanna smiled at her.

Selina looked about the room, wide-eyed. "There she is, she added. "Let us go and talk to *her*."

"Who?"

"Her." Selina tucked Joanna's hand under her arm and started off across the room. "Must find out."

Before Joanna could protest or stop her, Selina had walked directly up to Adrienne Finley, who was crossing the room opposite them.

"Good evening," said Selina truculently.

Adrienne looked faintly surprised, and far from pleased, but she returned the greeting. Joanna, embarrassed, murmured something incoherent.

"How is your hermit?" asked Selina, in what Joanna felt to be an over-loud voice.

Adrienne stiffened a bit, and the color in her cheeks deepened. All at once, Joanna felt sorry for her. Something in her eyes suggested that her arrogance and affectation had been shaken. "Oh, had you heard?" she replied lightly. "Yes, he has gone; he didn't care for the job after all."

"Really?" exclaimed Selina. But it was clear that she had heard this news before. "How unfortunate. Have you found another?"

Adrienne blinked. "No, I am not sure we shall . . . that is . . ." She stopped, at a loss for the first time since Joanna had met her.

"Shall what?" pressed Selina unmercifully.

Adrienne looked at the floor.

Joanna could bear it no longer; she said the first thing that came into her head. "I suppose it was the rain."

The other two women turned to look at her.

"Perhaps he didn't care to be outside in it. I do wish it would stop so that we might go on with our work. Has your brother told you about our digging at the Abbey, Mrs. Finley?"

Adrienne nodded warily.

"Of course, he thinks we are all a little mad on the subject, I believe, but he must find it interesting also, he comes so often. Where is he tonight?" As soon as she said this, Joanna wished she hadn't. She did not care a fig where Sir Rollin was, and as an attempt to shift the conversation onto less uncomfortable topics, the remark was a mistake. Adrienne's chin came up, and her jaw hardened.

"He is occupied with his own affairs this evening," she answered coldly.

"Ah," said Joanna helplessly.

"Really?" added Selina. She did not quite dare ask what these affairs might be, but her tone was clearly inquisitive.

"Yes," answered Adrienne, losing her previous unease. "He may be leaving us soon, and there are things he must do first."

"Leaving?" Selina, undeterred by the setdown in Adrienne's tone, pressed on. "For Brighton, I suppose?"

Recovering some of her old manner, the older woman glared at her. "I really haven't the faintest notion. My brother does not confide in me. He merely said he was leaving. And now if you will excuse me, I think my husband is signaling." And she swept away before Selina could speak again.

Oblivious, Selina watched her go. "So the hermit did leave," she murmured, "I knew it."

Joanna turned on her. "Selina you were abominably rude to Mrs. Finley. And I think you have had too much champagne."

Astonished, the other girl stared at her. "Rude? To her? But she is nothing . . ."

"She is our neighbor, and Peter's wife. Your conduct was despicable!"

Selina's face crumpled. "Oh, Joanna."

Realizing uneasily that Selina was quite capable of breaking into sobs before everyone, Joanna began to apologize, but she had hardly said two words when she was cut off by a commotion outside the drawing-room door. And in the next minute, Frederick, more dirty and disheveled than she had ever seen him, hurtled through the archway and stood blinking in the light.

"Frederick!" she exclaimed. She saw her mother start toward him, and she too stepped forward.

But Frederick was scanning the crowd. In a moment, he found what he sought. "Mr. Erland," he said. "He shot Valiant. I saw him. He had a pistol under his cloak and he shot him through the head. I chased him, but he got away from me."

Jonathan Erland came forward and put a hand around Frederick's shoulders. "What is this? You are soaking wet."

The boy brushed him off impatiently. "I know that, it's raining. But we must go after him. He *shot* Valiant."

"Yes, yes. But first you must take off these wet things."

"He certainly must," agreed Mrs. Rowntree, coming up to them. "Come Frederick, Mrs. Williston will have something you can change into."

Frederick clenched his fists. "Will no one *listen* to me! We must go after him. He may be back at the Abbey even now."

"Surely not, if you chased him away," soothed Erland. "Go and change, and then we will talk."

Protesting, Frederick was led away by his mother. Joanna came up to Erland anxiously. "Can it be true?" she asked him.

He shrugged. "Apparently. Things grow more serious."

"But why should someone shoot the dog? To break into the house? If the treasure . . ."

Erland threw up his hands. "Deuce take the trea-

251

sure. How could this stranger know where it is? My uncle was a senile old fool to leave his money so."

There was a short silence, then Erland took a breath. "Pardon me. I should not have spoken so, but it puts me in a flame to see Frederick endangered over my uncle's ridiculous *treasure*."

Joanna nodded and put a hand on his arm.

He looked down at her, and they stood so for a long moment. Then Frederick came back, in dry clothes and a filthy temper, and they turned their attention to him.

"I have half a mind not to tell you anything at all," snapped Frederick when Erland and Joanna came up to him. "That blackguard has probably broken through by now and gone off with everything. Serve you right, too."

Smiling a little, Erland said, "Softly." He turned to the group of guests who had come up at Frederick's arrival. "Would you excuse us? This appears to concern the Abbey alone." After this, the others were forced to move off, though Jack Townsend looked very disappointed. Joanna stayed where she was. Let them try to fob her off!

But they made no such attempt. Erland led Frederick to a sofa by the wall, and the three of them sat down.

"Now," said the man, "let us hear it all in order, and slowly."

Frederick looked down. "Well, after everyone went off tonight, without me, I decided to go to the Abbey to work on . . . that is to check on things." He looked at them defiantly, but Erland only smiled. "So, well, I was . . ." He paused.

"Perhaps you had gone in to check the cellars?" offered Erland blandly.

Frederick glared at him, then at Joanna, but he finally agreed. "Yes, well, I did. And I had come up for a moment to, ah, to get something, when I heard a shot, as plain as could be."

Erland nodded. "And then?"

"Well, I ran out to see what was happening, of

252

course. And . . . and it was then I found Valiant." He swallowed again.

"You are a brave lad, Frederick," said Erland, "but not perhaps an overly wise one."

"Indeed, you might have been killed," added Joanna.

"Pooh! I am not a poor dog, to be shot out of hand. He would not have dared!"

"That is probably true," agreed the man. "Did you see him?"

Frederick nodded. "But not very clearly. He was at that spot in the ruins again, where you have been working. He had some sort of great hammer and was trying to break through. I shouted, and he ran off. But he may be back there by now." The boy made as if to rise. "We have to stop him!"

"If that is what he is at," said Erland, "there is no hurry. I have labored over that pavement for days, Frederick. No one knows it better, and I tell you that no single man could break through it, not if he were Hercules. That is why I did not rush right out when you brought the news."

"Oh." Frederick thought about this. "Perhaps you're right. But it still makes me mad as fire that he can roam about as he pleases. And Valiant!" Frederick paused again, his throat suddenly thick with tears that he strove to hide.

Erland gripped his shoulder. "A villain indeed. And we shall lay him by the heels, never fear."

Joanna watched the two of them for a moment, feeling her own throat tighten.

"He made no attempt to get into the house?" asked Erland then.

The boy looked up at him. "No. He must believe the money is under the church."

The other looked at him. "Do you think he is right?"

"I did not at first, but now . . ." He stopped, looking uncertain.

"Indeed." Erland was thoughtful. Joanna gazed at first one then another.

"I knew he would come back," blurted Frederick, "but no one would listen to me."

"And you were right," said Erland. "We were all fools."

This drew a small smile from Frederick. "Well, I was. But I couldn't catch him by myself."

"No, we shall have to do that together." Once again, Erland put an arm around Frederick's shoulders. The boy looked up at him hopefully, and he smiled. Watching them, Joanna felt an intense wave of tenderness. They must find this treasure and make everything right. They must! They were both so . . . she found herself unable to finish this sentence, or to identify the strong feeling that possessed her at that moment. Just then, Erland looked up, and their eyes held.

"What is this—what is this?" exclaimed someone behind them. "Another vandal. Why was I not told immediately?" And Mr. Rowntree came bustling up to them, indignant at this new incursion upon the site. "Frederick, what happened? Clearly, now."

The boy retold his story willingly.

"Disgraceful!" said Mr. Rowntree when he was done. "This sort of thing really cannot be tolerated. We cannot work with method if outsiders tamper with our materials. It must stop." He subsided into grumbling, offering no suggestions as to how they could stop it.

After a moment, Erland began, "We might . . ."

But Rowntree interrupted, oblivious. "This settles it. We must get back to work tomorrow, rain or shine. A little damp will hurt none of us. And we must finish our current excavations." With this, he got up and went over to speak to Gerald, without another glance at them.

"That does seem the best thing to do," said Erland thoughtfully. "I can think of no better way of forestalling the thief." He looked down. "But before that, you and I must have a very serious talk, Frederick."

The boy looked up at him. "I didn't want to," he began.

"I know that, and I understand why. But now, things are a bit different."

Frederick considered this. "I suppose they are. After what happened to Valiant." He shivered.

"That, and other things."

The boy frowned, then nodded. "Yes, you are right."

"Come, I will take you home now, and we can talk on the way." They rose.

"What about me?" asked Joanna. She wanted to hear this talk.

"I fear we must leave you to make our excuses to the Willistons. But I daresay, the party will be breaking up soon. If we are to dig and pry at stones in the rain tomorrow, everyone will want his rest."

"Pooh," put in Frederick. "It's not as if it were cold." And with this, they walked away.

Joanna stood watching them go, indignant at being left out of their plans. After all she had done, was she to be excluded at the end? It wasn't fair!

Twenty-two

As if giving way before their determination, the rain trailed off during the early hours before dawn, and the following day was overcast but not wet. The Rowntree party arrived at the Abbey immediately after breakfast, finding Jonathan Erland awaiting them there.

"The young men from Oxford will be along in a bit," he told them. "I sent a note round."

Mr. Rowntree waved this aside. "We cannot wait. Come along, come along."

The grounds were very muddy, and there was water standing here and there in the ruins, several patches near where they would work. The two younger men looked at them unenthusiastically.

"What did you do about Valiant?" Frederick asked Erland in a subdued voice.

"The stableboy wrapped him up well. I am waiting to ask Carstairs what he would like," replied the man quietly.

Frederick nodded.

"Here we are," said Mr. Rowntree. "To work." He knelt beside the paving stone they had been loosening and began to tap at the mortar ineffectually. Gerald got a chisel and joined him, while Erland looked for a larger tool.

Joanna glanced about in hopes of finding a dry place

to sit, but there was none. With a sigh, she spread her cloak on a wet rock and sank down there. She felt rather useless today. She could not dig, and there would be no sketching, at least not until the stone was raised. And she was also annoyed. Frederick was so smug after his "talk" with Jonathan Erland, that he would not tell her what they had said or decided or any more about the passageway he had discovered. Watching Erland and Gerald bend over the rock, she grimaced. It really did not seem fair that she should be excluded now.

As she morosely watched the men gouge out mortar, a movement off to the side caught her eye. Frederick was making his way off across the ruins, in the direction of the house. Hurriedly, Joanna got up to follow him.

"Frederick!" she called commandingly.

The boy started and turned as she came up with him. "What is it?"

"Where are you going?"

"I shall be back in a while. I must see about something."

"In the house? What is it? Your passage?"

"Oh, Joanna, do let be. I'll be back in . . ."

Joanna set her jaw. "I'm coming with you."

"You can't!"

"Oh, can't I? Why not? There's nothing for me to do here; I'm perfectly free to help you. Are you going to clear out the passage?"

Her brother glowered. "Never mind what I am going to do. I don't want you."

"Well, perhaps I shall go and tell the others all about it then. I'm sure Father would like to see what you have found."

Frederick sighed. "Do just as you please. I don't care. But Mr. Erland will be mad as fire if you spoil everything now."

"Does he know where you are going?" asked the girl, dismayed.

"He knows all about it."

As if to confirm this, Jonathan Erland called to her at that moment. "Miss Rowntree, could you help us for a moment?"

Slowly and reluctantly, she went to him. He wanted nothing more than that she hold one of their tools briefly, but when she turned back, Frederick was gone.

Frowning, Joanna looked back at Erland. He seemed oblivious, but she was certain he had intentionally kept her from Frederick to allow him to get away. So. They thought to leave her out of the most exciting part of the treasure hunt? Joanna's chin came up. She would see about that!

The work that day was actually quite dull. Gerald and Erland chipped and chipped at the mortar around the paving block, occasionally aided by Mr. Rowntree. At about eleven, Carstairs and Templeton arrived, and there was a pause while Valiant was mourned and his final resting place decided. By then, it was time for luncheon, and since Mr. Rowntree resolutely refused to go home, Erland gave them cold meat and fruit in the Abbey dining room. There was barely enough for the seven of them, particularly with Frederick making his usual inroads on the meal.

They went back to the ruins at two—all but Frederick, who managed to slip away in spite of Joanna's watchfulness. The ground was beginning to dry a bit, and Carstairs joined the other two at the chiseling. Joanna began to hope that they really would finish that day. Indeed, by late afternoon, the mortar was out, and they all stood around looking at the great paving block, now denuded.

"It is large," said Joanna doubtfully, and it was: at least six feet long and nearly three wide.

"It's the depth that worries me," said Erland. "It goes down eighteen inches, if not more. It must weigh hundreds of pounds."

"How shall we raise it?" asked Templeton eagerly. "It is just like Stonehenge."

Erland grimaced. "A rope, I suppose . . . and braces. We'd best go looking for some."

"Let us search your cellars," offered Joanna sweetly. "I'm certain I saw a great deal of lumber there."

Erland glanced sharply at her, the corners of his mouth twitching. "I think the tool shed will do," he replied. "It's nearer."

"I don't mind walking to the house," responded Joanna.

"Thank you, but there is no need."

"Come along, then," put in Mr. Rowntree. "Let us go to the tool shed and look."

They all joined the hunt. What Erland called the tool shed was more like a small barn, and they picked through piles of trash and broken furniture, calling back and forth to one another as they came across likely pieces of wood or rope. It took nearly an hour to assemble the necessary equipment, and by then they were all covered with dust and heartily sick of the paving stone and all its history. All but Mr. Rowntree and Templeton, that is. They reveled in the castoffs and dust, standing back and directing the others in their search. And they urged them back into the field as soon as the things were bundled together.

When they emerged at half past four, Joanna was tired and longed for a good wash and a cup of tea, but she followed the others determinedly across the lawn. As they reached the pavement again, they were all surprised to see someone standing there. The man was bent over, examining their work, but he straightened quickly when he heard them approaching.

"You have made progress," said Sir Rollin Denby when they arrived. "I congratulate you. I only just heard that you were back at work."

If this were meant as a reproach, no one heeded it. Sir Rollin looked them over, amusement in the back of his eyes. And Joanna was suddenly much more conscious of her dirty gown and disheveled curls. "You are well prepared, I see," he added. "Do you mean to raise the stone today?"

"We do," answered Mr. Rowntree. And he bustled around to examine the paving.

Sir Rollin eyed the younger men. "It will be a great work," he said. "I should think you might wish to leave it until tomorrow." He smiled very slightly. "You look done up."

Carstairs shifted from foot to foot uncomfortably, but Jonathan Erland said cheerfully, "Oh no, we cannot give up now. We are so close." And he walked over to lay a coil of rope beside Mr. Rowntree.

The latter looked up. "We must pry a little first, I think, to get some space for the rope. After that, it won't be difficult at all."

Erland smiled.

"We'll need something narrow but strong to get in under the stone," agreed Gerald, coming up to them.

"There's an iron pike here that should be just the thing," replied Erland. "I'll get it."

In a moment, he returned with a metal bar nearly six feet long. "Here we are."

"Just the thing," said Mr. Rowntree. "Put it here." He indicated the widest crack between the stones.

Erland inserted the bar, pushing down as far as he could. Then he and Gerald leaned on it with all their strength. The stone did not move.

Carstairs joined them, and Mr. Rowntree grasped the top of the bar. "Once again," he cried.

They all pushed: nothing.

Frederick chose this moment to return from wherever he had been. When he saw what they were doing, he pushed forward. "Let me help, too." He inserted himself into the middle of the group and curled both hands around the lower part of the bar. "Come on."

But even the full efforts of all five of them did not move the great paving block an inch.

Mr. Rowntree stood back. "Hmmm," he said.

"You want a pair of oxen," said Sir Rollin with amusement. He stood to the side, looking as fashionably immaculate as ever, smiling slightly.

"Perhaps you'd care to take a hand?" retorted Gerald sharply.

"Yes," agreed Joanna. "Why don't you help instead of standing about being odiously sarcastic."

Everyone looked surprised at this. Erland glanced at her sharply.

Raising one eyebrow, and seeming amused still, Denby replied, "Alas, my young friends, I fear I am only an observer at life."

There seemed to be nothing to answer to this.

"How about you Templeton?" said Erland.

"Of course, of course." Templeton came over to them and raised his hands. "How should I hold it? I was watching you all, trying to get some notion of how it is done." He gestured ineffectually at the bar.

"Just grasp it and pull," answered Erland.

"Yes, to be sure. But, ah, I don't quite know . . ." Templeton took a gingerly grip on the pike, moved his hands up, then down, and finally pulled weakly. "Oh, I say, it really is lodged, isn't it?" He stood back, panting.

"We need more leverage," said Mr. Rowntree decisively. "I suggest roping up the pike and all of us pulling on the rope."

After some discussion, this idea was adopted, and they moved to secure the pike in place and tie a stout rope to its top end, in a way so that it could not slip down. This took some time. It was well past tea time before the rope was rigged to Mr. Rowntree's satisfaction, and Joanna was wishing more than ever for a hot cup of tea.

But at last, all was ready. Erland, Gerald, Carstairs, Mr. Rowntree, and Frederick picked up the rope and moved away until it was taut. Then, on Mr. Rowntree's signal, they all heaved mightily. With a grinding sound, the paving block moved slightly.

"There we are," cried Mr. Rowntree. "It moved at least an inch. Try again."

They did so and once again the stone moved an inch, then sank back.

"Come along Templeton," said Joanna's father. "You will have to help us."

Reluctantly, Templeton came. They all heaved again, and with excruciating slowness, the rock lifted, first one inch, then two, then all at once a foot or more.

"A brace," yelled Frederick. "Joanna, a brace! Put in a brace."

Horribly afraid of doing something wrong, or of being crushed by the precariously balanced rock, Joanna nonetheless ran forward, snatched up one of the pieces of wood they had readied, and tried to thrust it between the rock and the rest of the pavement. "It's too long," she cried despairingly.

"Put it in sideways, idiot," replied her brother, "and hurry!"

Convulsively, Joanna pushed the timber sideways into the crack. With a collective sigh, the men let go of the rope, and the stone sank down on it. The wood creaked and flattened a bit under the weight, but it held, leaving a crack about five inches wide.

"Bravo," said Sir Rollin from behind them. Frederick looked at him in disgust.

Mr. Rowntree came forward rubbing his hands together. "Splendid. The rest will be much easier. We can get a rope around it and rig a system of pulleys. Nothing could be simpler."

"Yes, indeed," agreed Jonathan Erland. But he looked around at the now lowering sun and added, "But perhaps we should wait until tomorrow for that. We are all tired out."

"And I must get back to Oxford," put in Carstairs. "I have an engagement."

"Nonsense, nonsense," answered Mr. Rowntree.

"Of course we can't stop now," agreed Frederick,

full of contempt for the faint hearts. "We are nearly done."

"Nonetheless," said Erland, "I say that we put off finishing until tomorrow."

As he spoke, everyone was suddenly reminded that this was, after all, his property. Something in his tone and bearing informed them, very politely, that they were being asked to leave.

Sir Rollin Denby smiled. "A guinea on the lord of the manor," he murmured to himself.

Mr. Rowntree was frowning at their host. "But see here, Erland, what can it matter to you? You needn't do anything."

The other man smiled gently. "If you'll pardon me, sir, I think that unlikely. I shall have to find the necessary materials for rigging a pulley, and Gerald and I have done most of the heavy work so far." Joanna's father started to speak, but he held up a hand. "And I am very ready to go on. Tomorrow."

"A flush hit," murmured Sir Rollin.

"No!" cried Frederick. "I won't give up now. We cannot leave it all open this way for any . . ."

"Frederick," interrupted Erland, "I should like to speak to you." He beckoned commandingly. Frederick frowned, looked at him, then went.

Joanna joined her father but couldn't decide if she would have preferred to go on with the work tonight. She was dirty, tired, and hungry, but now that the stone was really being raised, the excitement about what might lie beneath it offset these things. However, clearly, they could not argue with Erland on his own land, so she said, "Mother will be wondering where we have got to today."

Mr. Rowntree appeared to struggle with himself for a moment, then, reluctantly, gave in. Joanna looked, without much hope, to Frederick and found him transfigured. Whatever Mr. Erland had said to him had dissolved all his objections in a moment.

They all walked back to the house together, Templeton and Carstairs taking their leave, Sir Rollin following them. While the Rowntrees were waiting for their carriage to be brought around, Joanna went to speak to their host.

"What did you say to Frederick?" she asked. "I was sure he would make a great fuss over leaving."

Erland smiled down at her. "We have an agreement, he and I."

"But what is it?"

"Oh no, I may not tell."

"Just as you may not tell me what he was doing all day in your house?"

"But how would I know that?"

"You know. Frederick told me you did. I must say I think it is horrid of you, both of you, to plot without me. I was in this from the beginning, and now you won't tell me what is happening. Frederick was clearing out his secret passageway today, wasn't he? Did he find anything?"

Erland shrugged and smiled.

Joanna's eyes flashed. "It's too bad of you to treat me this way!"

Seeing that she was really angry, the man said, "Miss Joanna, this could be a dangerous hunt, you know, now that we seem close to whatever my uncle left. I don't think you should be involved."

Joanna tossed her head. "But my young brother should? A mere boy?"

Erland smiled again, then suppressed it. "I will watch over Frederick. Believe me, I shall take care."

She glared at him. "If it is safe for Frederick, it is for me as well."

Erland looked uncomfortable. "Well, we also thought it best to keep our progress as close as possible. All through this affair, too many people have known . . ."

"You think I will tell tales then?" exploded Joanna, now thoroughly enraged. "You think I can't keep a se-

265

cret?" She nearly walked away from him then, but some-how she could not. She wanted to show him just how mistaken he was.

The man reddened. "I did not mean . . ."

"Have I done so before?" she continued quickly. "Am I branded as a tattlebox then?"

Erland's brows came together. "I never said that. But . . ."

"But what?"

"Well, I believe you have mentioned several things to Sir Rollin Denby that we would have preferred . . ." He trailed off in embarrassment.

Joanna opened her mouth to confound him, and realized that he was right. In her foolish infatuation, she had told Sir Rollin nearly everything. She crimsoned. It could not matter what Denby knew, but it mattered very much indeed that Mr. Erland knew she had told him and what he thought about that fact. "I . . . I didn't," she stammered. "I didn't mean . . ."

"Of course, you meant no harm," said Erland quick-ly.

"No, and I . . ." Joanna struggled with pride and her intense desire to have this man respect her. "I didn't understand," she managed. "I was mistaken in him."

"Mistaken? In Sir Rollin, you mean?"

She nodded. "I thought he was so splendid, but he is *not!*"

"Not?" Erland looked down at her, some emotion growing in his eyes, and in that moment, Joanna realized that she wanted more than respect from this unusual man. She wanted love. He was nothing like the figure she had set up as her ideal short months ago, but she saw now that he was everything one could desire in a partner—intelligent, brave, kind, and principled. How stupid she had been not to see this before, how silly and young and stupid. "Oh, I wish I could do something to help you," she cried.

Erland held her eyes for a moment, then took her

hand. "You help me simply by existing," he answered, and he brought her hand up and kissed it.

"Oh, how can you say so, when I have been so foolish?"

"Never foolish, sweet Joanna, perhaps only a bit inexperienced."

She gazed at him, too affected to reply.

"Come, Joanna," called her father from the carriage. "If we are going, let us not dawdle."

She started and turned. "Oh, yes, Papa."

Erland released her hand and walked with her to the vehicle. "I shall see you tomorrow," he said. Everyone agreed and said goodnight, but somehow Joanna felt that this remark had been addressed chiefly to her.

the corridor. "Are you sneaking out of the house again,"
Aunt Mother anxiously remarked.

Twenty-three

When she went to bed that night, Joanna had trouble sleeping. She could think of nothing but Jonathan Erland and the way he had smiled at her as they drove away from the Abbey. Tomorrow seemed full of promise, but also terribly far off. At eleven-thirty, she arose, put on her dressing gown, and went to sit by the window. The clouds were breaking up at last, and a half moon showed through the gaps from time to time. Joanna wondered what they would find under the great paving stone tomorrow and what would happen if Mr. Erland did indeed gain a fortune. This last brought a slight smile to her lips, and she was looking out over the garden and smiling when she heard a sound in the hallway outside her bedroom. Cocking her head, she frowned and listened. The noise did not come again, but she was certain there was someone in the corridor.

She walked over to the door and opened it. At the far end of the hall was her brother Frederick, fully dressed but carrying his shoes. He was tiptoeing toward the stairs with exaggerated caution. "Frederick!" exclaimed Joanna, and he jumped a foot in the air, dropping his shoes.

"What are you doing?" she continued, coming into the corridor. "Are you sneaking out of the house again? After Mother expressly forbade you?"

"Shhh," responded her brother in an agonized whisper. "You will wake everyone."

"I most certainly shall wake Mama if you do not go back to bed immediately," said Joanna.

"Joanna, I can't. I am going to the Abbey. Mr. Erland asked me to come."

She stared at him, astonished. *"Asked* you? Frederick, you . . ."

"He did. He is sure the thief will come back tonight, to try to pry up the stone. That's why he hurried everyone away today. He means to trap him. And I am going to help!"

This seemed to Joanna a very queer way of taking care of Frederick, as Erland had promised to do. "That will be dangerous."

"Mr. Erland says thieves are cowards."

"But he shot the dog and . . ."

"Yes, but Mr. Erland says that is not like facing another man. He does not think there will be any great danger."

Joanna was getting a little tired of what "Mr. Erland said." She put her hands on her hips and looked down at her brother. "Well, that is beside the point. I forbid you to go. Go back to your bed this instant."

Frederick looked stubborn. "I shan't, and there's no way you can make me, Joanna. I am going now." He turned and started toward the stairs again.

"I can call, Mama," replied Joanna, raising her voice.

Frederick stopped. "What's the matter with you? Don't you *want* to find out who has been hanging about the ruins? *And* who killed Valiant? We mean to catch him and turn him over to the constable." He eyed her. "I'll come to your room as soon as I get back and tell you all about it," he added, with the air of one offering an irresistible inducement.

Joanna considered. She did indeed want to find out these things, and about the treasure as well. But in spite of everything, she still resented being shut out of Frederick's and Erland's plans. Why, Frederick was nothing but a child. She came to a decision. "All right," she said, "but I shall go with you."

Frederick was appalled. "Come with me? You can't do that!"

"Why not?"

"But, well, you just *can't*. You weren't invited," he finished triumphantly.

This only made Joanna more determined to go. "I'm going to get dressed," she said, turning away. "You will wait for me here, or I shall wake Mother and send someone after you."

"You will spoil the whole . . ."

"Not if you wait for me," snapped Joanna, and she went into her bedroom and began to pull clothes from her wardrobe.

It took her only a few minutes to dress. She put on an old gown and drew a cloak over it. It was not cold, but the grass was still damp, and besides, the cloak was dark gray and would be effective concealment. Joanna's heart beat faster as she thought this. Here was an adventure indeed.

Frederick was at the head of the stairs when she came out. She had been a little afraid he would be gone—she did not really want to wake their parents and betray him. But he was there, and in a moment they were hurrying down to the ground floor.

"I go out through the library window," said Frederick sulkily at the foot of the staircase. "That way I needn't leave a door unbolted. I don't see how you can climb out with those skirts."

"I shall manage."

She did, though her skirts were definitely a hindrance. Frederick caught her when she tripped on them and steadied her for a moment, then they set off on a footpath across the fields. In two minutes the hems of Joanna's cloak and gown were wet and dragging. She started to complain, then held her tongue when she thought what Frederick's reply was likely to be.

The walk to the Abbey was not short, but going through the fields, it took only about half an hour. And the occasional emergence of the moon helped them see their way. They reached the ruins at about twelve-thirty, and Frederick grasped her wrist.

"Come along," he whispered. "I shall lead you to the place."

He guided her around rocks and behind a section of wall to a place where two walls still stood to form a corner. In one of them, a window gave a clear view of the spot where they had been working earlier in the day. Joanna saw the paving block still propped up on the stick of wood she had thrust in. "This is where we wait," whispered Frederick. He crouched down on a fragment of stone, oblivious to the wet, and adjusted himself so that he could look through the window comfortably. After a moment's hesitation, Joanna did likewise.

"Where is Mr. Erland?" she whispered.

"He is over on the other side. He told me to keep watch here. You must be quiet, Joanna."

A bit offended, she turned away from him. She pressed her lips together and began to watch.

In half-an-hour, she was heartily bored. No one came to the site, and there was nothing to observe. "When do you think he will come?" she whispered to Frederick.

"Do be quiet!" he hissed back, ignoring her question. "Girls! Why *did* you come?"

Angry, she sat back. But in a few moments, they heard a movement behind them and whirled to find Jonathan Erland there. "Joanna!" he exclaimed when they turned. "What are you doing here?" Realizing he had spoken aloud, he lowered his voice to a whisper. "Frederick, what are you about, bringing your sister?"

"I didn't!" the boy hissed indignantly. "She brought herself."

Joanna added, "He could not stop me. I wanted to join the adventure. It is not fair to keep me out." Her face felt hot as she remembered their previous conversation.

"You must go home," replied Erland.

"I won't. If Frederick is allowed to be here, so am I." Joanna met his eyes defiantly. "I must watch him."

Frederick made a disgusted noise.

"I don't think you should have asked Frederick to come in any case," added the girl, pressing her point. "If there is some danger, he could be hurt."

His eyes twinkling appreciatively, Erland said, "I do not anticipate any danger, but I would still rather you went home."

Joanna crossed her arms over her breast and set her jaw.

Ignoring her, Frederick leaned forward and whispered, "Did you do it?"

Erland nodded, and before Joanna could ask about this cryptic exchange, murmured, "Listen!"

The others fell silent immediately. They strained their ears, and faint sounds of horses came across the grass.

Erland laid a hand on each of their shoulders and sank down on a rock behind them. Leaning forward, he could watch also, his head just between the two of theirs. "He's coming," he whispered very low.

Joanna trembled with excitement at the thought. They would actually watch the intruder at his work.

They waited; the sounds of horses came closer. There was more than one. Frederick opened his mouth to speak, but Erland put a hand over it and shook his head warningly.

An instant later, they saw the intruders. Two men emerged from the tumbled rocks at the left and moved toward the pavement. They were leading their mounts. The first was a burly individual in a freize overcoat. He had a coil of rope over his shoulder and a shapeless hat pulled over his face. Joanna did not think she had ever seen him before, but it was hard to tell in the dim light. She looked toward the other man, and at that moment, the moon came from behind a cloud. Joanna gasped. The second man was Sir Rollin Denby! Erland pressed her shoulder hard.

Numb with surprise, Joanna watched the two make their way to the propped-up paving stone and begin to secure the rope around it. This took some time, as the rope had to be worked through narrow cracks. She couldn't move; she could only stare. Was it really Sir Rollin? She couldn't believe it; yet, there he was. How could he do such a despicable thing?

Though Joanna had decided that Denby was perhaps not all she had thought him in the beginning, she had never expected him to do anything so wrong or dishonorable. Mutely, Joanna turned around to Erland. He met her eyes solemnly, sympathy in his own. He shook his head very slightly. Joanna turned back to the scene before them.

The two men knotted the rope around the rock. They did not speak; clearly, they had made their plan in advance. When the rope was secure, the burly man took the free end and went to the two horses; he began to tie it around one of the saddles.

Joanna watched him knot it, try it with a sharp tug, then go on to Denby's raw-boned hunter and repeat the process. In a few moments, the rope was secured to both saddles, the horses connected as if they were a team. The burly man went back to Denby, who was making adjustments to a dark lantern he had set on the ground near the stone. He tapped Denby's shoulder and gestured toward the horses; Denby nodded. He rose, picked up a large timber lying nearby, then nodded again. The other went to the horses' heads and urged them forward.

The rope stretched taut. The animals strained visibly. At first, Joanna thought that they would not be able to move the stone, but after a moment, it started to rise, first slowly then with a rush. Frederick took a deep breath, whether of chagrin or satisfaction Joanna could not tell.

Sir Rollin pushed the timber into the newly opened aperture. The hole was now at least three feet wide. He waved to the other man, who let the horses slack off. The timber held.

Denby examined it quickly, striking it once to make sure it would not slip, then he picked up the dark lantern and held it down into the hole. There was a thin rope tied around the handle, and as he paid it out, it became obvious that there was a space open under the stone. The burly man came over to peer down just as Denby stopped letting out rope. "I may be a few minutes," whispered Denby, and he disappeared through the opening.

The next few minutes were among the longest Joanna could remember. She had to remain perfectly still and quiet, for the burly man looked around watchfully, but she was nearly bursting with the need to talk. What did Erland mean to do? When would he descend on the thieves? Did he have constables waiting somewhere to leap out? Neither of her companions made a sign. They merely stared at the hole where Denby had disappeared. What would happen when he came back?

After what seemed an eternity, the light of the lantern shone up through the opening once more. She heard a shrill whistle, and the burly man knelt and leaned down, extending his arms. In another moment, he straightened, holding a metal box about eighteen inches square. He heaved it up and set it on the ground beside him. Joanna turned to stare wide-eyed at Erland. But he did not look at her, and she followed his gaze back to the scene. The man was now hauling up the lantern, and in another moment, Denby was vaulting out of the hole, pulling himself up with his arms. The other man helped him climb out and to his feet, then strode quickly to the horses, loosening the rope about their saddles. Denby bent and picked up the box, carrying it to the now unencumbered mounts. He held it before the pommel of his saddle and swung up.

Joanna turned again, desperately. They were getting away with the treasure. Would Erland do nothing to stop them? He met her eyes, smiled reassuringly, and pressed down on her shoulder. Surely he had some plan? She turned back.

Both men were mounted now, and they moved off

among the rocks. She watched until they were out of sight, then, unable to wait any longer, said, "You are not letting them get away? Is someone waiting at the gate? What are we going to do?"

"Shhh," hissed Frederick. "They might hear."

"*They* might hear!" She turned desperately to Erland. "Won't you go after them? They have your treasure!"

"There's no need," put in Frederick. "We . . ."

"No need?" exploded Joanna. "Why you . . . you dunce! Don't you understand how important this is to Mr. Erland? Don't you understand *anything?*"

Erland started to speak, but Frederick forestalled him. "Oh, I'm a dunce, am I? Well, it happens that I know quite a bit more about things than you, Joanna. We . . ."

"You don't know anything, either of you," retorted the overwrought girl. "All this watching and waiting, and now you have let them walk off with the chest without lifting a finger." And she burst into tears.

"Joanna . . . Miss Rowntree," said Erland.

"Girls!" said Frederick disgustedly. "If we had, what good would crying do? But we didn't. I told Mr. Erland where the treasure was, and he removed it this evening, before we came."

It took Joanna a moment to understand this statement. She went on crying, and Jonathan Erland took this opportunity to slip an arm around her and offer his shoulder as a headrest. In this comfortable position, she considered Frederick's remarks. All at once, she straightened.

"Removed it?" she cried. She looked accusingly to Erland. "*You* did?"

Taken aback at the outrage in her eyes, he merely nodded.

"And you did not tell me? You let me sit here, worrying, and did not tell me that there was no cause? How could you be so utterly unfeeling?"

"There was no time . . ." began Erland.

"And Frederick!" continued Joanna. "Frederick *knew* where it was, all this time? And he said nothing?" She stared at her brother accusingly. "I think you are both beasts."

Frederick squirmed a little under her gaze. "I was going to tell you," he said, "but then . . ."

"Well do so. Now," snapped his sister.

The boy looked at her, then grinned. "Very well. You guessed some of it already. I spent today clearing out that secret passageway I found. There was a deuce of a lot of trash in it. It took hours. But when I'd emptied it, I found that it led out this way. In fact, it came to this very spot. I had suspected that it might. Mr. Erland's Jacobite ancestors hid people under the old church."

"Very appropriate," murmured Erland. Joanna frowned at him.

"Well, I didn't have enough time to look around after I'd hauled out all the stuff," continued Frederick. "I wanted to go back after we pulled up that stone. That was when I came to tell Mr. Erland what I had found. He wouldn't let me. He made this plan instead."

" 'This plan' being that he would remove the treasure and then lie in wait for the thief?" asked Joanna.

Frederick nodded. "A really bang-up idea. We had the money safe, but no one knew."

"Was there money in that chest? Before, I mean," said the girl involuntarily.

"No," answered Erland. "Nor jewels, nor gold. It was very disappointing. There was only some papers, records of my uncle's bank accounts and investments. Dull stuff."

"But is it a fortune?" blurted Joanna.

He smiled down at her. "Oh, yes. Quite a large fortune."

Joanna suddenly became aware that she was nestled against her host. She drew back, pulling her cloak straight. "But what about them . . . Sir Rollin and that man? Oh, I can hardly believe it still. Aren't you going to chase them?"

"I have men posted around the walls," said Erland. "I daresay, he is caught by now."

Joanna looked up at him. "Did you . . . did you expect Sir Rollin? Did you *know* it was he?"

He shook his head. "I admit I disliked the man." He smiled. "For a number of reasons, not least that he outshone me on every occasion. But I did not expect him tonight. It did seem odd to me that he hung about our excavations, but I concluded he was bored, or after some other quarry." He laughed down at Joanna, who flushed.

"He's a blackguard," put in Frederick. "Anyone could see that?"

"Anyone?" Erland kept his eyes on Joanna.

As he looked steadily at her, a sudden realization flooded Joanna. Sir Rollin had not even been flirting with her; he had simply cultivated her in order to get information about Jonathan Erland's fortune and his progress in finding it. The whole of her relation with Sir Rollin flashed through her mind. He had begun to notice her after Thomas Erland's letter was discovered, and each time they had been together, he had questioned her closely about the hunt. There had been nothing, nothing, in his flattery but a wish to keep abreast of all new developments. And she, like a fool, had proudly told him everything.

Scarlet with shame, Joanna turned away. "I . . . I must go," she choked out and started to stumble off through the wet grass.

"Wait," said Erland, "I'll drive you."

"I c–can't." She met his eyes briefly, but she could not bear the tenderness she saw there. She had betrayed everything to a villain, and still he could look at her so! She turned and ran.

"I love you, Joanna," called Erland.

She checked, a thrill going through her that took her breath away.

"Why did you say *that?*" exclaimed Frederick disgustedly. "Come on, let's go look at the stone."

278

Joanna heard Erland refuse and an argument begin, and she hurried on. She could not speak to him tonight. She had to think. Tomorrow would be soon enough to face him.

Twenty-four

Joanna woke the next morning with a headache. She had tossed and turned for hours before she slept, thinking of her mistakes with Sir Rollin Denby and accusing herself of foolishness over and over again. As the hours passed, she became more and more ashamed, and by the time she finally fell asleep, she was wondering how she could ever face Jonathan Erland again, with this new knowledge.

She rose slowly and pulled on a dressing gown. Though she had fallen into bed very late, it was not yet eight. A glimpse of her face in the mirror made her groan: she looked heavy-eyed and tired, her dark curls limp.

"Enough self-pity," she told her reflection firmly. "If you have been a fool, that is no reason to continue to be one."

She washed vigorously and brushed her hair until her eyes watered. This in itself made her feel better, and she put on a delicate pink muslin gown that lent color to her cheeks. Determined to seem cheerful, she almost ran downstairs, causing her mother to look up in surprise as she erupted into the breakfast room and plopped into her chair.

"Good morning, Joanna," said Mrs. Rowntree.

"Good morning, Mama. It is a lovely day."

It was indeed, sunny for the first time in a week. "It

is," agreed the older woman. "What has put you in such spirits?"

"Why . . . why, today we discover the secret of the ruins," answered the girl, adding pointedly, "don't we, Frederick?"

Her brother, opposite her, and doing full justice to a large plate of bacon and eggs, choked, mumbling something through a mouthful of food. Joanna smiled sweetly at him and poured herself a cup of tea. For his part, he avoided her eye and said nothing at all.

Her father came in a few moments later. "Good morning, all," he said as he sat down. "Today is our great day, is it not? We shall open the crypt this morning. And we have fine weather for it, too."

When the gig was brought around a bit later, there was no sign of Frederick, so Joanna and her father rode over to the Abbey alone. Gerald was to come straight from Oxford. Joanna said little; her mind was too busy. Besides, Mr. Rowntree was never a great conversationalist.

They arrived in good time, and Jonathan Erland came out of the house to greet them. As he handed Joanna down from the gig, he said, "I must speak to you." The look in his eyes made her tremble. She wished desperately to tell him how she felt.

But Mr. Rowntree would brook no delay in their work, and he insisted that they all go out to the ruins at once. With a shrug and a rueful smile, Erland gave in. "Afterward," he told Joanna.

The state of their working place upset Mr. Rowntree acutely. At first, he thought that Erland had stolen a march on him and entered the crypt first, but when he was told that it had in fact been their thief, he demanded the rest of the tale.

Erland obligingly told it, leaving Joanna and Frederick out of last night's events.

"Ha," said Mr. Rowntree when he paused, "and so the fellow is laid by the heels? Serves him right, too. Pretending to be interested in our excavations."

282

Erland smiled a little, but he shook his head. "I fear not, sir. I had men posted, but he rode like the devil himself and got away from them."

"Got away!" exclaimed Joanna involuntarily.

"Outrageous," agreed her father. "Send after him."

"They gave chase, but I fear they failed once more."

"Incompetence," snorted Rowntree. "The world is being overrun with it these days."

"Yes, sir." Erland grinned at Joanna.

"Don't you care?" she whispered. "He tried to take everything."

The man shrugged. "Well, he got nothing, and I didn't really relish the idea of putting him in prison."

"Come along, come along," said her father. He had relented a little after hearing Erland's story. He still seemed to take the moving of the stone as a personal affront, but he no longer blamed anyone present. And when he realized that they could now descend directly into the crypt, without further efforts, he became almost cheerful.

A lantern was fetched, and Mr. Rowntree disappeared below the pavement. Erland was approaching Joanna purposefully when the Oxford party arrived—Gerald, Templeton, and Carstairs—and the story of last night's adventure had to be repeated yet again. When they had marveled sufficiently, the young men found another lantern and joined the explorations. Joanna heard her father call out, "There are inscriptions here, and a funeral plaque."

"Coming, sir," cried Templeton, tripping and nearly pitching headlong into the opening.

The others helped him down, but before they could advance far into the crypt, Mr. Rowntree shouted again, angrily, "Here, who is that? Who is there?"

"What is it?" called Gerald.

"There is someone else down here. Perhaps one of those blackguards from last night," replied his father.

There was a great clattering and confused shouting

below as Joanna and Erland looked at one another. "What can it be?" said the girl.

"I don't know. Unless . . . ah, yes."

"What?"

He started to reply, but was interrupted by another voice at their feet, crying, "No, Papa. Papa, it is I. Frederick. Don't!"

The confusion intensified. "Frederick!" exclaimed Joanna.

Erland smiled. "Yes, I just remembered. He came over early this morning and disappeared into his secret passage."

"Come, Father," they heard Frederick say then, "I will show you where the passage connects with the crypt. Mr. Erland thinks his family hid Jacobites here."

"He does, does he?" replied Mr. Rowntree. "Well, we shall see about that. This is all very slipshod."

The noise below lessened. Joanna and Erland smiled at one another.

"They will be occupied for some time," he said close to her ear. "Come in." Nervously, Joanna followed him toward the house. They walked together into the library, and he offered her a chair. She took it, folded her hands, and looked at the floor.

Erland cleared his throat. "Ah, last night," he began. But before he could go on, someone called from the hall.

"Hello, is anyone here?"

Joanna blinked. "That sounds like Peter," she said, amazed.

It was. In the next instant, Peter Finley looked around the corner of the door and came in, leading his wife. "There you are, Erland," he said. "We have been looking for you."

"Well, you have found me," said the other, with some asperity. Joanna looked at Adrienne Finley. Did she know about her brother's outrageous conduct? The other woman's expression was so stricken, Joanna thought she must. But what was she doing here in that case?

"I've brought Adrienne to apologize to you," said Peter briskly. "There was no stopping Denby, of course. The man is mad, I think. But he's fled to the Continent. He won't bother you again."

Joanna stared. This was a new Peter. She had never seen him so grim.

"You know?" asked Erland.

Peter nodded. "Denby's accomplice told everything when it became clear that there were no spoils from the night's efforts. He was quite bitter." He smiled thinly. "As was my brother-in-law, I fear. You were very clever, Erland, whatever you did." He took a breath. "At any rate, we are both here to make our apologies to you for this incredible invasion. Aren't we Adrienne?"

The woman nodded brokenly. "Yes."

"But it has nothing to do with you," replied their host.

"We brought the man here, and he is a member of my wife's family. That is responsibility enough. I take it no damage was done?"

"None."

"Good. Well, that is that, then. You will let me know if there is anything I can do. Perhaps you think I should have held Denby for the authorities, but I couldn't. He was berserk. And now, he is gone."

Erland shrugged. "I don't look for vengeance."

Peter nodded once, then turned to go. "Come, Adrienne."

His wife followed him meekly out of the room. The other couple stood mute until they heard the front door close behind them.

"Well," said Joanna, stunned.

Erland smiled. "Quite a change. Mr. Finley has gotten from under the cat's foot forever, I should say."

"It is so strange."

He nodded, then came toward her. "But we have something else to talk about, something more important." He took her hand. Joanna looked down. "Do you remember what I said to you last night?"

She nodded, still looking at the ground, then blurted out, "I don't deserve your regard, however. I have been so foolish."

"What do you mean?"

"Sir Rollin," choked the girl. "I thought he cared for me, but he was only *using* me to find out about your fortune. And I told him. He nearly got your money, and I . . ." She choked again. "I am so ashamed."

"You?" He sounded so outraged that she looked up. "*You* are ashamed? Nonsense. Only one person in this affair has done anything to be ashamed of, and that is Sir Rollin himself."

"But I was completely taken in, and I told him . . ."

"You were young, and a blackguard took advantage of your inexperience; that is all. And that is nothing to be ashamed of. You did nothing wrong. Do you hear me, Joanna?"

"Yes, but . . ."

"Nothing."

He was so positive that she could not argue, though when she remembered Sir Rollin's kiss, she was still uneasy. But the warmth of his feelings and the relief that he did not blame her were too great. She felt as if some great burden had been lifted from her shoulders and smiled tremulously up at him.

"That's better. Now then, my fortune is assured, Joanna. I shall be able to renovate the Abbey and live in high style. Will you come and help me? Will you be my wife?"

She laughed shakily. "Well, now that you are rich, of course I will."

"Vixen."

"Well, what else can I say when you propose in such

a way? How I wish you had asked me before, so that there could be no question of money."

"I could not ask you when I was practically penniless. I am not such a cad." He smiled. "Though I nearly did, didn't I? You were irrestible." He looked at her. "You know, I have none of what they call 'town bronze', Joanna. I daresay I never shall."

Thinking of all that had happened, Joanna blushed fiercely. "I could not bear it if you did. I have seen what it is worth, and I am over my foolishness. I did not see what was really important until now."

"What?" he teased. "But I took your strictures so to heart. I meant to have a season next year, when you go to London, and to put all my efforts toward becoming a town beau." His eyes twinkled. "With padded coats and collars so high I cannot turn my head."

"No, no," cried Joanna. "You must not change a whit."

"No? Would you not be happier if I were a fashionable suitor?"

"Never! I love you dearly just the way you are!"

With that, she found herself swept willy-nilly into his arms and crushed in a kiss such as she had never experienced before. A part of her marveled a moment at how different this was from Sir Rollin's unwanted embrace. That had been decidedly unpleasant, while this was, well, wonderful. Then, her arms crept naturally around his neck, and all thought was gone.

Neither of them heard the library door open or noticed Frederick come in. He stood for a moment, staring at them in outrage, then turned away. "Girls!" he exclaimed with loathing. "They spoil everything."

Regency Romances

___**IN FOR A PENNY**
by Margaret Westhaven
(D34-733, $2.95, U.S.A.) (D34-734, $3.95, Canada)

A tomboy heiress suspects her handsome
suitor may be a fortune hunter, until he proves
his love is not just for money.

___**THE MERRY CHASE**
by Judith Nelson
(D32-801, $2.50, U.S.A.) (D32-802, $3.25, Canada)

A spirited young woman becomes embroiled
in complications with her irascible neighbor
and his titled friend.

___**DIVIDED LOYALTY**
by Jean Paxton
(D34-915, $2.95, U.S.A.) (D34-916, $3.95, Canada)

Lady Judith Hallowell arrives in America and
is swept up in the social whirl of the area—and
into a rocky romance with an unpredictable
young man.